When Sam hired Christy, he'd thought she would solve all his problems

Instead, she'd added one more distraction to his life.

He thought about telling Christy that talking to the workmen was not a good example for Meggie. Weren't they trying to teach the child to be cautious around strangers? He thought about telling her that he preferred she not accept dates while she was on duty. He thought about telling her a lot of childish things, but he didn't. This wasn't Christy's fault. It was the men who were coming on to Christy—that was plain to see. A couple of them had evidently worked up the nerve to ask her out.

The truth was, he wanted Christy Lane, with her soothing hands and musical voice and sunny smiles and homey cooking, to be waiting in the kitchen when he got home. Waiting for *him*. Not standing at the curb talking to some tanned gorilla of a construction worker, giggling up at him and twirling a blond curl around her index finger.

The truth was, he wanted to ask her out on a date himself. Which was precisely what he intended to do.

Dear Reader,

One of my favorite expressions is: "Plan like mad, but take it as it comes."

Most of us have had an experience similar to that of my hero, Sam Solomon. Like Sam, we plan our lives (like mad), but then fate throws us an unexpected curve and we are forced to "take it as it comes."

I like to think that when unexpected circumstances force us to adapt, our true character is revealed. I like to think that if we are made of the right stuff, we grow with each challenge, reaching new levels of clarity, wisdom and joy. I like to think that love, in all its forms, is the reward for such growth.

Architect Sam Solomon is a good man who is about to grow and learn some powerful lessons. When his mentally challenged daughter, Meggie, comes to live with him, Sam discovers the meaning of sacrifice. And as a result, he is rewarded with the unwavering love of Meggie's invincible nanny, Christy Lane.

I want to thank my brother Rick, an architect, for his technical advice on this story. My mother, who delighted in all of my books, would have especially enjoyed this one because of Rick's input. But she will never read this story, because less than twenty-four hours after I completed writing *No Ordinary Child* Mother died unexpectedly. We must take it as it comes. So I am counting on you to read this one for her.

My best,

Darlene Graham

I love to hear from my readers. Visit me at www.superauthors.com/Graham or write to me at P.O. Box 720224, Norman, OK 73070.

No Ordinary Child

Darlene Graham

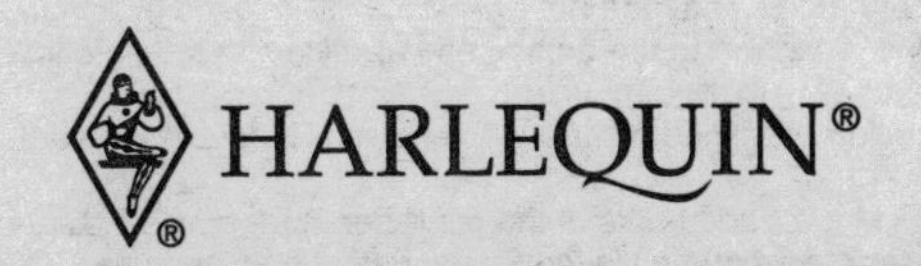

TORONTO • NEW YORK • LONDON
AMSTERDAM • PARIS • SYDNEY • HAMBURG
STOCKHOLM • ATHENS • TOKYO • MILAN • MADRID
PRAGUE • WARSAW • BUDAPEST • AUCKLAND

ISBN 0-373-71126-3

NO ORDINARY CHILD

This edition published by arrangement with Harlequin Books S.A.

Visit us at www.eHarlequin.com

Printed in U.S.A.

To Antonia Mae.

The sound of your voice reading Tennyson to me
will echo in my heart for as long as I live.

CHAPTER ONE

BENEATH THE DARK, GLASSY surface of the still water, Sam Solomon imagined he could see his future, waiting.

He had studied the old photographs and maps long and hard and knew well the intricacies of the rock formations and antiquated stone structures of the old ghost town that had been put to rest under the lake. He could picture every twist and turn, every trailing meander of the rough stone pathways. The way they veered up and down, their many steps. He was familiar with the dimensions of the old concrete retaining walls. He knew the shape of the arched stone bridge, the semicircular pattern of the seats in the tiny amphitheater. All of it vanished under tons of water when the Greer Dam was erected in 1939, a temple to the god of electricity. But the resulting lake had ultimately grown too large, gobbling up stray fingers of property. And in the process, the tiny town of Moonlight Grove, an abandoned hamlet in a narrow valley, had been covered by the flooding water.

Back then, nobody cared.

But now Sam Solomon cared. He could hardly wait to see what actually remained of the stone ruins. Most of the structures in Moonlight Grove had been built of native sandstone and would withstand the test of time. The water, however, was a more treacherous foe. Sam could not be sure of what he would find.

Soon enough, this shallow branch of Broken Arrow Lake would be drained. Soon enough, the restoration Sam had long envisioned would begin.

Restore. Reclaim. Resurrect. Excitement coursed through his veins at the very words. Sam Solomon loved fixing things—big things—in a *permanent* way. Maybe that was because in his life, there had been so many things that he could not fix, so many things he could not reclaim, could not resurrect. Maybe that was the whole reason he'd become an architect in the first place. To create something that could not be torn away in one cruel instant, by one cruel twist of fate, one tiny aberration of nature.

He squinted out over the lake, determined not to relive the tragedies of his past now, when his dream was coming true at last. His overachieving family of doctors and lawyers had always made Sam feel he had to prove himself every step of the way. But this project wasn't about them. Moonlight Grove was about *him.* Sam, the one who restored, resurrected.

''An architect?'' his old man had chided in disbelief when Sam announced his plans to return to college after marrying and becoming a father, too young, too recklessly.

''What you need to do is get your law degree and go to work for the firm, like your brother David. You need security, liquidity. You have responsibilities,

Sam. You have Meggie to think about now. And I shouldn't have to remind you that Meggie is no ordinary child. Her needs are only going to become greater as she grows.''

Why had his father felt compelled to talk like that? No one needed to remind Sam that his Meggie wasn't like other children. He had thought about that fact every single day of his life since the day she was born.

Sam closed his eyes, momentarily shutting out the lake and the sunset, remembering how his father had always made him doubt himself. An architect. The way his father had acted one would have thought Sam had chosen to become a park-bench bum. And when Sam had focused his energies on historic restoration instead of high-rise office construction his dad had mocked him all the more.

But now he had finally amassed the financial backing and the restoration experience to make his dream a reality. He opened his eyes again. Too bad his father had passed on before he could see Sam's vision become a reality.

He braced his legs wide on the rock ledge where he stood, his stance bespeaking the boldness of his plans. He ran his fingers through his hair and raised his eyes to the blazing Oklahoma sun that seemed to touch the edge of the water. For Sam it wasn't hard to see Moonlight Grove as the beautiful resort that would rise from this setting a year from now. Always, during any project, Sam kept his eye on his final vision.

The surface of the water, a black satin sheet moments before, was now lit with the torched hues of the fiery evening sky.

Sam drew and released a satisfied breath. Verandas on the main hotel would face southwest, affording guests this stunning view at eventide.

Sam's schedule as controlling partner in Solomon Architectural Masterpieces did not allow many moments like this, and, predictably, his cell phone bleated, interrupting his daydreaming.

He scowled at the little black intruder clipped to his belt, expecting to see his partner Josh's cell number—or the number from the office. But no, it was a California area code, which instantly raised a ripple of unease in him. He didn't recognize the number, but this had to be Andrea—he didn't know anyone in California except his ex-wife and her parents. Normally, Andrea left her cold, businesslike messages on his home answering machine. Why would Andrea be calling on his cell phone? Unless…something had happened to Meggie. He unclipped the phone and snapped it open.

"Andrea?"

"Yes. Hi, Sam."

"Uh, hi." His tentative greeting echoed the tone of his ex-wife's. She sounded strange.

"I hope I'm not interrupting something important." Her politeness only increased the feeling of dread building in Sam's chest.

"It's okay. What's up?"

"Sorry to disturb you at work. Your secretary gave me your cell number. I hope that's okay."

"I said it's okay." Sam didn't mean to sound abrupt, but he wanted Andrea to just get to the point. Prior to their divorce three years ago, they had been married for eight intense years, and—dammit—he could tell when something was wrong. "What is it?"

"Meggie's fine, Sam. You need to know that first."

Sam released the breath he hadn't realized he'd been holding. *Meggie's fine.* Okay. Maybe something had happened to Lorna or Bud. Andrea's parents were nice folks, and he wished them well. "That's good. So what's the matter, Andrea?"

"I...I have a kind of an emergency."

"Okay. You need my help?" His anxiety level dropped a notch. Maybe she only needed money. This wasn't the first time he had given Andrea a little help beyond her alimony and Meggie's child support. He didn't mind. He found that sending them extra money actually lowered his guilt quotient.

"Yes. Yes, as a matter of fact I do need your help. I need to have Meggie live in Tulsa with you for a...for a little while. At least, I hope it's only for a little while."

Sam drew in a cautious breath. Held it. This was a bit of a shock. Then he frowned, as consternation and suspicion set in. After all the times he'd begged Andrea to let him have Meggie half the year, to let him make some kind of life for his child with him here in Tulsa, difficult as that would be. And now, suddenly, Andrea was calling, asking him in this strange voice to take their child. *Not now.* He couldn't quash the unbidden selfish thought. *Not now, when I'm finally getting ready to start on my dream project.* Maybe he could negotiate with Andrea and make the move easier on everyone, maybe even negotiate a permanent joint custody of Meggie—only later. *Later.* Like a year from now.

"Andrea, listen. You know I'm always willing to have Meggie with me—to share the burden. But this is a really bad time right now. I'm starting a restoration project that involves nothing short of resurrecting an entire town from the bottom of a lake. I'm not sure I can meet Meggie's special needs while I'm trying to finish a project of this magni— "

"Sam, I'm sick," Andrea interrupted.

"Sick?" What did she mean, *sick?* Sam's chest tightened.

"Yes, I'm...I'm afraid I'm actually very sick." Andrea's voice, normally controlled and cool, sounded incredibly soft now, even vulnerable. And kind. Too kind. As if she wanted to soften the blow for him, as if this were an apology. "You see, I have cancer."

"Cancer?" At the word Sam's heart sped up, but still he hoped against hope that Andrea was dramatizing or something. She sometimes did that, except, of course, when it came to Meggie. And this was about Meggie, wasn't it? Or was it? Suddenly he hoped there was some big mistake, some miscommunication. His mind flashed around in denial. His ex-wife, the model-sleek beauty who had snagged him straight out of high school, the overprotective mother of their needy child Meggie, simply *had* to be okay. Meggie was the one who was not okay. Ergo, everybody else *had* to be okay.

"Cancer?" he repeated. Weren't there all kinds of cancer? One of the junior architects had beaten malignant melanoma only a couple of years ago. "What kind of cancer?"

"The doctors call it soft-tissue sarcoma."

Sam was so stunned that he lowered a hand to the rock ledge. "Is that…is that really serious?" he said, already sensing that it was. There was a brave finality about Andrea's voice.

"I'm afraid so, Sam."

He sat down, knees raised, head lowered, holding the cell phone to his ear, staring at the mossy lichen growing on the rock between his legs, thinking, *No.*

"But there's good news." Andrea altered her tone, lightened it—clearly a front, which scared Sam all the more. "The doctors tell me it is treatable."

Every time she used the plural of the word *doctor,* his anxiety level kicked up. What kind of cancer was this soft-tissue sarcoma that Andrea needed doctors, *plural,* to treat it? "What do you mean, it's treatable?"

"I mean, it's treatable," she said lightly. But she didn't sound convinced. She sounded scared. "I'm going to the City of Hope in Los Angeles tomorrow." Suddenly, her tone changed again and she sounded weird. Calm. Mature. Not like the Andrea he knew. Irrationally, he longed for the whiny, temperamental woman he had once called his wife. But she allowed herself only a cleansing sigh before she continued. "But my treatment won't be easy. First extensive surgery. Then some pretty heavy chemotherapy. That's why I need you to take Meggie for a while. The treatment that will save my life is going to take a lot out of me at first, I'm afraid. And Daddy hasn't been well, so Mother and Daddy and I discussed it, and—"

Save her life? Save her life! Good Lord, what was Andrea facing? But he suppressed his own panic and concentrated on listening to her.

"—and I don't think I can keep up with our daughter. You know, with her needs."

Sam did know. The familiar guilt clenched his gut. When it was his turn to have Meggie with him in Tulsa, life slowed down to her pace, the pace of a severely damaged child forever stuck in the chaotic world of a three-year-old. In short, when his daughter Meggie was visiting, he got next to nothing done.

"Andrea." He fought to keep the emotion in his voice under control. Was he going to cry? He sure as hell felt like it. "I...I'll help you in any way I can. You know that. You know I...I still care about you."

"I know that, Sam. You're a good man. You always have been. I know you care. And I know how much you love Meggie. So, here's how you can help me. Take her."

His answer was resolute. "Sure. Anything."

"I'm putting her on a plane tomorrow afternoon."

"Tomorrow?" As soon as he uttered the word, Sam regretted it. He wasn't going to complain about or question anything in this deal, dammit. He was going to help.

''Yes. It seems the timing is critical, and I am checking into the hospital very early in the morning. Actually, Daddy will take Meggie to LAX airport in L.A. I really hate putting her on a plane by herself in these uncertain times—'' At last Andrea's voice grew emotional, but she quickly recovered. ''You'll need the flight number and arrival time. Got a pen?''

Sam patted the pockets of his windbreaker. ''I do, but it's in my car. I'm out at a building site.'' Sam didn't wanted to tell her that he had been standing on a rock overlooking a beautiful lake, dreaming his dream, when she called with her terrible news. ''Where are you? Can I call you back?''

''I'm staying at Mother and Daddy's house in Huntington Beach. We're going to have dinner now, but just call me back anytime this evening. Meggie will arrive about 7:00 p.m. your time at Will Rogers.''

''Will Rogers? Down in Oklahoma City?''

''Yes. It was the only way to put her on a direct flight. There was nothing from here to Tulsa.''

''That's fine.'' It wasn't. Tomorrow afternoon he had an important meeting with the developers of Moonlight Grove that would undoubtedly run late. But what could he say? ''It's just fine.''

''Sam, I know this puts you in a bind, as far as child care and all. Maybe your mother could help you out.''

Andrea and his mother had always been friendly. His mother had once proclaimed Andrea the perfect daughter-in-law. These days they shared a mutual love and fierce protectiveness of Meggie. But his mother had her own life now—she was scheduled to leave for Central America on a photographic expedition in one week.

"We'll be fine. If Mom can't take care of Meggie, I know of a very nice older lady who can. Mrs. Waddle has baby-sat for me a couple of times. Very nice. Very grandmotherly." This was a somewhat rosy description of Cloretta Waddle.

"Okay. Call me back later tonight."

"Andrea?"

"Yeah?"

"When did you find out about this?"

"About a week ago."

Oh, God, he thought. A life could change so dramatically in only a week. Hadn't Andrea Haynes Solomon suffered enough in her life? First, bearing a severely brain-damaged child when she was only twenty years old, then having her marriage fall apart. And now this. Cancer. "Andrea, I'm so sorry. We will get you through this, all of us. Don't worry about Meggie. I promise I will take very good care of her."

"You always do."

"Yes, well. I love her. She's my baby." He was glad he hadn't said, *She'll always be my baby.* Andrea didn't need reminders of Meggie's shortcomings any more than he did, certainly not now.

"I know, Sam. Call me back when you're somewhere where you can write the plane information down. I'm really sorry to spring this on you so suddenly. I just didn't want Meggie to have to see me in the hospital, you know? I don't think she would understand any of this.''

''Does Meggie know you're sick?''

''We told her I have to have an operation. She had a friend who had her tonsils out, so she understands that much. I told her she would probably get to stay with her daddy until I'm...until I'm well.'' Andrea rushed on, her voice artificially bright again. ''She was very excited about seeing you and her nonnie.''

Sam closed his eyes, but somehow the hot orange light of the sun seeped through his lids, anyway, egging on the tears. ''I'll call you back,'' he croaked, trying not to choke up, ''in a bit.''

''Okay. I'll be here.''

Sam punched End and stared out over the shimmering apricot surface of the water again, feeling as if the world had suddenly shifted on its axis.

How could life change so completely in only a few minutes? Then again, hadn't he learned already that life *could* change just that fast? Suddenly, completely, horribly. In those few tense moments when Meggie had been born, those tortured moments, he had wanted to rip the cord from his child's neck with his own hands. Those moments had taught him that everything, positively everything, could spin out of control in an instant. When the nurses forced the mask over his tiny baby's blue face and she did not breathe, hadn't he seen, with his very own eyes, how in the span of less than five minutes, a life and all the lives around it could shift forever?

Soft-tissue sarcoma. Andrea was dying. *No.* He would not even think such a thought, would not even allow such a possibility. He would get on the Internet tonight and look it up, and he would find out everything he could about this...disease. He would help the mother of his child fight for her life. By God, he was a man who fixed things—restored things—and he would find a way to fix this, too.

But first, he had to find someone to drive to Oklahoma City and pick up Meggie at Will Rogers World Airport at seven in the evening. There was really no question as to who that someone would be.

GAYLE SOLOMON STOOD STARING out at the runways, thanking God that Will Rogers World Airport was quieter than most. Set on a grassy plain south of Oklahoma City, Will Rogers was a typical, vast, unadorned airport. At least here the parking lots were uncrowded and the traffic flowed smoothly. Even at seven o'clock on a Friday evening at the start of the Memorial Day weekend there weren't that many people. Maybe Meggie wouldn't be too scared, arriving in a relatively calm place like this. But the drive to Tulsa would seem unbearably long to the child, so Gayle had come armed with sing-along tapes. Meggie loved to sing.

The jet that carried her grandchild taxied in from a distant runway. She hated to think of little Meggie in a plane that big all by herself. She wondered if any of the other passengers had shown an interest in Meggie, if they'd talked to her. If they'd been kind.

Of course they'd been kind. People were always kind to children, weren't they? But even if they were kind, they would still be expecting Meggie to behave like what she appeared to be—a normal ten-year-old. When in reality, the specialists estimated that Meggie was, at most, mentally a three-year-old. Meggie could fool people. She wasn't slack-jawed or slow-moving. She was beautiful, thin and graceful. She moved like a tiny gazelle. And she could parrot the most astounding words, making her seem brighter than she actually was.

For an instant Gayle thought she saw Meggie's bewildered little face framed in one of the oval windows of the plane, but in the next instant, the glare of the setting sun obliterated it. Envisioning her granddaughter's face reminded Gayle of how simple, how sweet Meggie could be. Well, Meggie could be sweet if she wanted to be. At least when her routine wasn't disrupted. Gayle sighed. Being separated from her mother and having to fly across the country was certainly a major disruption.

Not for the first time, Gayle wished Andrea hadn't taken the child off to California. What was Sam supposed to have done? Abandon his struggling architectural partnership when it was just taking off? Building a reputation as a specialist in restoring historic buildings took time and persistence.

Gayle walked around the passengers waiting at the gate, positioning herself directly in front of the door of the boarding ramp, thankful that the airline security had allowed her to come this far down to meet Meggie.

Airports, Gayle thought, had become such somber, anxious places these days. The long, brightly lit corridor around her, with its boarding gates fanning out in a semicircle, felt subdued, vacant, compared to her last visit to Will Rogers.

Gayle walked over to a rounded bank of windows and folded her arms across her middle. The heat from the prairie sun setting low over the vast tarmac radiated through the glass. The holiday weekend promised to be a scorcher. Gayle watched as the blue-and-white jet aligned its door with the boarding ramp. Meggie was in there. She hoped her baby wasn't scared. Meggie would remember her nonnie, wouldn't she?

A stream of passengers emerged from the doorway. A little family. Some college students. A few tired-looking businessmen. Soon the area was filled with passengers. People assembled their parties, then rushed toward baggage claim. Gayle's view became blocked by a large man. She ducked around him, but she still couldn't see any sign of Meggie. In no time the stream dwindled to a trickle. Still no Meggie.

Anxious, Gayle took the paper on which she'd written Sam's instructions from her purse. Flight 1292. She looked at the digital display behind the boarding desk. She was at the correct gate. She stepped toward the ramp and peered down the tunnel toward the door of the plane. Not a soul was in sight. What should she do? Surely they hadn't let something happen to the child. Gayle's mind flashed to the time her elderly mother-in-law had been left sitting in a wheelchair while her connecting flight took off in Salt Lake City. Her palms grew damp.

Sam should have flown to Los Angeles to pick up his daughter. Gayle had told him that in no uncertain terms.

In defiance of the rules, she was about to march down the ramp and look into the plane herself when she heard a shriek and then a child's howling protests.

Behind Gayle, a small cluster of people had formed under a large sign that read Oklahoma City, the new Agenda for Business, next to a stunning blowup of a fire-red Oklahoma sunset. But there was nothing sunny about their faces as they turned anxious expressions toward the sound of the shrieking child.

The suspended alertness of the group fractured as they all heard the young child plainly yelling, "Help! Help me!"

As one, everyone rushed forward, expressions horrified. Gayle was overcome by a sinking feeling. Meggie was acting out again. Out of the corner of her eye, she saw security officers jogging down the concourse.

A man in a straw cowboy hat standing next to her muttered, "What the hell?"

"I think it's my grandchild."

Sure enough, around the corner came a flight attendant, tugging a screaming Meggie by the hand. Meggie, clutching her beloved stuffed companion, Mr. Bear, and wielding a pink Pokémon backpack at the flight attendant's arm, dug in her heels and stopped their progress.

Meggie was incredibly strong for such a thin child. Gayle had to smile, though she was mortified that Meggie was making such a scene. The child did have a will of her own. Her little face was so red with exertion that it made her blond hair look almost white. Like the unfortunate flight attendant, Gayle herself had often been jerked to a halt when Meggie didn't want to cooperate. There was no reasoning with a three-year-old in a ten-year-old's body. The flight attendant bent forward at the waist, obviously trying to reason with the struggling child.

"Meggie!" Gayle called, "Meggie! It's Nonnie!" Gayle put on a brave smile and waved frantically, trying to get the child to calm down and see that everything was okay. Nonnie was here.

The flight attendant turned. "Are you Mrs. Solomon?"

"Yes!"

Gayle was relieved when she was waved down the ramp. "Meggie, it's okay, honey." She tried to speak calmly above Meggie's screaming as she took hold of the combative child. "Nonnie's here."

"I going back to Cal-forna!" Meggie screamed while trying to tug her hand out of the attendant's grip and twisting her thin body away from Gayle, back toward the plane.

"She refused to get off the plane." The woman had to holler to be heard above Meggie's crying.

"I...want...my...*mom*-meeee!" Meggie wailed.

"Meggie, listen!" Gayle dropped to one knee and bracketed her hands on the child's flushed, tear-streaked cheeks. "Remember Nonnie?" Gayle brushed back Meggie's thick blond curls and tried to look into her eyes, but they were squeezed shut. "And Daddy? Daddy wants to see you. Remember? And Brutus. Brutus wants to see you. Remember Brutus?"

Gayle hated to use her poor little schnauzer as bait, but what choice did she have? It always worked. Instantly, Meggie's body relaxed and her eyes opened wide.

"Bootus?" she said in quiet awe.

"Yes. Remember Brutus?" Gayle encouraged.

"Bootus?" Meggie repeated softly. She hiccuped innocently, then graced the hapless attendant with an angelic smile. The poor woman cautiously released Meggie's hand, then wilted as if she wanted to slide down the wall of the tunnel to her backside. "You go with your grandma now," she sighed, "okay, Meggie?"

"My *nonnie,*" Meggie corrected with an evil glare.

"Yes. Your nonnie. We'll have fun the next time you fly with us." The look on the flight attendant's face said, *Which I hope is never.*

In a singsong voice, Meggie started chanting, "Boo-tus. Boo-tus. I gonna see Bootus."

Gayle stood up and took Meggie's free hand. "They did tell you that my granddaughter is mentally challenged, didn't they?"

The attendant nodded, looking sheepish but exhausted. "Yes. Her mom gave us plenty of instructions. But they didn't mention the *t-e-m-p-e-r.* I let her eat several doughnuts. She refused to touch any healthy snacks and it was a long flight. It was the only way to get some orange juice down her."

Gayle smiled wanly and patted the woman's arm. Sugar certainly didn't help Meggie's moods. "It's okay. I'll feed her some protein on the way home. She loves McDonald's."

With that, Meggie changed her chant to "IckDonald's! IckDonald's! I gonna go to IckDonald's!" as she tugged on Gayle's hand, dragging her petite grandmother down the exit ramp.

"Thank you!" Gayle called over her shoulder.

"I'm sorry she got upset," the flight attendant called after them. "I did get her to take a two-hour nap during the flight."

Great, Gayle thought, *that means now she won't fall asleep until after midnight. Not an auspicious beginning on her first night in her daddy's house.*

CHAPTER TWO

GAYLE SOLOMON WAS USED to answering distress calls from her youngest son. And since his pleas for help invariably involved her darling Meggie, she felt she had to heed them. She *wanted* to heed them.

She was used to coming into Sam's house and making herself right at home—if one could make oneself at home in such a stark, cold atmosphere. And why her son favored so much black was an inconsistent mystery. Couldn't the man at least get some green plants?

In his work Sam favored color, lots of it. Persian blue and misty mauve and hot tangerine. He restored Victorian houses in lavish colors, calling them "painted ladies." The interiors he designed always felt rich, cozy and golden. But in his own home it was unrelenting black. Black, black and more black. Black leather couches. Black granite kitchen counters. Even a black shower curtain upstairs. Sam's home looked as stripped and clinical as a dentist's office.

Gayle sighed. What her son needed was a wife. Sometimes she wondered if Sam would ever really get his act together. He worked too much, for one thing. Tonight he looked exceptionally frazzled, exceptionally tired.

She watched him as he trudged down the open stairs into the kitchen, one loose-hipped step at a time, removing his tie.

Sam was an undeniably handsome man. Beautiful, in fact. Although that was a word she would never use aloud to describe any of her very masculine sons. The Solomon Sons. All gorgeous, but Sam had indeed been the most beautiful of all her children except, of course, for— She forced herself to smile up at Sam, focusing her love and attention on him.

Of all her sons, Sam was the most like her late husband, Edward, which had made the constant father and son friction all the more troubling and confusing. She watched as he ran his long fingers through his hair, a habit from childhood that, for Sam, could signal anything from frustration to shyness to happy excitement. The full head of curly white-blond hair from his childhood had deepened to a burnished gold with rich taupe undertones. He wore his hair in a casual lionlike mane, curling behind his ears, touching his collar, stubbornly raked straight back from his brow and temples, an occasional lock falling forward.

At thirty-one, he already had telltale sprigs of gray lacing his sideburns, though his body was still athletically honed and his face had only grown more handsome as he reached full manhood. His forehead was broad, his nose straight, his jaw square, and his deep-set dark blue eyes were as compelling as a midnight sky.

"She's finally asleep." He slumped when he got to the last step.

"Have you eaten?" Gayle asked.

"Only the finger food we served to the investors."

"I'll make you a sandwich," Gayle said, turning toward his kitchen.

"I can make it myself," he said as he followed her. "Mom? Do you remember that woman—the one the Barretts used for child care before their kids were old enough for school? You know, that older lady? The one you got to take care of Meggie a couple of times for me on Saturday nights? Mrs. Waddle?"

"Cloretta?"

"Yeah. I wonder if she's available now?"

Gayle turned to him with a look of horror. "You aren't considering Cloretta Waddle as a possible full-time caretaker for Meggie?"

"Why not? Bob Barrett always talked about how efficient she was. He said she was clean. Sensible. I think he even told me the woman used to be a nurse."

"That woman used to be a Panzer tank," Gayle practically shouted, "and just because she's strapped an apron around her middle that doesn't mean she can take care of my grandchild on a daily basis!"

"Shh. You'll wake Meggie."

"Sorry. But you listen—" Gayle hissed, grabbing Sam's arm and hauling him around the corner into the kitchen as if he were still five years old. She flipped on every last one of the recessed lights. Sam knew his mother hated his dark, sleek kitchen. But he liked the shimmering stainless steel, the professional chef-style gas stove, the massive nickel fixtures.

Gayle whirled to face him. "Cloretta Waddle ran

the Barrett household like an absolute drill sergeant. You cannot possibly be serious about bringing her into your home.''

Gayle watched as Sam rammed his fingers through his thick blond hair again. His frustration level was definitely peaking. Putting Meggie to bed could try anyone's patience, but it was this whole situation that was killing him. In the twenty-four hours since he'd found out Andrea was ill, he'd probably repeated that gesture so often that it was a miracle he wasn't bald.

He flipped off several of the lights, then jerked open his massive side-by-side—black, naturally—built-in refrigerator and started pulling out shaved ham, cheese, mustard. ''As I recall, Bob Barrett told me that Mrs. Waddle is a licensed practical nurse who is trained to care for children.''

''Trained to care for children is one thing. Doing it kindly is quite another.''

He turned to his mother, his rugged features, highlighted by the cold light from the refrigerator, looking older than his years. ''Mom, look. I can't exactly be picky here. Meggie is upstairs right now—'' he pointed at the kitchen stairs ''—and just getting her tucked in wore me out. I have got to have somebody here—tomorrow. The investors are in town. Men like Mr. Yoshida do not understand the concept of a family crisis, and they do not like to be ignored.''

Gayle's heart clutched at the worry and sadness etched in her son's face. He had withstood so much. *Lord, when will it end?* ''Don't worry,'' she assured him. ''*I* will keep Meggie tomorrow.''

"And what about the next day? And the next? Andrea is going to be sick for a long time and you can't stay away from your work forever. Now, let's think. How can we find out if this Cloretta Waddle is still around Tulsa?"

Gayle took the sandwich things from him and placed them on the center island. "We simply must find a better solution." She tried to keep her tone from sounding overbearing, but she knew how her son tended to act in a crisis. Just like his father. Efficient to the point of ruthlessness. And sometimes that efficiency vanquished things of greater importance—like Meggie's contentment and happiness, for example. Putting Meggie in the hands of Cloretta Waddle would be like putting a wild bunny rabbit in the hands of an ape. "Sam, that woman is not an appropriate match for a sensitive child like Meggie."

"Then exactly what do you suggest?"

"I told you, I will keep Meggie myself." She found a knife in a militarily neat utensil drawer.

Sam sighed. They had tried this arrangement before on one of Meggie's summer visits. His mother had raised four rowdy sons almost single-handedly while his father had been off building his legal dynasty. Sam, being the youngest of the Solomon sons, felt the most strongly that his mother deserved some peace and quiet—or at least the luxury of pursuing her own interests for once in her life. It bugged him that he was the one who seemed to call on her for help the most often. His brothers and their wives were all too involved in their high-powered careers to help with

Meggie. His mom seemed like the only one in the family who had time for Meggie and her problems. Yet, every time Gayle took over with Meggie, Sam ended fighting a roaring case of the guilts.

"Mom, are you telling me that you are going to drive across town to my house at the crack of dawn every weekday, then haul Meggie around to school and her therapy and her various activities in your minivan?"

"Absolutely." Gayle calmly spread mustard on two slices of bread.

Sam threw up his hands, then planted them on his belt. "And then I suppose you'll go home and somehow find the energy to pursue your photography, which, I'd like to remind you, is going rather well these days."

"Oh, poo." Gayle flapped her palm at him. "Let's be honest. My photography is merely a hobby."

"You've been winning awards, selling some stuff at art fairs. And what about your trip to Belize?"

"My photography is not going so well that I'd turn my helpless granddaughter over to a battle-ax like Cloretta Waddle."

"I hardly think the woman is a battle-ax." Sam rubbed his brow. But that was a lie. Three hundred pounds if she was an ounce, Cloretta sported kinky gray curls that looked rubberized, wore hideous flowered polyester pantsuits and size-twelve white nursing oxfords. She topped it all with a perpetual scowl. Okay. So what if Cloretta was a bit of a stereotypical battle-ax nanny? ‘‘It wouldn’t hurt Meggie to come under a firm disciplinary hand for once.’’

‘‘Oh, really? What good would that do? Discipline or not, Meggie is always going to be age three, mentally.’’

‘‘But she doesn’t have to be a bratty, unmanagable age three,’’ Sam argued. He had long worried about the fact that Andrea spoiled their child to pieces, but he felt powerless to change that when he only had Meggie for short visits three times a year. But now, for the foreseeable future, their little terror Meggie was going to be his sole responsibility. He didn’t exactly have a ton of options here. ‘‘I’m calling Bob Barrett.’’

Gayle stopped making the sandwich and clapped her hands once. ‘‘Wait! I know who we need!’’ She darted in front of Sam on his way to the built-in kitchen desk. ‘‘Christy Lane! Do you have a phone book?’’

‘‘Who?’’ Sam followed his mother as she turned and charged to the desk. The name Christy Lane had a familiar ring.

‘‘The Pearsons’ nanny. That child is delightful! Very creative. Does origami and stuff like that with the Pearson children. Why, she actually gives those kids piano lessons.’’

‘‘Mom, Meggie doesn’t need piano lessons and origami. She needs constant management and close supervision.’’

‘‘Meggie has the right to have fun just like any other child. And from what I hear, Christy Lane is an absolute bundle of fun. Lou said she is adorable.'' Gayle was rapidly opening and closing cabinet doors above the desk.

''Lou who?'' Sam said.

''Trustworthy. Kind. Talented. Lou can't say enough good things about her. The girl is a regular Mary Poppins.''

Finding Sam's cupboards predictably bare, Gayle started opening the desk drawers. ''Where on earth do you keep the phone books in this house?''

Sam wondered how his mother knew so much about this Christy Lane woman. ''If this nanny is so special, won't the Pearsons be determined to keep her?''

''Oh, for heaven's sake. The Pearsons don't actually *need* a nanny. All Amy Pearson does is shop. Ah-ha!'' She pulled a Tulsa telephone directory out of a drawer.

''I swear, every time I pass through Dillard's at Utica Square, there's good old Amy,'' Gayle muttered as she flipped the pages of the phone book. ''Pawing through a sale table or examining some ridiculous little purse as if it were an archeological find. It wouldn't hurt that woman to stay home with her children once in a while. And I saw Christy running a register at Wal-Mart the other day, so I'm thinking the Pearsons probably don't employ her full-time. I'm sure she'd much rather work for *you.*''

Again, Sam wondered how his mother could possibly know what Christy Lane would rather do. ''Mom—'' he slapped his palm onto the open phone book "—I refuse to hire somebody else's nanny right out from under them."

"This—" Gayle yanked the phone book out, jerking Sam off balance "—is a family emergency. Besides, I'm not calling Christy Lane. I'm calling Lou Allen—" She flipped the phone book open.

"Lou who?" Sam asked again.

"Lou Allen. Amy's mother? I'll talk to Lou and then she'll talk to Amy and then Amy will talk to Christy. It's how these things get done—with a little finesse. Before I'm through with them, the Pearsons will feel like they've done a great kindness for us." She glanced at his skeptical frown, then started punching numbers into the phone. "Sam. Your situation is dire, even if it is—" She paused with her finger above the phone and gave Sam's face a searching look. "This *is* only temporary. Isn't it?"

Sam didn't know what to say. The thought that it might not be temporary had snaked across his mind, but he'd banished it. Andrea would get well. Andrea *had* to get well. She would get well and they would all return to their former lives—patched together and painful as those lives sometimes were.

How he longed at this moment for his former imperfect, sometimes hectic life. Drumming up enough projects and contracts to keep a business with twenty employees thriving. Keeping track of a handicapped daughter who lived all the way across the country. Staying at the office until the wee hours to finish the drafting on a project. Sometimes he got lonely, but now that his imperfect life was about to be torn to pieces, he decided it hadn't been so bad, after all. He could visit the remote building sites whenever the mood struck. He could indulge in late-night dinners and drinks at the Polo Grill with his buddies. He never had any trouble arranging the occasional date with an attractive young woman. But now…now his solitary life was about to become totally disrupted. His mother's meddling couldn't possibly make it any worse.

"Okay," he said, caving in, "call your friend Lou and ask her to see if Amy Pearson might be able to loan me this Christy Lane woman for a while. Let's say just for the summer."

"Yes. We can make it through the holiday weekend on our own." Gayle Solomon was already punching in the final numbers. "And then Christy can start next week."

CHRISTY LANE SMILED AT THE next customer. Smile. Smile. Smile. It's a good thing she had perfected that little habit. The average patron at Wal-Mart seemed to be in sore need of a smiling face. Especially on a Memorial Day weekend when the crowds were crazy.

This next guy was a fat old sourpuss who whomped a very corroded battery onto the conveyor belt beside the shiny new one he obviously intended to buy. "I'll want the battery deposit refund," he announced to the whole store. "You got any idea how to do that?"

"Sorry. You'll need to stand in our special battery-deposit-refund line on the other side of the store for that."

His face shot red and his fat lips dropped open, ready to spew out a diatribe, no doubt, about how he'd already been standing in line for half an hour, or whatever. But quick as a flash, Christy tapped his rough hand with her pen. "Just kidding." She winked. "Five bucks, coming right up."

If her smile didn't work, a little touch usually did. The old sourpuss grinned, visibly relaxed.

A little girl in the line started whining about needing to go to the bathroom, so Christy punched the necessary keys lightning fast. "Here you go." She dismissed Mr. Sourpuss with his receipt, the refund and another quick smile.

Christy treated every customer special. Every customer got her full attention. Her friendly, laid-back style was deceptive. Christy's line actually moved faster than the other checkers'.

The next lady, a slender, petite woman with stylishly bobbed graying hair, smiled and said hi. Christy could sum people up pretty fast, and this one was not your typical Wal-Mart maven. She wore an expensive-looking gray silk outfit with a tiny black alligator shoulder bag strapped across her chest. She was buying a bunch of kiddie stuff, and while Christy ran the items over the scanner, the woman leaned forward confidentially. In a strange, low voice she said, "Christy?"

Christy glanced up from her work with her habitual smile. Her name tag read Christina, so how did this woman know she preferred to be called Christy? "Do I know you, ma'am?"

"No, you don't," the lady said. "I'm a friend of Amy Pearson's."

"Oh!" Christy relaxed. "Yeah. Mrs. Pearson." The beep of the scanner continued rhythmically. Some little kiddo was sure getting a load of stuff. Beginner coloring books, Barney videos, musical cassettes, preschool toys. Maybe she was shopping for two kids, because there were also socks and underwear big enough for a school-age child.

The woman leaned in a little more. "I called Amy a couple of days ago, asked her to give you my number. Did she?"

"Me? No. Not that I know of. But I haven't been home enough to check my machine." Between this Wal-Mart job at night, her part-time nanny job in the daytime and writing her songs, there was little time to take care of details at her own humble apartment. Lately, Christy had been praying for a breather.

Beep. Beep.

"I'm Gayle Solomon."

Christy's hand halted and so did the beeping. *Solomon.* As in Sam Solomon? This woman, though incredibly well preserved, certainly did look old enough to be his mother. Christy took a closer look. As a matter of fact, the deep-set dark blue eyes were amazingly similar.

"Do I know you?" Christy said again, although she already knew that the answer was no. If she had ever met Sam Solomon's mother, she would have surely remembered it.

"No, you don't know me, but I believe you went to high school with my son."

Gayle Solomon decided to leave it at that. She didn't add that she'd had a soft spot in her heart for Christy Lane ever since she delivered a new coat to Christy's house on behalf of the Junior League. The beautiful, tiny blond child who had answered the door had caused Gayle's breath to catch in her throat.

"Are you the coat lady?" the child had said with the sweetest little smile.

Gayle hadn't been able to stop herself from staring. The delicate little girl before her could have been Lila's twin.

Through the years, Gayle managed to find ways to encounter Christy over and over, always from a distance, always with a strange mixture of longing and curiosity and sorrow. At the Junior League vision screening in third grade, when it was determined that Christy desperately needed eyeglasses, Gayle quietly arranged to pay for the eyewear herself. She had seen the conditions at Christy's home firsthand—there would be no money for glasses in that impoverished family of four children. Later, Gayle had come to the same conclusion about braces.

And years later, when the arts council was choosing its scholarship recipients, Gayle had squared Christy's application in front of her on her mahogany desk and reminded herself to remain strictly impartial. Then she opened the folder and stared at Christy's senior photo, at her pretty, round blue eyes, her sweet smile. She remembered thinking, *Is this what Lila might have looked like?*

Through the years, Gayle had managed to keep track of Christy's progress, and her struggles. And through the years, Gayle had kept Christy close in her heart, wishing the best for her, as if she were her godchild or something. As if she were her lost daughter.

And now here they were, face-to-face in Wal-Mart. If only Amy Pearson had cooperated and allowed Gayle to do this behind the scenes, the way she'd done everything else for Christy Lane.

The beeping started again.

"Your son? Is his name Sam?" Christy smiled her famous smile again. But she imagined it looked just a touch uneasy now. She could never think about Sam Solomon without getting a little confused. She'd actually written a song about him once, to get him out of her system: "I Should Be Over You." It never sold.

"Yes. My son's name is Sam Solomon." The beeping finished and Gayle swiped her card to pay. "Do you remember him?"

"Kinda."

"I was wondering if I could talk to you when you get off work," Gayle said while Christy finished the transaction.

"That won't be until midnight." Christy handed Gayle the charge slip to sign.

"That's okay," Gayle said while she scribbled her name. "Would you mind giving me a call then?"

Christy frowned. ''What is this about?''

''My son needs a nanny.'' The woman looked up, and Christy thought her eyes had grown sad. ''For his little girl.'' She fumbled in her slim shoulder bag.

''I'm sorry, but I'm not looking for another nanny job.'' As much as Christy loved kids, being a nanny hadn't been as undemanding as she'd imagined. Originally, she had wanted to free up her mind and her time to concentrate on her songwriting, but she'd ended up funneling all of her creativity into her little charges. For her, this mindless Wal-Mart job was a better fit.

''My granddaughter is special,'' the woman said as she withdrew a card from her purse. ''Sam will pay you very well.''

To Christy's astonishment, the woman snapped the business card onto the counter along with the signed charge slip. Christy separated the receipts, then picked up the card, examining it. It had unusual angular lettering slashed across thick gray paper.

The center read:

Solomon Architectural Masterpieces
Samuel Solomon, AIA, Restoration Architect

''I'm staying at my son's house,'' Gayle Solomon explained. ''Call the number in the right-hand corner. It forwards automatically.''

The customer in line behind Mrs. Solomon shoved her goods toward the register with an impatient scowl. Christy smiled apologetically at the woman, remembering that the little child with her needed to go to the rest room. She started scanning the stuff as fast as she could.

"Okay," she said as she worked, "I'll call you." Mrs. Solomon picked up her plastic bag, bulging with kids' stuff, and they smiled at each other one last time.

Later Christy slipped the card into the pocket of her blue Wal-Mart vest. Life was so weird, she thought. Who would ever imagine that she'd be standing here, minding her own business, scanning stuff at Wal-Mart, and suddenly Sam Solomon's mother would appear and say "Call me."

Sam Solomon, the blond Adonis that Christy had fantasized about all through high school. Christy hadn't thought about him in a long time. Well, at least she'd tried not to think about him. Christy had heard, somewhere, that Sam had gotten some sorority girl pregnant and they ended up married. End of fantasy.

But Sam Solomon remained stubbornly imbedded in Christy's heart, in her dreams. And if she was honest, she'd have to admit that over the years he had become the haunting benchmark for all other men. And now she was going to work for him?

CHAPTER THREE

CHRISTY SURVEYED THE STARK interior of Sam Solomon's home with a mixture of dread and awe. She was actually going to be Sam Solomon's nanny, in Sam Solomon's house.

She wasn't exactly sure how that had happened, except that Mrs. Solomon—Gayle, the woman kept insisting—had been very persuasive. She had shown Christy pictures of Sam's beautiful daughter, and Christy had recognized Sam in the child's wide blue eyes. And then when the grandmother had told Christy about the child's disabilities, about the fact that this darling child's mother was gravely ill, Christy's heart had melted.

So, here she was.

The outside of the arts-and-craft-style house in this historic Tulsa neighborhood had actually looked inviting. But the inside…

Mrs. Solomon had gone upstairs to get the child, Meggie, and so Christy took a moment to explore the surroundings before they got down to business.

Her mama always said you could tell if a person was happy or not by looking at their home. And from the looks of this place, Sam Solomon was not a happy man. His home looked as cold as the lobby of a bank.

The more she looked, the more she wondered if she'd made a huge mistake. What kind of man lived in such a home? Uptight? Austere? Controlling? Cold?

So much black. So much black that even the banks of bare mullioned windows failed to brighten the place. Even the floor where she stood was painted black. Everything seemed dark, shiny…slick. The man actually had an entire wall of his foyer covered in smoky mirrors.

But Christy was adaptable, she had proved that. Flexible. Creative. Sunny and positive under any circumstances. The fact that her new charge had been brain-damaged at birth did not deter Christy in the least. But *this house*…that was another story.

A little girl was living here? Already Christy was formulating plans to get the child out of this place as much as possible.

She peeked around the corner into the living room. It was spacious, airy. Really high ceilings. At least the walls in here were painted off-white. But still, starkness prevailed. Black marble fireplace. Black leather couch. A big old painting with slashes of hot red, yellow and lavender in birdlike shapes. As her eyes traveled over it, she realized the thing spoke to her on some level. She supposed she could live peaceably with the painting, at least. She really liked art.

Oh.

Oh, my.

In an alcove of windows draped in gray velvet

gleamed the most gorgeous black-lacquer grand piano Christy had ever seen.

She went to the keyboard as if drawn forth in a Sleeping Beauty-like trance.

She slid onto the bench and plucked a few keys with her delicate fingers. The notes resonated, perfectly tuned, like sounds from heaven. Magnificent! This piano would surely be her salvation in this bleak house. Impulsively, she drifted into a few bars from Chopin's Nocturne in E-flat major. Then she cut loose, momentarily filling the barren room with trilling sounds of magical notes.

''Hello,'' a man's voice called above the music.

She swiveled her head with her fingertips guiltily poised on the keys. ''Hi,'' she said, a little breathless. He'd startled her.

''You must be Christy Lane,'' he said as she straightened and stood. ''Mother said that you play.''

Christy examined the man—a tall, blond man with Nordic good looks—leaning against the doorjamb with his arms crossed over his chest. He wore tasseled loafers and a smooth black mock turtleneck tucked into sharply creased chinos. Were it not for his wild mane of caramel-and-cream hair, his appearance would be as stark and forbidding as his house.

''Or did I see that on your résumé?'' He slipped on a pair of wire-rimmed spectacles and perused the piece of paper in his hand.

He was still in great shape, but it was a surprise to see Sam the Athlete in reading glasses. She supposed since he was an architect he spent a lot of time at the computer.

"I love music," she said. "This is a wonderful piano. Do you play?"

"No. I got a good deal on it and thought it looked great in the alcove."

"I hope it's okay that I tried it out." She trailed her fingers over the keyboard. She felt a little self-conscious about playing Sam Solomon's piano before she'd even been introduced to him. But his mother had said he was out of town, up at some place called Moonlight Grove. She thought about explaining herself. But the explanation would be long and complicated. She certainly couldn't tell her new employer how she had chosen to subsist in a series of undemanding jobs so that she could pour her creativity into her music. "You must be Sam Solomon."

She marched toward him with her hand stuck out. As she came closer, she suspected that he didn't remember her. It was important to make a good first impression, if, in fact, this was Sam Solomon's first impression of her. She hoped to goodness it was. She didn't enjoy being associated with her sad past.

For one protracted second he held her hand too tightly, then dropped it. "Yes. I'm Sam Solomon."

"Yes. You're Meggie's daddy."

From up the stairs a child's protesting wail curled through the house.

Christy watched Sam Solomon wince and run his fingers through that thick chamois-colored hair and thought, *This man looks stressed.*

Hmm.

''Sounds like Meggie's having a bad day,'' he said. ''She didn't want to come to Oklahoma. And she didn't get to bed until very late last night.''

''I know. Your mom told me.''

''I hope you know what you're getting into, Christy—may I call you Christy?''

''Sure. Listen, Sam—may I call you Sam?—don't worry about me. I've been a nanny to some world-class brats. And I've also been a waitress, a Merry Maid, a vet's assistant and, until yesterday—'' she made a wry little grimace ''—I was a checker at the local Wal-Mart. I think I'm up to this job.''

''But do you have any experience with mentally challenged children?''

The wailing broke into one long, eardrum-piercing shriek. Miss Meggie was apparently giving her granny hell.

''No. But there are worse things. And I like to think I'm patient and that I am very intuitive about how to handle people.'' The shrieking upstairs stopped abruptly. ''And, Mr. Solomon? Sam?'' She smiled at him. ''I love kids, even the kind that scream at you.''

Gayle Solomon burst into the room then, looking careworn and surprised to see her son. ''Sam! What are you doing here?''

''I live here.''

Mrs. Solomon gave him an irked look. ''You know what I mean. I thought you went out to Moonlight Grove.''

"I just popped in for lunch. I wanted to see how the new nanny was working out."

Mrs. Solomon raked her silver hair back with the exact same gesture her son had used. Christy wondered if either one was aware of the similarity. With her fingers still in her hair, the woman shot an apologetic glance at Christy. "Yes. Well, I'm afraid we haven't even gotten acquainted yet. Christy just got here."

"We introduced ourselves," Sam said.

"And I've already played a little Chopin for him," Christy added brightly. She smiled at her little joke. But neither of the Solomons did. *Oh, boy.* This family was going to be so much fun.

"Meggie won't come downstairs." Gayle Solomon remained tense as she explained the situation to Sam. "Sometimes, with Meggie," she explained, turning toward Christy, trying belatedly to compose her face in a smile, "patience is required. Sometimes it's better to just let her decide things for herself."

Christy seriously doubted that. Easier, maybe, but not better. Behind his mother, she saw Sam Solomon roll his eyes.

"Why don't both of you have a seat." He indicated the couch across the room. Then he disappeared into the foyer. He returned carrying a briefcase.

They settled onto the leather furniture—Mrs. Solomon sinking into an overstuffed armchair, leaving Sam and Christy to position themselves uneasily, side by side, on the low couch.

Sam reached into the briefcase and pulled out some

papers, then he reached in front of Christy to lay them on the glass-topped coffee table. When his shoulder came near hers she felt a wave of attraction. In high school, they had never gotten this close except for that one time when they'd bumped shoulder to chest between class periods. The hallways of Central High were so overcrowded that no one ever excused themselves in the jostling. Except Sam. He'd looked straight into Christy's eyes and said, "'Scuse me." She had felt the impact of that incident for days. Now the memory came over her like a spell. He even smelled the same. Overwhelmingly clean and fresh and strongly masculine.

She forced herself to concentrate on the papers. Before her was an actual contract. He was thorough, she'd give him that. After they agreed on the terms and signed the thing, Mrs. Solomon scurried into the kitchen to make lunch.

"You realize I have hired you to take over for my mother," Sam explained after his mother was gone. "Which won't be easy. Mom's a dynamo who'd rather do things herself than turn matters over to somebody else. She's already made arrangements to continue Meggie's speech therapy here in Tulsa." He raised an eyebrow, skewering Christy with an assessing blue-eyed gaze. "She's also a hoverer."

"I suppose that's natural when you have a granddaughter with disabilities."

"Yeah. Well. My mom was a control freak long before Meggie arrived. The truth is, my daughter can be a holy terror. So much so that hardly anyone can stand to be around her.''

Christy wondered if that included the child's own father. ''How sad.'' She did not make a habit of glossing over the truth. And if what Sam Solomon had just said was true, it was, indeed, sad. There was no other word for it.

''I take it you haven't met my daughter yet.''

Christy smiled and she shook her head. ''No, but I've heard her.''

Again, he didn't smile.

Goodness. Maybe she was losing her touch.

''I'm going up to try to reason with Meggie now. Want to come?''

''Sure.''

AS SOON AS THEY OPENED THE door of a sunny upstairs bedroom, Christy sensed that here was big trouble. The child, who was jumping in the middle of her rumpled bed, leapt off of it and into her father's arms, almost knocking the big man over.

''Dad-dee,'' she whined as he hitched her up over his hip, ''I don't want no nandy!'' She glared at Christy, who stood a discreet distance away, just inside the doorway.

''Now, Meggie,'' Sam chided. ''Christy seems nice.''

Christy smiled, opened her mouth to introduce herself, but the child shrieked, ''I don't *want* that nandy!'' From behind a wavy fringe of bangs, she skewered Christy with intense navy-blue eyes. A dominant Solomon trait, Christy decided.

Sam chastised his daughter again. ''Meggie!''

''It's okay, Sam,'' Christy said mildly. ''Is this your new room, Meggie?'' She stepped inside.

Though the underlying decor was minimalist like the rest of the house—mullioned windows with white plantation shutters covering them, black lacquered floor, mission furniture—the childish debris made it look as if a tornado had just passed through. And the child in Sam Solomon's arms looked as if she had been at the center of that storm.

She was lanky, painfully thin, actually, still wearing rumpled pajamas at noon, and her wild, frizzy blond hair was tangled and matted. She buried her head under her father's chin and continued to regard Christy with an openly hostile stare.

Christy stepped farther into the room and bent to pick up a stuffed brown bear that had all the threadbare markings of being loved to pieces.

''Who's this?'' She raised her eyebrows at Meggie.

''Mr. Bear,'' Meggie answered uncertainly.

''Mr. Bear—'' Christy regarded the impassive stitched face ''—did you make a mess of this room?''

Meggie giggled.

Sam Solomon looked mildly astonished.

Watching Christy's eyes as she took in the child's face, then her hair, Sam said, ''Meggie, let Daddy brush your hair so we can all go down and have a nice lunch now.''

''No!'' Meggie screamed, and struck her father's

shoulder with her skinny fist. "I don't wanna comb my hair."

"Meggie, stop that." Sam clutched her thin little fingers. "You may not hit Daddy."

"No!" Meggie repeated, and pummeled his shoulder with three more thumps. "I don't wanna eat no yucky old lunch. I want IckDonald's."

Christy only smiled. "Ooh," she cooed in a soft, low voice as she sidled farther into the room. "I *love* McDonald's. Big Macs and chicken nuggets and ooey, gooey sundaes."

"Me, too!" Meggie reared back from her father, suddenly distracted. With obvious relief, he dropped his daughter to her feet. "And fench fies." The child's eyes lit up as she walked toward Christy and stuck her thumb into her mouth with an expectant look.

Christy reached out and smoothed back the child's untidy hair, then gently withdrew the little thumb. At her touch the poor little baby actually blinked in surprise, then, predictably, became as docile as a kitten. Christy, who loved to calm people with her touch, tucked a strand of hair behind Meggie's ear.

"Well, then," Christy crooned as she stroked Meggie's hair back, "maybe we can have McDonald's for supper...to celebrate my first day with you in your house."

At first Meggie only nodded docilely, but then her eyes snapped and she jerked away. "This ain't *not* my house."

Christy could fully understand the child's resistance to calling this sterile black box ''home.'' Why hadn't the father done more to make this vulnerable child comfortable? But it was too late—or perhaps too soon—to change that now, and Christy had her ways of smoothing over unpleasant things that couldn't be helped.

''So. McDonald's for dinner. Would that be okay?'' Christy addressed the question to Sam, who didn't answer immediately because he was staring at Meggie, who was now actually leaning toward Christy. ''I guess so,'' he said absently. ''Sure.''

''All right. Now.'' Using a light touch, Christy fanned out Meggie's tangled hair. ''Let's brush your hair until it's all pretty and then get dressed in something nice so we can see what kind of delicious surprise Nonnie has fixed for our lunch. I'm starving!''

''Me, too!'' Meggie echoed.

''Okay. Then let's find your brush.''

Again, Sam stared at his daughter as she lurched around the room, searching high and low in the mess. Then he stared at this strange new person that had invaded his home like a pixie sprinkling fairy dust. She was bent at the waist, peeking under the bedskirt. Her shapeless clothes did little to disguise her curvy figure.

When he had paused in the doorway downstairs, listening to the music, studying the tiny woman perched at his piano playing with such expert energy, he had experienced a moment of disorientation. Watching her now, he realized he should never have trusted his mother's judgment. He should have called

Bob Barrett and tracked down the dependable, matronly Mrs. Waddle on his own. This little imp of a woman before him was so beautiful that she could have passed for a model, except—his gaze traveled down over her garish outfit—she was dressed like a...well, there was no other word for it...like a clown.

Her masses of curly light-blond hair were smashed under a wide, hot-pink polka-dot scarf, which was tied behind one ear in a big floppy bow. She wore a long, flowered skirt with a baggy denim shirt atop it, buttoned—strangely—right up to her neck. The shirt was cinched at the waist with another scarf, this one actually decorated with fringe and sequins. Striped socks peeked out over ankle-high red boots. The overall effect was definitely of a clown, perhaps a slightly demented one, recently escaped from the circus.

But when Sam had taken Christy Lane's hand and looked into her impossibly blue eyes, he had experienced the most amazing sensation. An electric thrill, as they say. No, it was much more than that. He felt an unmistakable lightness somewhere in the vicinity of his chest. At the same time, he had been seized by a sudden urge to hold tight to that tiny warm hand.

Weird. He'd never felt anything quite like it.

"I can't fine it!" Meggie whined, ready to give up.

"Let's keep looking," the nanny said. "Nonnie's waiting."

How had this woman already discovered that Meggie called his mother Nonnie? It was the kind of small detail that mattered, that would win over Meggie's childish heart—that apparently already had. As he squinted at Christy Lane's backside, he tried to figure out why she seemed so familiar. Realizing what he was doing, he cleared his throat and looked away. It didn't matter. What mattered was, in less than five minutes, this impish woman had gotten through to Meggie. Sam felt a pang of something like jealousy as Meggie called out, "I fine it, Christy!" with a note of cheery cooperation that he had never heard from his own daughter.

He watched in utter disbelief as Meggie fairly skipped across the room, retrieved her brush from the rumpled bed and proudly presented it to Christy Lane.

CHAPTER FOUR

CHRISTY'S FIRST FEW WEEKS in Sam Solomon's household flew by in a kaleidoscopic swirl of change. She had determined on the very first day that there was much to be accomplished in this odd situation. She had gone home and made an extensive list on a large yellow legal pad. Each day she hauled the pad around with her and took delight in scratching items off.

-Give Meggie a thorough bath and grooming. (Trim her bangs?)
-Teach her to pick up her room before dinner and at bedtime.
-Straighten her closet. (Get suitcases unpacked!)
-Launder and press all her clothes.
-Get some cash from Sam in order to stock the pantry with nutritious food to entice a child.
-Establish a routine naptime for Meggie.
-Write a song especially for Meggie.

And last but not least on Christy's list:

-Have some fun.

Fun was a big priority for Christy Lane. And the Solomon household seemed to be sorely lacking in that particular commodity. In fact, it was obvious to Christy that the Solomons were so overwhelmed with the unexpected arrival of Sam's mentally challenged daughter that fun was the farthest thing from their minds.

She had learned from Gayle that Sam usually arranged not to work at all during Meggie's brief visitations. It sounded like he went into some kind of survival mode until he could ship the child back to California. Just as Christy had suspected, this was not a household that accommodated the needs of a small child easily.

But Christy loved a challenge.

By Friday of the third week, her to-do list had shrunk nicely. She was sitting at the bowed window by the dining room table, feeding Mr. Charlie, the betta fish she'd bought Meggie that day, when Sam Solomon's black Suburban pulled into the circular driveway. Meggie was upstairs, konked out. A pot of mildly seasoned spaghetti sauce simmered on the stove. Quiet classical music drifted from the CD player. Brutus lay like a warm pillow across Christy's feet. Mr. Charlie swam to the surface of his fishbowl and snagged a pellet. "What a good fishy-wishy you are," Christy cooed.

She glanced up, watching Sam climb out of his Suburban. She had seen little of the man all week. He usually left the minute she arrived at 7:00 a.m., long before Meggie was awake, and many nights he didn't get home until Meggie was in bed for the night.

Christy was determined to fix that situation, hoping that Meggie's new routine of an afternoon nap would allow her to stay up later so she could get to know her daddy.

For the last few days Christy had also been debating about whether or not to tell Sam that they went to high school together. He didn't seem to remember her at all. She got to thinking that since she had allowed three whole weeks to pass without bringing the subject up, it would seem silly, even self-conscious, to suddenly mention it now. As if it were a big deal or something. As if she expected him to remember her. And he clearly *didn't.*

Better to be cool about it. Maybe the whole thing would come out naturally at some point. Or maybe he'd remember it on his own. It was not important. What was important was Meggie.

She heard his key in the lock and said, ''Gotta go, Mr. Charlie.''

Brutus jumped up, barking like a maniac, and ran to the front door.

Christy dropped one last pellet into the fishbowl, then stood to gather her things: a giant red bag she'd made herself from one of her grandmother's old quilts, the yellow legal pad, some books and tapes she'd borrowed from the library for Meggie. Dealing with Meggie had proved a challenge, but the child was already coming around nicely. Now, if Christy could only find a way to get Meggie's daddy to spend a little more time with his daughter.

WHEN SAM ENTERED HIS FOYER, he almost tripped over that barking Brutus, then over a large paper box decorated with cut-up construction paper. "Brutus," Sam snapped, "will you kindly shut the heck up?"

The dog flipped to his back, showing Sam his belly.

The box looked like a little red choo-choo train. While he rubbed Brutus's tummy, he peered inside. Toys. One lonesome dirty sock. A torn, scribbled-on storybook. Meggie's flotsom and jetsom. Did it have to sit right here, smack in the middle of the foyer?

He spotted Christy through the double doors of the dining room. She was cramming stuff into that hideous red bag she hauled around with her. He stepped over the box, put on his glasses and started flipping through the mail as he strolled into the dining room with Brutus sniffing at his heels. "Hello," he said without looking up.

"Hi."

"What's the deal with the box in the foyer?"

"I hope you don't mind a few changes around here. I'm training Meggie to pick up her clutter before we go out. She pushes the choo-choo train around and puts her toys and so forth inside. Then we end up at the station—the foyer—and we're ready to go. It's working."

"Really?" Sam couldn't help giving the nanny an approving glance. Hers was a simple, but clever, idea. He continued to flip through the mail. "And she does this willingly?"

"She does if she knows we're going someplace

fun, like swimming, and if I tell her we can't leave until the train is in the station.''

He shot Christy a look over the rim of his reading glasses. *''Swimming?''*

''Yes. I'm teaching Meggie to swim. In your mother's pool. You should drop by some afternoon and watch her.''

''Meggie isn't coordinated enough to swim.''

''Of course she is. It's just a matter of persistence.''

''We'll talk about it later.'' He went back to checking the mail, but inside, he was battling a rising anxiety. He didn't want Meggie attempting anything dangerous or difficult. But why? Because Andrea was already in danger? That wouldn't be fair to Meggie.

Christy finished gathering her stuff. ''Well, I'm off.''

''Where is my daughter, by the way?''

''Asleep.''

He stopped sorting the mail and frowned. ''Asleep? So early?''

''It's only a short nap. I think part of the reason Meggie is cranky is because she doesn't get enough sleep. I'm trying to get her to take a short nap at the same time every day. She watches her favorite TV show when we get home from speech therapy and then she drifts off. It's working. I was thinking the two of you could have dinner together when she wakes up.''

''I see.'' He quirked an eyebrow and, without thinking about what he was doing, looked her up and down.

She tugged at her patchwork broomstick skirt and fiddled with the drawstring of a hideous red georgette peasant blouse, then raised her chin.

"Before you go, would you mind telling me—" he tilted his head at the fish bowl "—what is that?"

Christy bent down to look at an orange fish swimming around in a small, cheap glass bowl. "I think it's a man-eating shark, but I'm not sure." She grinned.

Sam frowned.

"This is Mr. Charlie." She peered into the side of the bowl, addressing the fish. "Say heh-woe to Sam, Mr. Char-wee."

"I hope you don't talk like that around Meggie."

Christy straightened and faced him, looking puzzled. Her startled, defensive expression seemed to ask if she'd said something wrong.

"Meggie's speech certainly isn't going to improve if you use baby talk around her."

Christy bent to address the fish again. "But Mr. Char-wee *is* a baby. Baby talk is the only wang-widge Mr. Char-wee understands." She glanced up, this time with a slightly defiant gleam in her eye.

Sam Solomon didn't favor her with even the hint of a smile. Meggie was his daughter, and though it was a small thing, this baby talk concerned him.

"Okay," the woman sighed. "No more baby talk. Mr. Charlie—" she bent to speak to the side of the fishbowl again "—as of this moment, we shall speak nothing but proper Queen's English in this household. Understood?"

Sam managed a wan smile. She was kind of cute. ''Christy,'' he said as he finished sorting the mail. ''I don't mean to sound ungrateful. It's nice that you bought Meggie a fish. And I also want you to know—'' he tossed the last letter onto the table ''—that I appreciate everything else you've done for my daughter these past three weeks. And you can do whatever you want with the house as long as it benefits Meggie.''

''I appreciate it that you appreciate it.'' Christy smiled, but then her expression grew serious. ''I enjoy my work.'' She dug around in her bag for her keys.

''I can see that,'' he conceded. She had done many small things to make Meggie's life better. She certainly fed the child well. She deserved to hear a compliment. He rotated his head toward the kitchen. ''Something smells good.''

''It's my secret spaghetti sauce. The pasta is cooked and drained, dressed with a little olive oil. There's a magic salad chilling in the fridge.''

''*Magic* salad?'' Maybe he should have chosen something other than her culinary skills to compliment.

''I call it magic so that kids will eat it. Orange Jell-O with carrots and cottage cheese stirred in.'' She smiled brightly again.

Carrots and cottage cheese? Sam eyed her and decided Christy Lane's smile was almost reflexive. Why did she smile so much?

''And then,'' she went on as if it mattered, ''I fold in a little Dream Whip to disguise everything. That's the—'' she made quotation marks with her fingers ''—magic part.''

Sam suppressed the urge to say, ''I'll pass.'' He sensed that he'd probably come on a little too strong about the baby talk and he didn't want to hurt this sweet young woman's feelings again. He tilted his head at her. ''Magic, huh? My mom used to call it orange-Jell-O-with-carrots-and-cottage-cheese salad. Guess that explains why I never ate the stuff. Maybe if she had called it *magic,* I would have scarfed it up.''

She smiled again, almost a laugh. A bit self-consciously, he thought. Unsure. Maybe she thought he was being sarcastic. He was actually trying to be nice. Had he become such a drudge that he'd forgotten how to just *be nice?* What was the matter with him, anyway? A mess a minute out at the Moonlight Grove site this week, that's what was wrong with him.

Still, he couldn't stand the idea of hurting this sunny young woman's feelings, even unintentionally. She had been working so hard, making amazing progress with Meggie. And managing his household in unconventional ways he hadn't counted on. He was astounded at the amount of food she'd managed to purchase with the money he'd given her. Pasta, beans, croutons, cereal, whole-wheat crackers. Three kinds of rice. Salmon, chicken, peanut butter. Flavored vinegars. Olive oil, canola oil, real butter. Tortillas and bagels. Fresh garlic, basil and cilantro. Yogurt and cheeses and fruit spreads and even a jar of carrot juice. The truly amazing thing was, Meggie apparently relished Christy's simple cooking. Her color had improved and she looked less thin lately.

Magic, indeed.

"It was nice of you to cook for her again tonight. Thank you."

CHRISTY WONDERED WHY Sam Solomon acted so amazed every time she prepared a little simple food for the evening meal. She only wanted Meggie to start eating something besides McDonald's. It wasn't as if she was trying to impress *him.* She doubted Sam Solomon had even noticed that his pantry was now well stocked.

In any case, for Christy, cooking was no trouble. Preparing a meal simply added more zest, more creativity, to her day. For her, it was as natural as breathing.

In her hand she had already singled out the key to her little Ford Contour. She clutched it between thumb and forefinger, staring down at it.

She glanced up and saw that he was frowning at her outfit again. Christy got the distinct impression that Sam Solomon did not approve of the way she dressed. She never discounted these intuitive vibes of hers. But who was Sam Solomon to judge? A man who lived in a cold black house? Sam Solomon had been an easygoing, fun guy in high school. What had happened to make him so dour?

He was still handsome. If anything, he had grown more handsome, more interesting, with the years. And every time Christy looked into Sam Solomon's deep-blue eyes, she felt like biting her lip. But she didn't. She stood there, smiling calmly like a good nanny.

He loosened his tie. "Can you stay a minute? I've been so busy the past few weeks that I haven't had time to get to know you at all. I know it's Friday night, and you've probably got plans."

"Not really. In the summer, I usually try to go for a run before the sun goes down."

"Then why don't you stay for dinner? In fact, would you join me for a little glass of wine? We can discuss Meggie's schedule."

"Uh, sure." Christy shrugged, surprised by his invitation.

As chance would have it, she didn't have a date with Kyle tonight—her boyfriend was on duty—but she couldn't imagine that a man as good-looking as Sam Solomon was content to sit here without a date on a Friday night. She supposed with Meggie around maybe he'd been forced to alter his lifestyle a bit.

He led the way into the kitchen and removed a bottle of red wine from a small wrought-iron—black, of course—wine rack. "This okay?" He held the label out for her inspection. It read pinot noir, which meant nothing to Christy.

She shrugged again. "I don't drink much wine. Anything's fine."

"Have a seat." He indicated a high black leather bar stool pushed up under the counter. He reached into a tall cabinet with glass doors and took out some crystal stemware.

She climbed onto the stool and slid her lumpy red

calico bag off her shoulder and onto her lap, gripping the thing to her front. She told herself not to act nervous. He was only being nice to the baby-sitter who had worked so hard to make his busy, high-powered architect's life a little easier these past weeks. It wasn't like he was really interested in her as a person, or anything.

"So. How was your day today?" he asked as he drove the corkscrew into the cork with brisk, muscular twists.

Sheesh, Christy thought. He hadn't bothered to ask that all week. And now, today of all days, he decides to ask how their day was. Of course, she could conceal the truth from him, gloss it over. But that wasn't Christy's style. She held firm to her policy that the parents of her charges deserved the truth about every detail of their children's daily lives. The absolute truth, the good stuff and the bad stuff, the cute and the worrisome stuff. "Uh. Well, actually we had a little...an incident."

"An incident?"

"Yeah. I took Meggie to an art showing—they had some cute black-and-white photographs of animals at the Philbrook—and...and she...well, she got upset and knocked over a small statue."

Abruptly, he stopped twisting the corkscrew. His shoulders slumped. "Oh, no. What kind of statue? Was it damaged?"

"No." Christy held up a palm in a gesture of peace. "No damage. It was a sturdy bronze."

"Even so, that must have been difficult for you."

"And for Meggie," she reminded him.

"Yes. For Meggie. Of course. I'm sorry." He sighed as his shoulders slumped even farther. "I seem to be saying I'm sorry a lot these days."

She frowned. "Why's that?"

"Long story. Things are behind schedule out at Moonlight Grove—my job site. And I haven't been able to help Andrea at all. I dunno. I just feel like I'm—tell me about Meggie. What did the museum staff say?"

"Oh. They couldn't see any damage. They even called a curator to look at it while we waited in a little office. Still, I felt we had to leave the premises right away. I didn't want that security guard following Meggie around all day."

He pulled the cork and poured some wine in each glass. "Did you explain to them that Meggie is special?"

"Of course," she answered quietly. Christy studied his movements, seeing it all so clearly. How it was, how it had always been, for Meggie's parents. Every day, she imagined, they hoped for progress, or a least a little bit of normalcy, in the life of their little girl. But every day this is what they got. It was worse than two steps forward, one step back, because it was *always* one step back. As Meggie grew physically older but remained in her limited mental state, they were continually losing ground.

"Here." He handed her a wineglass. Then he dragged the other bar stool around the bend of the counter and settled himself up on it with his muscular thighs spread wide, facing her. An undeniably masculine pose that stretched the fabric of his expensive wool trousers across his pelvis.

Christy turned squarely toward the bar and leaned forward so she wouldn't be so aware of him. She clutched her bag tighter to her middle and took a tense sip of her wine.

Sam watched her for a moment, then said, "How long do you think she'll sleep?" He jerked his head toward the stairs before sipping his wine.

"I don't know. She needs a good nap, today of all days. All in all, it was—" Christy tasted her wine "—kind of a stressful day."

"Yes, I imagine that kind of thing would wear her out." He twirled the base of his wineglass on the counter. "Poor little Meggie."

He looked so defeated that Christy felt driven by compassion, by a fierce protectiveness almost, to give him some tidbit of joy about his daughter to hold on to. "Some nice things happened today, too."

"Oh?"

"After we left the museum, we went by your mom's to pick up some more food for Brutus. Meggie perked right up when she saw him."

Sam couldn't believe his mother had given Christy Lane a key to her luxurious home only four days after he employed the woman. Then his mom had zipped off to Belize, leaving her beloved pet in Christy's care, to boot.

"Meggie certainly loves that dog." Christy smiled.

"She certainly does. Good old Brutus." He eyed

the spoiled dog, who answered Sam with a belligerent chuff.

Christy giggled, and Sam did smile then, warmly and genuinely, and Christy relaxed.

Outside, the sky was turning charcoal gray and the wind was kicking up, buffeting the tree branches outside the kitchen windows.

"It looks like it's going to storm." Sam clicked the power button on a small TV next to them on the kitchen counter and found the local weather.

Areas of the map around Tulsa were highlighted in bright orange, signaling a tornado watch.

"Is it coming this way?"

"Looks like it." Sam tapped a finger over the greenish satellite images of clouds skittering over the screen. "Maybe you shouldn't drive home just yet," he reasoned. "Man!" He snapped his fingers. "I forgot to show you the safe room."

"I found it when I was teaching Meggie how to play explore."

"Explore?"

"A game that keeps kids occupied, and teaches them how to be curious about their surroundings." Christy and Meggie had peeked inside the tiny area with a steel door and a reinforced ceiling next to the washer and dryer in a corner of the basement. There she found two plain wooden benches and some shelves that were well stocked: flashlights, bottled water, rain ponchos, a weather radio, warm clothes for Meggie. Sam Solomon was as prepared as any Boy Scout.

"Was that room already here when you bought this house?"

"No. I built it after the F-5 blew through O-K-C a few years back." He jerked a thumb toward the southwest, where the killer tornado had cleared a path through central Oklahoma. "My firm went down to the city and did some of the restoration work."

She frowned, remembering the pictures on TV and in the papers. "That must have been hard."

"Seeing devastation like that makes a believer out of you. I installed a safe room before I moved into this house. Besides, I figure it's my civic duty. No self-respecting architect would resell a house without a safe room. Bad example." He grinned.

"Are you selling this house?" Maybe, she thought, that accounted for the barren feel of the place.

"I thought I was. My plan was to remodel one old home after another—living in each one while I did the work. Then sell, make a handsome profit, and repeat the process all over again."

"But..." She supplied the word because he'd said it as though his plan was history.

"But now I've got to consider the possibility that..." He sipped his wine.

"That Meggie may be living with you permanently."

"Yeah." He winced.

Christie couldn't decide if his discomfort was because he didn't want to be a full-time dad or if he was thinking that Andrea might not survive. She hoped it was the latter.

"I suppose there's always Meggie to consider."

His eyes shadowed and he downed more wine. "Yes. Meggie."

"You expect to have Meggie past the summer?"

"Who knows?" His expression grew darker, like the clouds outside. "The truth is, I don't know how long I'll have Meggie. Her mother's pretty sick. It could…it could go badly for Andrea."

"I understand. Mrs. Solomon—Gayle—told me a little bit about it. Poor Meggie. And poor…what did you say your ex-wife's name is?"

"Andrea."

"Poor Andrea."

"Yes. Andrea's illness still seems very surreal to me, you know?"

"Has she always been healthy?"

"Well, healthy…no, that's not the word I'd use. She's always been way too thin…like Meggie. But still, you don't expect something like this."

Christy nodded. "Were the two of you married for a long time?"

"Eight years. It felt like a very long time."

"Oh?" Something in his tone sounded so sad that Christy didn't think he meant to be bitter or unkind toward his ex-wife, only honest.

"Andrea and I were like the proverbial oil and water. There's nothing worse than being married to the wrong person."

Christy absorbed this frank statement about his former marriage for a moment with accepting silence. Personally, she had made up her mind to never, ever divorce. Not after the childhood she had endured, watching her mother having to beg for every penny from her distant father. Though it was sometimes hard, especially when one of her friends got married, she had remained firm in her resolve not to settle until she found a man she could love forever. ''I have always imagined,'' she said softly, kindly, ''that being married to the wrong person would be a torment. But at least you got Meggie out of the deal.''

''Yes,'' Sam admitted, seeming glad that someone understood that he treasured his daughter despite her limitations. ''I got Meggie.''

They sipped their wine, and there passed one of those silences that sometimes follow the speaking of a profound truth.

''I've always thought where a person lives affects them in subtle ways.'' Christy decided to lighten the conversation by returning to the original topic of selling his house. ''To me, a home isn't just an investment.''

He ran a hand through his hair, and the gesture had the look of relief this time. ''I suspect you're right. Where do you live?''

''In an apartment.''

''Your résumé said you're single. I take it you've never been married?''

''No.''

''Just haven't found Mr. Right?''

''Oh, I've met my share of Mr. Rights. Just haven't found Mr. *Perfect.* I do have a boyfriend right now, in fact,'' she added, realizing she sounded almost defensive. Was it because she wanted Sam Solomon to know that she had prospects, despite her lingering crush on him? But that was silly, because Sam didn't even know about the crush.

"Oh?"

"Yes. Kyle. He's really very sweet."

"And what does Kyle do?" Sam shifted uncomfortably on his stool.

"He's a cop."

Sam grinned. "A *sweet* cop?"

"Yeah. Aren't they all?" Christy grinned back.

His eyes studied her with curiosity. "How old are you, if I may ask?"

Christy wondered if her cheeks were turning as pink as they felt. Here was the perfect moment, if ever there was one, to tell him that they'd gone to high school together. He had given no indication, over this entire three weeks of her employment, that he remembered her at all. In fact, this was the first time they'd actually sat down and talked, face-to-face.

"Oh," she evaded, "I'm old enough to have a boyfriend."

Sam chuckled despite his confused emotions. Why was he feeling this twinge of disappointment to discover that Christy Lane was attached?

He smiled to cover his discomfort, then squinted at her, studying the woman sitting across the counter from him. She was actually quite pretty, quite feminine, despite the funky clothes. She had the kind of looks that made it impossible to judge her age. Flawlessly smooth skin. Long, lush, naturally curly blond locks. A petite, curvy figure. Full. Very feminine. The more he looked at her the more he thought there was something fascinating—and something oddly familiar—about Christy Lane. He'd been with lots of pretty women since his divorce, and the truth was, they all seemed the same. But this Christy Lane...she was...absolutely unique. Her face looked flushed, and he wondered if he'd embarrassed her, prying about her boyfriend that way.

The phone on the counter trilled, defusing the charged moment.

Automatically, Christy snatched up the portable unit near her elbow. "Solomon residence," she answered with a smile in her voice, the way her mama had taught her to.

The woman's voice on the other end of the phone sounded young, but weak and weary...and maybe just a touch *wary,* too. "Hel-lo. Uh. Who is *this?*"

"This is Meggie's nanny."

"Oh." There followed the kind of stillness that indicates some small mental shift. "Of course. Then you're...Mrs. Waddle?"

"No. I'm Christy Lane."

"Oh. I see." But it sounded like she didn't. "This is Meggie's mother, Andrea Haynes Solomon. May I speak to Sam, please?"

"Yes. He's right here."

Christy handed the phone across the counter. "It's Meggie's mother."

Sam frowned, took the receiver, eased off the stool and ducked his head. "Andrea?"

Christy slid off her bar stool and crossed to a set of glass-paned garden doors that looked out over a small brick courtyard that opened onto the sloping terraced yard below.

"Yes. She's Meggie's baby-sitter," Christy heard Sam saying. "No. No, Mrs. Waddle didn't work out, remember?"

After a pause he said, "She's very good, Andrea. Very caring and creative."

Then he said, "Is it really? It's seven o'clock already? She's still sleeping. She takes a little nap before supper almost every day now. It gives me more time with her in the evenings, actually. She's still in bed by nine o'clock. Don't worry, Andrea. Meggie's fine. She's gained a little weight, actually. She's better than I've ever seen her, in fact I'll have her call you when she wakes up." He paused. "What's wrong?"

He listened for a long time.

After a while he said, "Oh, no," very softly.

After another long pause Christy heard him expel a shaky sigh. "Oh, no," he breathed. "I'm sorry. I'm...so sorry."

Christy folded her arms over her middle and stared intently at a lilac bush, heavy with blooms, slapping against the wooden fence in the brewing storm winds. She felt uncomfortable, as if she shouldn't even be hearing this strangely telegraphic half of a conversation between her employer and his ex-wife. She glanced back at Sam to see if she could catch his eye and excuse herself. But his head was bowed, and he rubbed his brow fretfully, the fingers of his large hand shading his eyes. She didn't want to interrupt such intent concentration, and she didn't feel right about leaving without saying goodbye, so she stayed put. She tried to direct her thoughts elsewhere, but her mind insisted on replaying the woman's breathy, startled tone when she had said, "Who is *this?*"

And Christy couldn't help overhearing him murmur more urgent things like "Oh, no" and "What does your other doctor think?" Obviously, something had gone wrong. Then she heard him say "Clinical trial?" questioningly, and her gut tightened with apprehension.

"Wait," he said anxiously, "I want to write this down so I can look it up on the Internet." He fished his glasses out of his pocket and wrote something on the scratch pad on the counter.

Gayle Solomon had made it clear to Christy that her former daughter-in-law's prognosis wasn't good.

"Is something wrong?" she asked Sam as soon as he hung up.

He sat staring at the phone in his hand.

"I...I mean," she stammered, afraid she'd overstepped her bounds, "is there anything I can do to help?"

Sam put the phone on the counter, stared at it another moment, then raised sorrow-filled eyes to Christy. "Do you have to leave right now? Would you stay with me? I mean, would you stay here until Meggie wakes up? Would you help me give her the bad news?"

"The bad news?" Christy echoed.

"That was Andrea—my ex-wife."

"I know." Christy's voice was almost a whisper.

"She's...she had bad news."

"What?" Christy waited.

"You are aware that she has a pretty aggressive cancer?"

"Your mother told me about it before she left for Belize."

"Well it turns out that she...the new treatment didn't work, after all."

"*What?* Why not?"

"The second round of chemotherapy they gave her apparently damaged her heart, and now the doctors don't think her heart is strong enough to withstand more, at least not now...or maybe ever. They are going to try some kind of vaccine on her."

"Oh, Sam. I'm sorry. And so what does this mean?"

"I'm afraid—" he ran his fingers through his hair in that tense gesture that Christy was becoming all too familiar with "—I'm afraid that it ultimately means that Meggie's mother probably won't live to see Meggie grow up."

CHAPTER FIVE

UPON HEARING SAM'S TERRIBLE assessment of Andrea's situation, Christy found herself frozen in place next to the garden doors. She should go to him, she thought. Comfort him somehow. Here was a man who had just gotten terrible news about his daughter's mother. He was a man who needed a caring human touch. A man who needed *her* caring touch.

But something stopped Christy from going to Sam, from gently laying a hand on his shoulder or his arm as she would any other human being in his situation. Was it because he was her employer? Or maybe it was because she felt a strong taboo about touching this particular man…maybe she'd kept her fantasies about Sam Solomon too carefully sealed away for too many years.

With his elbows braced on the counter, he took off his glasses and pinched the bridge of his nose, his face lowered. "This is a nightmare," he mumbled toward the granite counter.

Christy's heart tightened for him. She could hardly stand to see the bold and cocky Sam Solomon of her youth suffering this way, reduced to this. What must he be thinking now? Surely he'd loved Andrea once.

They'd had a child together. They'd seen that child irreparably harmed. And now this.

"Sam..." she started.

But he held up a palm. "Just give me a minute." He voice sounded as if it was about to break, as if he was on the verge of tears. He kept his head down.

Feeling helpless, Christy looked around the quiet kitchen that she had carefully put in order after Meggie went down for her nap, unable to think what to do next.

Steam from the bubbling pot of spaghetti sauce drew her eye to the stove. Thinking that more wine probably wouldn't be such a good idea right now, she decided to make him some herbal tea. She crossed the kitchen, moving gently and quietly, like a person tiptoeing around in a sick ward, because, she told herself, surely Sam Solomon was sick. Sick at heart.

Carefully, she lifted one of her aprons off a hook beside the refrigerator, slipped it over her neck, tied it behind her back and took the teakettle to the faucet to fill it.

Mama always said that a simple cup of tea was often the best medicine.

By the time she'd put the teakettle on and lit the burner, Sam had recovered his composure. He raised his head.

When she turned to face him, he made such a sad picture.

He had put his glasses back on. Behind them, his deep-set eyes, staring at the granite countertop, reflected a pain that Christy could hardly bear to witness.

"You loved her once," Christy said.

The sound of her kindly words breaking into the protracted silence caused him to blink, like a man waking from a bad dream.

He looked up, squinting at her. "Yes, but it's a lot more complicated than that."

"Do you want to tell me about it? I'm a good listener."

"I'm sure you are. But some things are just…too sad. There's no point in reliving it."

She went to the pantry and took out the tin of Tension Tamer Wellness Tea that she'd brought along with her on her second morning in the Solomon house. She placed two mugs on the counter and put the tea bag in one and a dollop of honey in the other. "Would you like some honey in yours?"

He nodded.

She squeezed honey into his mug to the side of the tea bag, poured steaming water in both mugs, then used the one bag to make two cups of tea.

"What will we tell Meggie?" she said as she dipped the bag back and forth. At least, Christy decided, she could help him problem-solve about his daughter.

"Meggie." He breathed. He stood and walked to the garden doors and looked out with his hands jammed in his pockets and his shoulders bunched with tension. "Sometimes I feel like Meggie was the beginning of everything."

Christy frowned as she offered one of the mugs to him. ''What do you mean?''

He sighed and took the tea. ''Before Meggie was born, Andrea and I thought we had the world by the tail. Even though she got pregnant, we had decided to finish college. Her dad had helped us move into a nice house. Then...'' He took a sip of his tea, but not as if he was enjoying it, or even tasting it. It was clearly a way to postpone saying something difficult.

''Then Meggie was born,'' Christy supplied.

''You can't imagine. One minute we were expecting a healthy baby girl, and the next minute the cord was strangling her, cutting off the oxygen to her brain.''

Christy closed her eyes. When she opened them, he was looking at her, no longer bothering to conceal his pain from her.

She was looking so deeply into his eyes that she was able to see a startling rim of black surrounding his blue, blue irises.

''Our marriage started to break down under the weight of that blow.''

Christy lowered her head, looking down at the tea in her mug, wondering what she could say. He had warned her it was sad.

''We were too young to understand the full impact of what had happened yet. But even then, I think Andrea felt like I ran away, buried my grief under a mountain of work, of ambition. After Meggie was born I changed my major from business to architecture. I had to have something that was meaningful to *me,* you know? Then, when Meggie was two and that bomb went off in Oklahoma City, I hurried up and got my business going and I took contract after contract, did a lot of the restoration work down there. I don't know, maybe Andrea was right. Maybe I did it just so I wouldn't have to see Meggie falling further and further behind with each developmental stage.''

Their gazes collided, then, too intense, shifted away.

Slowly, carefully, they both sipped their tea. Christy had told him she was a good listener, and she was determined to be, refusing to offer him any pat consolations, any easy answers. Refusing to gloss it over.

''And then again when that huge tornado struck,'' Sam went on, ''I gobbled up all the work I could handle. More than I could handle. I was never in Tulsa, always in Oklahoma City. I think Andrea started to think she had a lifetime of that ahead of her, being left alone with her damaged child. Finally, she went to California to be with her parents. I can see all of it so clearly now, how it happened. But back then, I told myself I was building my business, trying to be a super success so I could always take care of Meggie.''

''And now this.''

''Yes. Now this. How do you tell a virtual three-year-old that her mommy is really, really sick? That her mommy can't take care of her?''

''I think for now you keep it simple.'' Christy tried

to sound reasonable, reassuring. "I wouldn't tell her any more than she has to know right now."

Sam looked up, nodding hopefully, seeming to accept Christy's guidance with surprising trustfulness. "You're right. Meggie won't be able to go back to L.A. at the end of the month like we planned. So I'll just tell her that. I'll tell her Andrea needs to be in the hospital some more."

"Which is the truth. Do you think that would be okay with Andrea? You need to keep the lines of communication open with her so that we are all telling Meggie the same thing and your little girl doesn't get scared or confused."

He nodded solemnly, looking at Christy as if she had the wisdom of a sage.

"And I also think I'd wait a bit, Sam. If you tell Meggie tonight, she won't remember it, anyway. There is no reason for her to worry about her mother right now. She's just getting into her routine here, just learning how to have fun. She goes to her first softball practice tomorrow afternoon."

"Softball?"

"Yes. Over near Woodward Park. A summer league. With some other ten-year-old girls."

"Meggie can't play *softball,*" he said, as if they were talking about her becoming an astronaut. The admiration of a moment before had vanished from his eyes, and he was now looking at Christy as if her judgment was suspect.

"Of course Meggie can play softball. In her own way, of course. I talked to the coach—she coached the Pearson children when I kept them. She's aware of Meggie's limitations, and she agreed that the other girls will develop sensitivity and acceptance by having the opportunity to be around Meggie. I also met a couple of the mothers and they agreed to smooth the way with their daughters, educating them about the mentally challen—''

''I will *not* have my daughter hauled over to Woodward Park as some sort of lesson in compassion for a bunch of brats.''

''Sam, it's not like that. These are sweet girls. They call their team the Angels. Meggie is looking forward to participating. It will be good for her to do something physical. She needs to be with other children, to feel accepted for who she is—''

''Accepted?'' Sam stared at Christy as if she'd lost her mind, while in the distance thunder rumbled.

''Yes. Accepted. These girls are old enough to accept someone who is different. They need to be around Meggie just as much as she needs to be around them. It will teach them kindness.''

''How do you know they'll be kind? How do you know she won't end up feeling inferior?''

''She might end up understanding her limitations, but she'll have fun, anyway. I promise.''

''You can't promise any such thing! She may never understand what has happened to her—understanding her *limitations?* Meggie can't understand what *day* it is. Besides, she's not even athletic. Why does she need softball?''

''Why does *any* child need softball?'' Christy argued. Honestly, she was amazed how some parents—even educated, supposedly enlightened ones like Sam Solomon—could be so thickheaded. She recalled her struggle to make the Pearsons understand that their little boy needed to be in a transition class instead of first grade. And that child's father was a teacher!

''She has the Dayspring School,'' Sam was saying. ''She sees other kids there.''

''She is not exposed to mainstream children at Dayspring,'' Christy replied, standing her ground.

''Why in the hell does Meggie need to be in the mainstream? She is always going to be the way she is now. Andrea and I have accepted that for ten years now. And then you come along and suddenly she's got to sing songs and make art and play softball and learn to swim, for crying out loud.''

''Dad-dee! Stop yelling at Chrissie!'' It was Meggie, standing at the top of the kitchen stairs. Apparently their heated argument had awakened her.

''He wasn't yelling at me, honey.'' Christy rushed to the foot of the stairs, suddenly feeling as if she'd only made this family's dire problems worse instead of helping them as she wished to. Maybe she was pushing too hard. She had a bad habit of doing that—always seeing ways for people to be happier or healthier and then urging them to get with the program. *Her* program. Sometimes she needed to remember that everybody didn't think the way she did. Sometimes people just needed to feel safe. Especially when a family was facing a life-threatening illness and all the sad upheaval that came with it. ''We were only having a discussion…trying to figure out something important.''

''What's 'portant?''

''It means—'' Sam stepped up beside Christy ''—stuff we have to do now. Just some stuff we have to figure out before tomorrow, honey.''

''Oh.'' Meggie accepted his answer, then whined, ''Chrissie, I *hungry.*''

''I made spaghetti,'' Christy said brightly as she crossed to the stove. ''Why don't you and Daddy go wash your hands while I get the spaghetti dished up and the table set.''

''I gots strawberry soap in my baffroom!'' Meggie cried, and tugged at Sam's hand.

Over the child's head, Sam gave Christy a warning look that clearly telegraphed his intention to take up the topic of softball later, then he lumbered up the stairs behind Meggie. ''Strawberry soap, huh?'' Christy heard him say as he followed her.

Christy had no idea what went on while they were washing their hands upstairs. Meggie had a tendency to get a little carried away, making a mess with the scented soap they'd bought at Wal-Mart. She hoped Sam was being patient and gentle, yet firm. That approach was what the child responded to best. No, what Meggie responded to best was just plain *love,* and plenty of it.

Christy hurried around and did her best to set a cheerful table. She had scrounged up some brightly colored, mismatched paper party napkins at her house and she used these instead of Sam's elegant linen ones. She found Mr. Bear facedown on the living room couch and made a booster seat out of phone books and seated him in the fourth chair at the round kitchen table. She put some fresh pellets of food in Brutus's dog dish and moved it into the dining room. This was going to feel like a real family meal for Meggie, and she didn't care if Sam Solomon approved of her efforts or not. She even lit a small votive candle and placed it beside Sam's black salt-and-pepper shakers.

When they came back down the stairs Sam eyed her handiwork but said nothing.

Meggie spotted Mr. Bear and clamped her hands over her mouth in glee.

"Mr. Bear's ready for his dinner." Christy raised her eyebrows. "Now you hop up in your chair and get ready, too."

Meggie skipped to her seat.

Not for the first time since Christy had begun managing Meggie, a faintly astonished look passed over Sam's face, as if he couldn't believe his child was behaving herself. Christy turned toward the stove to hide her little smile. She was good with kids, she knew that. And she *would* find a way for Meggie to play softball. In her heart, she *knew* it was the right thing for the child. She just *knew.* After all, Meggie was doing quite well at swimming.

Just as Christy was covering the noodles with sauce, a huge flash of lightning strobed outside the garden doors. Christie glanced out at the terrace. The sky had taken on an unnatural darkness.

"Better check the weather again," Sam said, and looked at the small TV on the bar. He retrieved the remote and put it beside his plate.

A sitcom was on, but the map in the corner of the screen showed a tornado watch for Tulsa County.

"Looks like we might be in for some pretty severe weather tonight." Sam frowned at the image.

"Let's go ahead and eat, then." Christy fanned a palm toward the table.

"How was your day, Meggie?" Sam asked pleasantly as they passed around the garlic bread.

"Find."

"Fine," Sam corrected, emphasizing the *n*.

"Fine." Meggie glanced at Christy for reassurance.

"Tell Daddy where we went."

"We goed to a…a museum."

Christy smiled as she served up the salad. "And we saw some pretty pictures, didn't we?"

"Yeth."

"Did you have fun?" Sam raised his iced tea to his lips.

"Yeth. Until I peed my pants."

Sam nearly choked on his tea. He swallowed with an effort and shot Christy an accusing look for not telling him this little detail.

Christy smiled at him self-consciously and filled another salad bowl.

"When did that happen?" He dotted his lips with his napkin.

"After I knocked over that cowboy," Meggie said.

"The statue," Christy supplied.

"You didn't tell me she had an accident." Sam focused his intense blue eyes on Christy.

"It didn't seem that important."

"Is that why you left the museum so quickly?"

"Partly. And I told you. The security guard was being rather…judgmental about the whole thing. He made me uncomfortable."

"He was *mean,* Daddy. I peed my pants 'cause I was a-scared of him!"

Getting overexcited now, Meggie was talking with her mouth full again, but at least it was full of a healthy salad, Christy thought, congratulating herself on the progress she'd made with Meggie's diet. "But it all turned out okay, didn't it, Meggie?" she soothed. "We left and it was all okay. Remember? Now, don't talk with your mouth full, sweetheart."

"Okay." Meggie calmed down and swallowed. "It was okay," she said, echoing Christy's words to Sam.

Christy looked at Sam and saw that the muscles in his jaw were bunching into tight knots.

"You didn't happen to get that security guard's name, did you?" he asked quietly, then speared a hunk of salad as if he were trying to kill it.

"No."

"No?"

"No, Sam. I didn't. It's not important. The whole thing is over now."

"A 'mean' guard intimidates a preschool-level child? I hardly think that this is over."

"He had no way of knowing anything about Meggie," Christy reasoned, weighing her words carefully so that she didn't say anything to hurt Meggie's feelings. "As far as he was concerned he was dealing with a ten-year-old—"

"I *am* ten!" Meggie protested.

Christy shot her a smile and continued mildly. "The man was only doing his job. He was watching me, actually, because I did not watch Meggie."

"I was bein' good!" Meggie defended herself further.

"Yes, you were being good, sweetheart." Christy patted the child's hand. "You just didn't see that statue." She looked at Sam, widening her eyes in warning. "It was all an *accident,* and now it's over. So could we please drop it and have a nice dinner?"

"Fine," Sam said.

"Find," Meggie echoed. "I mean, *fine,*" she corrected herself.

Over the child's head, Christy smiled indulgently. Surely Sam Solomon could see what a precious child he had here. Couldn't he?

But Sam only gave Christy a tight smile as if to say, *We'll discuss this later.* The list of things to discuss later was getting longer and longer.

They ate in uneasy silence for a while, with Sam keeping an eye on the muted TV screen. When loud raindrops started to pock the skylight above the sink, he snatched up the remote and raised the volume.

The piercing *beep-beep-beep* of the National Weather Service Alert filled the room. At the sound, Meggie's eyes got huge. Coming from California, the child was not used to the alarming sound of severe-weather warnings. "What's dat?" she asked.

Sam shushed her sharply and Christy raised a finger to her lips and squeezed the child's hand. "Daddy and I must listen," she whispered.

"We have a wall cloud with a massive rotation," the intense young meteorologist was saying, "traveling extremely fast in a north-northeasterly direction from the vicinity of Okmulgee...."

On the screen the computer images grew more detailed as a map zoomed in with a large flashing green arrow showing that the developing twister would reach the Tulsa area in less than fifteen minutes. "All persons in the path of this dangerous storm are advised to seek shelter below ground immediately...." The map was replaced by a head shot of the meteorologist giving people instructions about how to save themselves.

Sam and Christy had heard the instructions all their lives. Without hesitating, they turned to each other.

"The weather radio and flashlights are already down there," Sam said.

"Water?"

"Yes."

"Cell phone?"

He patted his trouser pocket. "Got it."

"First aid kit?"

"Downstairs."

"Jackets? Pillows and blankets?"

"No. Better get some."

As she started up the stairs Sam grabbed Christy's

wrist and pulled her back to him. "Do you have any shoes besides those with you?" He tilted his head at the flimsy sandals she'd worn to the museum that morning, then he checked under the table to see that Meggie was wearing her Nikes.

"No, I don't."

"Then you can use a pair of my boots."

All of this was in anticipation of the worst—the possibility of crawling out of a hole in the ground and finding oneself in a wet, dark, chilling wind surrounded by demolished homes and twisted vehicles, and then having to walk over acres of cutting debris to reach shelter and safety.

Christy started up the stairs again, but Sam yanked her back.

"I'll get the stuff. You take Meggie and Brutus down to the basement and tune the radio to the emergency station." He bolted up the stairs.

Meggie was still sitting before her half-eaten plate of spaghetti with her big spoon poised in midair. Her wide, innocent eyes panned from TV to Christy in confusion.

"Come on, sweetie." Christy rounded the table to the child. "We have to go to the basement. A bad storm is coming."

"But I gots to finish eating." Meggie balked when Christy took the spoon out of her fingers.

"We'll take some snacks and have a picnic in the basement." Christy pulled Meggie up out of the chair.

"No time for snacks!" Sam yelled from up the stairs. "Get downstairs. *Now.*"

"We goin' to the safety room?" Meggie asked.

"Yes."

Christy thanked her stars she had shown the child the room that day. When they looked in the room Christy had explained how much Meggie's daddy loved her—enough to build a safe place to hide in a storm. Now maybe Meggie wouldn't be too terrified if the worst did happen.

At the door to the basement stairs, Christy shot one last glance at the TV where the meteorologist was announcing that the twister had touched down in the small town of Bixby. The helicopter shot showed a distant funnel of massive proportions grinding up barns and houses into toothpicks. South Tulsa would be next.

"Take shelter immediately," the TV meteorologist was saying.

Christy dragged Meggie down the stairway.

"Mr. Bear!" Meggie screamed.

Christy turned back, meaning to get the toy, but Sam came bounding down the steps with his arms full of sleeping bags, pillows and the boots for Christy. He cut Christy off at the basement doorway, grabbed her other hand and pulled her back toward the shelter. "Forget the bear," he shouted.

Meggie broke free from Christy's grip and scooted around them, running back toward the breakfast area. Both adults lunged after her. Sam reached her first and scooped the child and the bear up in his free arm. Christy readjusted her grasp of Brutus, and took some of his burdens.

Then the rain stopped and the air around them grew deathly quiet. The very molecules felt charged as the dim evening light grew eerily greenish with static and the lights and the TV went dead. Brutus started to howl.

"Come on!" Sam put his arm around Christy and pushed her across the room to the stairs. Finally sensing the real danger, Meggie buried her face in her father's neck.

Behind them they heard it. A deafening *clackity-clack* with a horrid rumble and a constant roar underneath. Like a train. Just like a train. Bearing down on the house. Headed right for them.

They plunged down the stairs into the dark basement. Christy felt her way along the wall. Against the crush of the building air pressure, Sam managed to yank open the heavy safety room door.

"Dad-deee!" Meggie screamed as Sam pushed them inside, onto the floor.

Christy tried to utter words of reassurance, but the pressure shifted abruptly and she felt her lungs struggling for air as her ears popped and all she could do was clutch the child and the dog against her chest. Above the sound of windows shattering, the roar became deafening and Christy did her best to protect Meggie's ears, while simultaneously keeping a grip on the frantically struggling little dog.

She could feel the house shuddering and shifting above them. She heard Sam grunting as he slammed the steel door against the wind and flying debris. She could not hear the dead bolts click, but she knew that's what Sam was doing in the next few seconds. Then, the beam of a flashlight lit their tiny haven.

The oblique rays illuminated waves of dust and debris sifting down through cracks as the floorboards above them split apart. Sam threw his body over Christy and Meggie, then pulled a thick sleeping bag over the top of all of them.

The air became suffocating and the stench of human fear rolled off of Sam, but his arms felt sure and strong and Christy's heart beat with gratitude for the feel of his massive protective weight on top of her.

Underneath her, Meggie was whimpering in fear, shivering like a frightened little fawn.

Sam pressed down upon Christy, and Christy in turn pressed herself over Meggie as their bodies were buffeted by incredible pressure from above. For those long, roaring moments when speech was impossible Christy's lips moved in one repeated litany. *Protect us. Protect us. Protect us.*

Then, it seemed like in only seconds, the whole thing was over. The shuddering stopped. The rumble and roar grew rapidly distant.

An eerie silence filled the close little room.

Sam eased his weight up and Christy rolled away from Meggie.

Sam threw off the sleeping bag and collapsed back against the wall. Christy was positioned between his legs with Meggie huddled on her lap. For a moment no one spoke as they all took great, hungry gulps of the dust-filled, oppressive air. After a minute Sam hugged them both to him and Meggie started to cry.

Sam leaned forward and kissed her hair. ''We're okay,'' he soothed as he panned the flashlight over Meggie's face, arms and legs, then over Christy's. ''Everybody *is* okay?''

Christy said, ''I'm fine.'' She scanned Meggie's body for injuries. ''She looks okay.''

Sam found the radio and turned it on. The reports were not good. The twister, almost half a mile wide, was demolishing parts of northeast Tulsa now. The towns of Claremore and Broken Arrow Lake were directly in its path, which meant the construction at Moonlight Grove was in harm's way, as well.

Sam tried not to think of the fresh structures at Moonlight Grove being leveled. All around them, people's homes were being destroyed and Moonlight Grove was unoccupied, and thus, irrelevant for the moment. All that would be lost would be an architect's chief commodities in such a project: time…and money.

''I wanna get out of here.'' Meggie sounded panicked. She started to squirm out of Christy's arms.

''Not yet, sweetheart,'' Christy murmured below the sound of the radio. ''We have to wait until the man on the radio says it's safe.'' Sam could see her casting around for something to keep Meggie occupied in the dark, confined space. He berated himself for not thinking to put some crayons or something down here.

Brutus was still shivering and whining, so Christy wisely said, ''Brutus is scared. Poor doggie.''

"Poor doggie," Meggie repeated as Christy showed her how to comfort and pet him.

When the dog calmed, Christy said, "Tell you what—" her tone was upbeat, bright "—I'll sing a song for you."

"'It's All Right to Cry'?" Meggie requested.

Christy circled her arms around Meggie and started to sing the soothing children's ballad from the CD she'd bought Meggie. Her voice hummed low, filling the small space, as sweet and lilting as an angel's.

Sam kept one ear tuned to the monotone of the weather announcer while part of his mind was captivated by Christy's soothing voice as she sang about a little boy who allows himself to cry when he is hurt. Right now, Sam wanted very much to cry himself. He wanted to cry because, undoubtedly, just above his head, his beautiful home lay in shambles. He wanted to cry because you could be arguing about softball and eating spaghetti one minute and hearing reports of your hometown being scoured into the ground the next. He wanted to cry because his baby had been so frightened. He wanted to cry because holding Christy Lane in his arms a moment ago, keeping her safe, had felt as right as anything in his life ever had. And he had no idea what to do with that stunning realization.

CHAPTER SIX

WHEN THE NATIONAL WEATHER Service announced the all clear, the three of them put on their rain slickers, Christy pulled Sam's big boots over her flimsy sandals, and they opened the safety room door. Sam panned the space with the flashlight and saw that the laundry room looked surprisingly intact. Puddles on the floor were full of splintered wood, crumbled drywall and broken glass from the two high narrow windows that had been blown out, but everything else looked pretty good. No leaking pipes, no collapsed floor joists from above. Just a box of Tide spilled on its side, mud splattered on a basket of unfolded laundry, and part of a tree limb sticking through the broken window. Sam sniffed the air for a gas leak, detected none. He turned back into the safety room and pulled his high-powered emergency halogen light off the shelf.

He flicked on the powerful beam and took Meggie's hand. Christy carried Brutus as Sam led them up the stairs and out into the uncertain night.

In the kitchen they found their dinner and Christy's charming table setting heaped in a pile on the other side of the room.

Many windows were blown out, but they could feel an especially strong gust of wet wind coming from the back of the house. "Come on," Sam said. The diffused light shifted to milky gray as they went back there, as if the space were opening up. It was.

The back wall, almost the entire back room, a small wing that had been Sam's spare room, was now missing. Sam fanned the flashlight over several large tree limbs lying across the yard. Residual clouds scudded away from the rising moon, they could see even more damage—a section of fence gone, someone's doghouse slammed into the ground on its peak. They backed away from the hole as raindrops splattered from the tree limbs onto their faces.

Meggie took it all in with wide, fearful eyes.

"It's okay, honey," Sam soothed her. "Everybody's all right. That's what matters." He put a hand on Christy's shoulder. "You want to call your family?" He pulled out his cell phone.

Christy nodded and took it. When she completed her calls across town, she said, "That was my sister, Kate. Their neighborhood wasn't hit. And my brothers are okay."

"What about your apartment?"

"Kate said as far as she knows it's fine."

"Good." He took the phone and called one of his brothers, who told him that they were not in the twister's path and that their mother's house was okay, as well. Sam thanked Jack, who said he would drive across town to help Sam with his damage. When he hung up, Sam fanned the high-beamed light over the ceilings and walls. "This area looks stable. Wait here." He handed Christy a smaller flashlight.

Then he cautiously trudged up the stairs, panning the high beam ahead of him. Christy hugged Meggie while they waited. Soon Sam came back down. "No big leaks that I can see. Sometimes these old hip roofs actually hold up better in a vortex wind than the gabled ones. Well, at least the main house looks sound. I guess we'd better go out front and check on the neighbors."

Out in the street, many vehicles were shoved askew, rolled on their sides, blocking the road. People had turned on the headlights of the functional ones. Christy's car had leaves and mud sticking to it but sat upright at the curb. Sam's Suburban, parked in the circular drive, looked about the same as it had when he'd left it an hour earlier.

Black holes from broken windows gaped in every house. Many homes had missing walls and missing roofs, but nothing in the neighborhood looked completely flattened. There were no streetlights, of course. People were out with flashlights, milling around and assessing the damage. Some were talking on cell phones. Some were quietly crying. Many were silent. In the distance sirens wailed and air horns blasted.

Some of the men had already organized themselves, going from house to house, checking for any trapped people or pets, giving direction to those who seemed unable to decide what to do next. Sam took Christy by the shoulders. "Can you stay with Meggie?"

"Of course." Now that she knew her family across town was fine, she wanted to stay here, where she was needed. She could see that there was going to be much to do in this neighborhood. She knew Sam would be invaluable, helping people decide if any given home was safe enough for occupancy through the night.

"Okay." He took the smaller flashlight from Christy. "Take this—" he gave her the halogen "—and go back into the dry part of the house, but stay in the front, downstairs, until I can do a thorough inspection on the damage in the back." Then he joined the other men.

Sam spent the next few hours helping people tar-paper over holes in their roofs. When he finally came in, it was past midnight and he had never felt so discouraged or exhausted. The electricity was still off so the house was dark except for his flashlight and a greenish glow from the battery-operated emergency lantern Christy had brought up from the safety room. He went toward the glow of the light in the kitchen. There, Christy stood holding the corner of a large black garbage bag that she had been filling with debris. She was still wearing his boots and had donned a pair of his heavy leather work gloves that he supposed she'd found in the utility room. She had pulled the hem of her broomstick skirt up in back and tucked it into her waistband, creating the effect of balloon pants. Again, he thought of a clown. But at the same time he thought how wonderfully unselfconscious she was about her looks.

"Your brother came," she informed him quietly, "and stapled a big sheet of plastic over the hole in the back of the house."

Sam hung his head. "I should have done that myself."

"You were busy helping people with their roofs. He helped me do some cleanup, then I told him to go home to his wife when it got late. I took care of Meggie. We were fine."

"Where is Meggie?"

"Asleep on the couch. Mr. Bear and Brutus are with her. All cozy. The front of the house seems okay. Hardly any damage at all. I didn't want to take her upstairs until you checked it thoroughly."

"Yes, of course. It's the back roofs on our side of the street that took the worst hit. There could be some damage up there I didn't see before."

"Was anybody hurt?"

"A few cuts and bruises."

"But no one was...killed?"

"Not that we know of."

Christy's shoulders sagged with relief and then the arm holding the garbage bag went suddenly limp. In the dim lantern light, Sam thought he saw a glimmer of tears forming in the corners of her eyes as he quickly crossed the room to her. He took the bag from her hand and set it aside on the floor, then he reached out and put a steadying hand on her upper arm. When she sank toward him, he folded her into his arms.

"We could have all been killed!" She dropped the chunk of drywall and clung to his neck in the same desperate way Meggie did when she was afraid or when her little heart was breaking over some small hurt. Only this was no small hurt and Christy Lane was no child.

The sob that escaped her throat tore at Sam's heart. Again, he was assailed by the urge to cry himself. He gulped back his emotions as she clutched the back of his neck with her gloved hands and pressed her forehead to his chest. He held her tighter.

"I can't believe it!" she cried. "We really could have all been killed!"

"But we weren't." He spread a palm on her back, steadying her, pressing her to him. He told himself he did it because she'd started to tremble.

"How can you be so calm?" She turned her head, and he felt her warm breath pulsing against the base of his throat. "I mean, one minute we were having a quiet little meal, and the next minute, the whole back of the house was getting sheared off..."

"Shh..." He pressed her closer, and again he swallowed. "I guess I've learned that sometimes life is unpredictable." He was suddenly thinking of the other times he'd been forced to respond to tragedy. One thing he'd learned—you stepped up to the plate with everything you had. You didn't hold back and you didn't look back. There was no point in saying, *If only this hadn't happened.*

"Not for me it isn't!" Christy's trembling turned to outright shaking. "I live a very pre-dictable, a very qu-quiet life."

He hugged her even tighter. Her breasts and pelvis

were pressed as tight as they could be against him, and yet he wanted to hold on tighter. "Shh," he murmured again. "It'll be okay."

But her shaking grew worse, and when she pressed her face into his shoulder, he cupped his palm to the back of her soft, soft hair. He felt her turn her face up, and it seemed like the weight of the world pulled his gaze down into hers. In the dim light her brimming tears made her eyes sparkle like dark sapphires. And then, somehow, in the next instant he was kissing her trembling lips. Later, Sam would examine that moment in hindsight, from every angle, and never be able to figure out exactly how it had happened, exactly who had kissed whom, although it was definitely his mouth that did the seeking. But it was definitely her mouth that did the imploring, the responding.

Instantly, Sam experienced the same expanding, out-of-bounds sensation that he'd had the first time Christy Lane had taken his hand on the day she'd come to work for him.

Only now, the taste of her lips hit him twice as hard—ten times as hard—as the touch of her fingers had. Those lips, soft and yielding, seemed to pull him in, while at the same time giving over something electric, something thrilling, something that he wanted to drink in—to devour before it escaped him. He turned his head for a better fit, unable to stop his mouth from seeking more of the taste of her. *More.*

As he assailed Christy's mouth with his tongue, she responded with a tortured moan that literally sent his mind reeling. In the dark kitchen his thoughts became a jumble of tender memory and dawning hope and urgent sensation, all mixed together. He thought, strangely, of a time back in high school when he'd glanced at a girl—who was that girl? He couldn't quite picture her face, but she'd been pretty, and something in the shy way she'd glanced away from his gaze had made him feel powerful, alive.

He could feel Christy's body—every inch of him was aware of every inch of her—but it was as if he were suddenly somewhere else, somewhere outside of his own body. It was as if the two of them were becoming surrounded by a bright, warm cocoon instead of the damp, dark rubble of the recent storm. It was as if they had slipped into some other world. A world where all things were possible, where everything was suddenly right, suddenly bright.

Christy yielded against him, seeming locked with him in this joyous state. It felt as if she shared his very thoughts as their mouths spoke one to the other.

He turned his head the other way and murmured, "Christy," before he plunged down for more of her mouth from a new angle.

But at the sound of her name, Christy startled, as if he'd broken the spell. With a little cry she twisted her mouth away from his still-seeking one.

Breathless, she drew her head back and stared up into his eyes as if they'd both done something horrifying.

"No—" he clutched her body to him, refusing to let her withdraw "—it's okay." He had no idea what he meant by that, except that this had nothing to do with her boyfriend, if that's what she was thinking. And it had nothing to do with the fact that she happened to work for him, if that's what she was thinking. This wasn't her fault. This wasn't wrong. It was meant to be. He lowered his head and tried to cover her mouth with his again.

"Sam." She twisted her face away.

No! his mind protested in reply. *Don't make us stop.* I haven't felt this way since...I haven't felt this way *ever.*

But when she pressed her gloved palms rigidly against his chest in the universal sign of female resistance, he released her. Sam was a big man. He had learned early on in life that he could overpower almost anyone, and therefore early on he'd also learned how to restrain himself. But letting her go, seeing her step back into the dark shadows behind the lantern—away from his arms—nearly killed him. His whole body thrummed with passion. And his chest actually ached for the feel of her. He spread a palm over that ache and started to say, "Christy—"

"No." She threw up a gloved hand. "Please don't say anything, Sam." She bent and picked up the black plastic bag at her feet and turned her back to him. After she'd gathered another couple of pieces of debris, she said, "That shouldn't have happened. I'm sorry. I guess it was just a...a moment of weakness."

No, it wasn't, his mind vowed, it wasn't just a moment of weakness. It was something important, something incredible. He'd never experienced a kiss like that before in his entire life and he knew it. Why didn't she?

"Christy, listen." He stepped toward her and grabbed at her hand, but she jerked it away, leaving him holding only the large glove.

They both froze, as if he'd torn off a piece of her clothing instead of an oversize leather work glove.

Without looking at him she whispered, "Could I please have my glove back?"

Sam looked at the thing for a moment, feeling like a character in some kind of silly Victorian melodrama. *This is crazy,* he wanted to say, *we're both adults. And we both know what we felt just now.* But maybe Christy hadn't felt it. Maybe for her that kiss really was only a moment of weakness, a mistake, just like she said.

She refused to even look at him, so he handed her the glove. With her back to him she pulled it on, then threw herself into the task of shoving more debris into the bag.

Sam, incredibly aroused, yet incredibly confused, stood surrounded by the dark disorder of his home, realizing that no matter what that kiss meant to Christy, for him, it meant that his whole life had changed. For some strange reason, he was overcome with the urge to laugh out loud. What in the hell had gotten into him? His whole life was turned upside down, literally, and he was grabbing his nanny and kissing her. He must be losing it. Sane people just didn't go around *doing* things like that.

AT SAM'S INSISTENCE, Christy had finally gone home to her apartment in the wee hours. He gave her his cell phone and told her to call him if she ran into any trouble on the way home. Sam would make a pallet on the floor beside the couch, not wanting to wake Meggie.

Christy slept fitfully, rose again at dawn, showered, and was back at Sam's house before seven. She wanted to be there as a comforting presence when Meggie woke up.

She used her key to let herself in the side door, which was ridiculous, she decided, since the whole back of the house was protected by nothing more than a sheet of Visqueen. The kitchen actually looked better in the morning light than it had in the eerie glow of the lantern. The refrigerator was humming steadily, cooling back down, so apparently the power had been restored at some point. So the first thing Christy did was make a pot of strong coffee.

The aroma filled the room and Sam appeared at the top of the stairs. He'd showered and was wearing baggy gym shorts and a loose T-shirt. Christy had dressed in a light sleeveless sundress herself, anticipating that even if the air-conditioning worked, it would be ineffective with a hole the size of a truck in the back of the house.

"You're here early," Sam said as he came down the stairs.

"I want to make Meggie a hot breakfast. Then, if it's okay, I thought I'd take her over to my apartment, away from the mess."

"Okay. I'll be hanging around here this morning. I'll have to arrange for an insurance adjuster, emergency repairs, stuff like that, and then I've got to go out to Moonlight Grove and see what's left of it. Can you work late this evening in case I get stuck out there?"

"Of course," Christy said, without looking up from the cantaloupe that she was cutting into the tiny bite-size cubes that Meggie preferred. "My boyfriend—the cop?—oh, he'll be working long hours, anyway, until things get back to normal."

At the mention of her boyfriend, the tension grew heavy in the room as Sam walked over to the coffeemaker and poured himself a cup. He leaned his backside against the counter and crossed one ankle over the other, sipping coffee while Christy's knife kept up its steady *click, click, click* on the cutting board.

She could feel him watching her. "There's your cell phone. I have your number in case I need you. And here's my home number." She'd written it on a Post-it note for his convenience.

"That's great." He took the little yellow square off the counter and put it in his pocket.

"The power's back on," Christy said brightly. Which was a dumb thing to say, with the fridge humming and the coffeemaker gurgling right next to them. But she was desperate to break the tension between them.

"That explains why the coffee's so hot."

She would have enjoyed the fact that he'd actually

made a joke if it weren't for the awful tension between them.

He took another gulp of his coffee, then said, "Christy."

The clicking knife halted.

"About last night."

"Last night was simply awful, wasn't it?"

"I'm talking about that kiss."

Christy kept her eyes down, but she wasn't seeing the orange pieces of cantaloupe against the white Plexiglas board. Instead she saw Sam's eyes, filled with meaning right before they closed, right before he sealed his mouth over hers. "I told you," she made herself say, "that was a mistake. Could we please just drop it?"

"If that's the way you want it." He said it so quietly that she knew the air had somehow gone out of him. She knew it wasn't what he wanted. She knew she had hurt him. Could it be that Sam had really felt something besides lust when he'd kissed her? Men had kissed her like that before—passionately—but she'd never felt the way she had last night. Later, while she'd tossed and turned in her bed, she'd admitted that to herself. She supposed it was that old high school crush coming back to haunt her. Which was bad—one stupid kiss from Sam Solomon and already it was making her question her relationship with Kyle.

"Yes. That's what I want," she said, although, truth be told, she did not know what she wanted at this moment. Oh, truth be told, she most certainly did know. She wanted to kiss Sam Solomon again. She wanted to kiss him so bad she ached. ''Please promise me you won't mention that...incident again.''

''All right.''

A beat passed.

She couldn't imagine *what* he must be thinking of her, throwing herself at his head and letting him kiss her that way in the first place, and now saying *don't mention it ever again* as if it was some kind of big shameful deal. He probably thought she was a little ninny, that's what.

He drained the coffee mug. ''I won't.''

Out of the corner of her eye she saw him frowning into the mug. After a moment he said, ''That's good coffee,'' as if nothing had happened, and, ''thank you.'' He walked to the sink and rinsed the mug thoroughly before carefully placing it in the dishwasher.

All this time Christy had stayed looking down at the chopping board, one hand stilled on a piece of cantaloupe, the other on the knife. Mechanically, she forced herself to start chopping again.

SAM CLOSED THE DISHWASHER door and watched Christy, chopping with such determination, and wondered if he'd misread that kiss, after all. All night he'd thought about that kiss, relived it. Even his short interludes of sleep had roiled with dreams of that kiss...and more. How could she just stand there and ask him never to mention it again? Weren't they even going to talk about it?

''Daddy! Lookit!'' Meggie hollered from the door

to the dining room, interrupting his dejected thoughts. "Part of our home got blowed away!"

Sam's heart, so wounded over Christy's rejection a moment earlier, did an astonishing about-face at his daughter's announcement, suddenly beating with unexpected joy.

His little girl had never before called his house "our home."

AFTER IT HAD DONE ITS DAMAGE to several neighborhoods in Tulsa, the twister had scoured its way across Moonlight Grove like a gigantic eraser, exposing the red earth.

Out there it had left only a bare track, stripped, twisted trees and the ghostly remains of the bedrock structures Sam had started with only two months earlier.

The worst of it was the flooding. Debris had obstructed the grate covering the huge drainage pipe that flowed into the lake, and the part of Moonlight Grove that had been drained was now under water again.

Sam would have to rethink and redesign his whole drainage plan. Businesses would not come to a vacation spot that was constantly flooding.

His beautiful vision had been obliterated.

He walked the grounds in silence, feeling an oppressive loneliness, wishing Christy were here. How could you miss somebody you hardly knew? He struggled to sort out his sudden strong feelings for this woman. But he couldn't. All he knew was that something had shifted during that storm, and the feelings he had for Christy Lane went way beyond his usual feelings for an attractive woman. Right now it would be a comfort just to hold her hand. It had felt so good just to hold her during the storm. And later, it had felt good to hold her in his arms and comfort her. To kiss her.

He tried to put that kiss firmly out of his mind and concentrate on his work, but he kept going back to it. He'd never imagined himself getting that swept away by a mere kiss. He found himself wondering about this so-called sweet cop, her boyfriend.

He'd wanted to ask her if the cop had come by to hold her, to kiss her, later that night. Had he? Sam wondered. An image flashed of a muscle-bound young man in a uniform, sweeping Christy Lane off her feet, holding her tight…bedding her. But the cop was undoubtedly out doing his duty while Sam was busy laying a lip lock on the guy's girlfriend. It was small wonder Christy had rebuffed him this morning. She had a sense of decency.

Sam told himself to keep his mind on his business. Disaster had struck. He certainly had more important things to think about besides Christy Lane.

CHAPTER SEVEN

SAM LOOKED UP FROM THE SET of plans he'd spread on the hood of his Suburban, and saw that the sun had slipped over the rim of the lake like an orange marble rolling over the edge of a table. With so much to do at Moonlight Grove, nightfall had taken him by surprise.

"That's all we can do for today, boys," he told the crew that had been hard at work bulldozing debris and clearing a new access road.

He climbed into the Suburban. Inside, he slipped the strap of his digital camera off his neck, unclipped the yellow tape from his belt, then his pager and his cell phone. Sometimes he felt like a walking electronics store. He drove the short distance back to the field office.

The inside of the trailer was cramped but orderly. File cabinets, low drafting tables, a rough board with labels above rows of nails that held the various keys. Sam's computer. He flicked on the fluorescent light and did a few wrap-up chores.

He was tired, sweaty and grimy from the long, humid day. His jeans and boots were completely mudcaked. He and his crew had repeatedly walked the perimeter of the old-town area, measuring and surveying, trying to figure out how to get enough fall in the drainage pipes and still raise the opening above the level of the lake so it would work. He only hoped the investors didn't see the place flooded like this. It would be hard enough to convince people from Japan that such a storm happened very rarely. He would have to get this problem squared away before Mr. Yoshida came to the States again.

He spread the massive plans—more than one hundred pages—on a low drafting table, then sat down in his creaky vinyl desk chair and considered what to do next. Then, it dawned on him. He hadn't called Andrea last night. She might be frantic if she'd heard about the tornado on the news. She hadn't called his cell phone, but she might have tried reaching Meggie, who had been at Christy's all day. He dialed his mom's number to see if she'd spoken to Andrea, but got her answering machine. He decided he didn't have time to go all the way home for a shower, because if he did it would be past Meggie's bedtime before he picked her up. And he didn't want to impose on Christy one minute longer than necessary. He closed up shop and headed straight to Christy's.

As he came into the city he exited on Riverside Drive according to Christy's directions and found her apartment complex easily enough. It was amazing to Sam how a tornado could flatten one end of a town, while on the other side everything appeared normal and intact.

Christy lived in one of those sprawling, modest

apartment complexes that looked out over the Arkansas River. He pulled into the first entrance, parked at the curb and fished out his phone and the little yellow Post-it note with her number on it.

"I'm here," he said when she answered.

"Oh, good. Come on up. Meggie's just now eating." She had a smile in her voice that made him feel instantly better after his long day. "She had an extra-long nap. I guess she didn't get much sleep last night."

"Which one is your apartment?"

"I'm on the front side, facing the city." She told him how to get there.

He found the building quickly. Bone weary, he climbed out of his Suburban and slammed the door, looking up at a third-floor balcony directly above his parking spot. It was heavily festooned with potted plants and wind chimes. Something told him that balcony had to be hers.

As he climbed the flights of stairs up to it, he thought how constantly climbing these stairs probably accounted for her great figure.

Her front door was adorned with a blue-and-pink welcome sign painted with pansies. He wondered if she'd made it herself. Probably. She was always doing crafts with Meggie.

She answered the door in a set of well-worn, comfy-looking lilac-colored sweats. He'd never seen her in anything but those flamboyant artsy getups she favored for daytime. She was barefoot and had her hair pulled back in a loose ponytail at her nape, and her makeup was completely removed. "Hi," she said.

"Hi."

"Come in." She smiled, pulling the door wide as she stepped back.

"I, uh..." He looked down at his mud-caked boots. "I don't want to mess up your place."

"Oh. Well, just take your boots off and leave them there." She pointed at a doormat next to a potter's bench. "No one will bother them. All of my neighbors are nice."

He tugged off his boots, trying to brush some of the dried mud from his jeans as well, then stepped inside to a smallish room that seemed overwhelmed by a huge upright piano crammed into one corner. The top of the piano was covered with framed photos. Her family, he supposed. Some of them looked like her. Sheet music littered the piano stand, the bench, the floor all around. He wondered how on earth she'd gotten the massive thing up those two flights of stairs. At a right angle to the piano was a computer desk with a home system and what looked like the keyboard of a synthesizer. And next to that sat a contraption on a tripod, three flat black hexagonal plates that looked like a space satellite.

The rest of the room had a lack of adornment that would have seemed austere except for a few touches here and there that bespoke an artist's life. Offbeat framed prints and stained glass ornaments and treasured rocks and scented candles. Every little piece was precious, he was sure, connected somehow to

Christy's wit, her soul. The serenity of the atmosphere surprised him, because when it came to her person, Christy seemed so lush, so exuberant, almost wild at times...anything but serene.

But this apartment, with its simple lines, rich textures and soft, natural earth tones felt as restful and homey as a woodland cabin. The living room windows were bare, showing their white mullioned panes to advantage, even against the night skyline of Tulsa. He supposed from her perch up here on the third floor, overlooking nothing but treetops, Christy didn't need to worry about privacy much.

"Hi, Daddy!" Meggie called from her spot in front of the TV where Christy had positioned the child on the Berber carpet with a little folding tray across her lap. She was eating fruit salad and macaroni and cheese and watching a Walt Disney movie. He bent forward and kissed the top of her head.

"Ooh. Daddy, you are so durdy."

"I know, sweetie. Daddy's been working out at Moonlight Grove."

"I wanna go to Moon-night Grobe wid you," Meggie whined.

Again, Sam worried about neglecting his daughter at this crucial time in her life. He dropped to one knee beside her. "Moonlight Grove is dirty, Meggie. And it's boring out there." He looked around the cozy apartment. "It's more fun at Christy's."

"I still wanna go," Meggie insisted, but she turned back to her movie.

"I'm sorry I'm so late," Sam said to Christy, feeling bad about the lateness of the hour, about Meggie eating Christy's food, ashamed that he hadn't even thought about what his child would have for supper.

"You look exhausted, Sam," Christy said. "Come into the kitchen. I'll get you a beer."

Christy's kitchen was the antithesis of his sterile one. The six-by-ten-foot area was crammed to the gills with food and gadgets. Cookbooks, a bread machine, a baking stone, fresh fruit and vegetables in huge ceramic bowls. The space, brightened with country touches, looked as if it was probably never totally clean and tidy.

"I should have given you some money for fast food," he said quietly when they were out of Meggie's earshot.

Christy gave him a funny look while she twisted the cap off a Coors. "Meggie doesn't eat much fast food these days, remember?" She said it calmly, as if it was a fact. A fact he hadn't noticed. "You pay me very well, Sam. I can afford to fix Meggie a little dinner." She handed him the bottle, pointed at a plain wooden stool and turned back to peer into her refrigerator.

He perched a buttock on the stool, one sock hooked over a rung to steady himself, self-conscious about shedding dirt all over her clean linoleum floor. He surveyed her surroundings, wondering how it would be to struggle this way, day to day, paycheck to paycheck. But though there wasn't anything luxurious or expensive about Christy's place, everything had a feeling of care and freshness, as if it had been recently touched or moved…accounted for. He didn't doubt that Christy Lane lived within her means, and he would bet she managed it happily, too.

For one second he felt almost envious. Despite the fact that she was obviously not well off, she was happier than he was. Maybe of the two of them, he was the one who worried about money more. Always striving to make an impression, to make his company grow, trying to attract investors, keeping his contractors on schedule.

Why was he doing it? he sometimes wondered. For Meggie's sake? She seemed supremely happy, sitting on Christy's carpet, absorbed in her movie, spooning simple food into her mouth.

"Well, thank you for feeding her in any case."

"No problem." Christy smiled over her shoulder.

A sudden thought hit him and he patted his pocket. "Shoot!"

"What?" Christy looked concerned.

"I left my cell phone out in the truck. I was going to have Meggie call Andrea. She may have heard about the tornado by now and—"

"She has."

"Huh?"

"I called her. I got her number from Gayle, who had already talked to her and told her that you and Meggie were not hurt in the storm, but I figured she'd need to hear Meggie's voice. We called her as soon as we got over here."

"Why…thank you." Sam was amazed that Christy had taken this upon herself, but he was beginning to learn that this was the way his quirky nanny operated—with thoughtfulness, with compassion. "Thank you so much. I'll reimburse you for the long distance charges, of course."

"Don't worry about it. I talked to Andrea quite a while myself. She seems so fragile, so very worried about her little girl. I hope I was able to reassure her some. I tried to fill her in on Meggie's progress. I hope that's okay."

"Of course." He studied Christy, transfixed, as she rummaged through her fridge. How could he thank her enough for all she'd done today?

"Andrea told me Meggie likes macaroni and cheese. How about you?" Christy broke into his reverie.

"Huh?"

"Are you hungry?"

"Oh. No. I'm okay." He was starving, but he wasn't about to impose and let Christy cook supper for him, not after asking her to work late and feed his child to boot.

"There's still some fruit salad, and I have some leftover chili. My special recipe." She smiled in that way of hers. It was seductive, being with her like this. The small kitchen was incredibly cozy, smelling of the recently cooked macaroni.

His stomach growled and he put a palm on his belly, abashed.

Christy only smiled. "You may not think you're hungry, but your stomach seems to think you are." She raised her eyebrows.

He smiled, feeling himself relax. ''A bowl of chili sounds wonderful,'' he admitted, ''if it's not too much trouble.''

''Oh, no trouble. You can go back there—'' she pointed ''—and wash up while I fix it.''

The apartment was so small that he had no trouble finding her tiny bathroom. Off of a hallway the size of a cardboard box, there were only three white doors. One led to a utility closet. One led to the bathroom. And one, standing open, led to her bedroom.

Sam couldn't resist a glance in. What he saw was a far, far cry from the clinical, futuristic feel of his own master suite.

The whole room seemed to be glowing. The walls were a soft shade of cotton-candy pink. The white woodwork was suffused by a pale lavender cast. The bed, unmade and lush with linens and pillows in a crazy mix of pale pink and blue and yellow florals and stripes, sat high above a ruffled white eyelet bed skirt. Two tiny wall lamps on either side of the mounds of pillows, both pure white, lit the small space with soft ivory light. Two huge white cabinets with louvered doors flanked the head of the bed like guardians of the woman who slept there. At the lone window above the plain white headboard, a simple shade, a simple pink-striped valance, created a feeling of privacy and balance. She had an alarm clock, some seashells and other whatnots, lining the sill. It was a room that smelled faintly of perfume and invited snuggling and reading in bed and long afternoon naps.

It was a room that beckoned: *Come in, lie down, don't worry.*

He turned away from it and jerked open the third door. In her bathroom he caught himself looking for evidence of a man sharing it, but everything was as simple and feminine as the rest of the place. He washed his hands and face in intentionally cold water and dried his skin vigorously. But it didn't help. That bed was still there, like a giant fluffy magnet, as he walked by.

As he passed through the living room, Meggie was singing along with the videotape, still content as a little lamb.

Christy made the food preparation seem effortless, as she did with everything. At her small oak table, she spread a black-and-white place mat printed with musical notes, then set before him a red bowl loaded with chili, onions and cheese. Next to the chili she placed a basket of tortilla chips, a plate of carrots and celery and a glass of cold milk.

Sam ate with relish. He didn't know if it was because he was so famished, or because Christy's chili was really that good, but when he'd scraped one bowl clean he accepted her offer of another.

He watched her, mesmerized by the sight of her slender fingers, gently sprinkling a few onions on top, then repeating the movement as she sprinkled the cheese, a bit at a time, with those delicate fingers until she was satisfied that she had layered on just the right amount.

Her hips swayed as she carried the bowl to the

microwave. She stood at the counter with her back to him, setting the cooker. He seized this opportunity to study her movements covertly. Even in the baggy sweatpants, her figure was stunning—petite, yet lushly rounded. Each movement accentuated a curve here, a hollow there. He remembered how perfect she had felt in his arms. She tilted her head to read the controls and he enjoyed the way her hair tumbled off her shoulder in a glittery golden sheet. It looked as if it would feel as soft as down, falling against a man's skin.

She stood watching the microwave as the time ticked down, saying nothing. It occurred to him that maybe he should fill the silence with chitchat, but he found himself preferring to continue to soak up the scene, to take it all in. The sound of the movie and Meggie's singing, the delicious aroma of chili... Christy in the unpretentious purple sweats. It was as if he'd stepped into an alternative world in this little apartment, a world where he felt the strongest sense of...belonging...that he'd ever experienced.

When the microwave beeped, she took the bowl out with a pot holder that also had musical notes on it.

She watched him eat, occasionally sipping a glass of tea, smiling as she made small talk, getting up once to busy herself around the tiny kitchen.

"What is the situation out at Moonlight Grove?" she asked him as she refilled his glass of milk.

"Terrible. The place is destroyed."

''Oh, Sam.'' She held the milk carton still. ''I'm so sorry.''

''It's not good. The builder's risk insurance will cover the damage, of course. But it's the lost time that will kill me. The investors were impatient as it was. They're the kind of people who don't like waiting forever for a return on their dollar.''

''But surely they understand that catastrophes happen.''

''Nevertheless, I'll have to double-time it now to keep from losing them midstream. We were scheduled to start pouring concrete on the second floor of the hotel at 3:00 a.m. next Friday—I was going to ask you about staying with Meggie—but now the hotel structure is destroyed, so that will be delayed at least a month.''

''I'm sorry.'' She frowned, puzzled. ''Why 3:00 a.m.?''

''It will take seventy truckloads to do the job and it's better to bring them down the highway before the traffic gets too thick. Also, once we start to pour, we can't stop.''

''Wow. I had no idea your project was so massive.''

''It's massive, all right, a massive mess now. Fifteen pallets of Indiana limestone got cracked in the tornado, the drainage pipes got covered by the lake and the part of the old town we'd uncovered is back under water.''

''I see.'' Christy gave him a sympathetic look.

"And your house—what is it like over there?" she asked.

"Messy. Muggy. The air-conditioning's going right out that big hole in the back wall. Cleanup has started. The cops are making patrols. I'm sure they'll cruise by with alley lights all night."

"I was thinking, why don't you let Meggie stay here?"

Sam frowned. He looked off into the living room at Meggie's thin back. She was jiggling in place, humming along with another song now.

"You look exhausted, and she'll only be in the way while you're getting the house livable."

"You don't have to do that." He was touched by her generosity.

"I want to. You've both been through so much." Her blue eyes were soft with compassion. "Maybe I can take her mind off things for a while. I'll make sure she has fun. She can take a bubble bath. I brought her jammies with us."

Sam twisted around, surveying her meager surroundings. "I don't want to impose. What about your boyfriend? Won't he object?" He wanted to take it back as soon as he said it. Because he knew why he was asking. He wasn't trying to be polite. He wanted to *know*.

"Kyle? I..." Her eyes darted away, looking troubled. "Well, he's busy with aftereffects of the storm, and besides he...he doesn't live here, you know."

No, Sam didn't know. But now he did. And he was ashamed to admit that that was what he had wanted to know. And he was ashamed to admit that he was glad to hear their relationship hadn't reached that point yet. Still, he wondered. Did Kyle share her comfy, inviting bed?

"Let her stay with me, Sam. She's happy."

Sam didn't have the heart to pull his child out of this cozy environment and drag her back to the side of town where only darkness and discomfort waited. He was reluctant to leave himself.

But he did leave. After Meggie hugged his neck, seeming all too willing to stay with Christy instead of going home with her daddy, he trudged down the two flights of stairs outside as if his legs were made of lead.

Back at the house the power had failed again, so the atmosphere was chaotic, dark and muggy.

He went into his lonely house—the first time he'd been alone in the place since Meggie had arrived a month ago—and found he didn't have the heart to do more cleanup work by flashlight. The living room was the coolest place in the house and he flopped on the couch there, tossing and turning with guilt about Meggie, with worry about Andrea, with anxiety about Moonlight Grove, finally falling into a fitful sleep, and dreaming, again, of Christy Lane.

TWO WEEKS LATER THINGS were beginning to return to normal on Sam's street, except for minor irritations. Such as Jim Holloway's shiny white pickup truck blocking the circular driveway when Sam got home, so that again he was forced to park out on the street. Sam liked Jim Holloway, the aggressive, hard-working owner of The Rainman, a fast-growing company that installed affordable inground sprinkler systems that preserved all of Solomon Architectural Masterpieces' elaborate and expensive landscaping. Sam respected Jim's great business instincts.

Sam had always wanted to add in-ground sprinklers to his own yard. The long, dry summers in Oklahoma almost required them if a homeowner was going to have any kind of landscaping at all. Since everything was torn up from the tornado, anyway, he'd decided now was as good a time as any to get the job done.

At the curb, the presence of the long, white, rectangular horse trailer where the work crew had been pulling out lengths of plastic pipe forced Sam to park even farther down the street. He pulled up in front of old lady Southard's, who would, undoubtedly, call and gripe about Sam's Suburban impeding the visibility from her drive. She'd already complained about the constant stream of trucks, about the Porta Potti for the workers, about the mess the many repairs around the neighborhood had created. In Sam's opinion, Mrs. Southard, who could barely see, could barely hear, and had the reflexes of a sluggish old cat, shouldn't be backing that boat of a Cadillac out of her driveway in the first place.

Sam felt a ripple of irritation about all of this inconvenience as he trudged back up the hill. He paused in front of Jim's pickup, which bore the Rainman logo—an energetic jet of blue water—on the door. The guy certainly seemed to be taking his sweet time about finishing up Sam's sprinkler system. He'd have to talk to Jim about parking his truck out of the way if he was going to keep showing up at the house unexpectedly like this. His irritation intensified as Sam wondered if Jim's diligence about this project had anything to do with Christy. Jim was single, and Sam guessed, in his mid to late twenties. He'd started his company after high school, about the same time Sam had formed Solomon Architectural Masterpieces, ten years ago.

Sam entered his foyer with a fresh wave of awareness that it wasn't truly his foyer anymore. Not at all. Rather, this house was becoming, day by day, hour by hour, Meggie's…and *hers*. All hers.

The mess after the tornado had been bad enough, but Christy Lane had a way of infusing her own special upheaval into the place. From the fish on the table to the rabbit cages on the patio to the hummingbird feeders hanging over the deck, to the half-eaten food overflowing in the fridge, now plastered with big plastic alphabet magnets, Christy Lane had taken over his household like a foreign army setting up bivouac. But he reminded himself that he'd agreed to all of this and that the changes were for the good of his child.

But grudgingly, he had to admit that despite the intrusion, the look of things had somehow improved. Well, not the *look*, exactly—for the look was decidedly more cluttered than he liked. But somehow the *feel* of the place pleased Sam. He couldn't put his finger on what, exactly, had been missing before, but since the arrival of Christy Lane, and right on her heels, the tornado, his home had, literally and figuratively, opened up, come alive.

He surveyed his once minimalist, almost sterile foyer. As usual, there sat the ubiquitous cleanup choo-choo box, crammed with toys. Sitting beside that was a pair of small sparkle-decorated flip-flops next to a pair of identical larger ones. A shopping spree at Wal-Mart again? Next to that were Meggie's swim flippers and goggles.

The smell of baking drifted from the kitchen. A cluster of tiny seedlings pushed up from dirt in foam cups along the low sill by the dining room window. Music drifted down from up the stairs.

"Christy?" he called out. He walked through the house, shoving aside the clear plastic barrier that shielded the intact part of the house from the damaged area under repair. He hoped they were home, though Christy wasn't expecting him for lunch. He told himself he only wanted to see Meggie for a little while. He didn't want to admit how much he also wanted to see Christy. But for the past two weeks, his mind, he admitted ruefully, had remained stubbornly preoccupied with seeing Christy Lane.

Maybe she was out on the deck, watching the guys installing the in-ground sprinkler system—or more likely, encouraging Meggie to watch the excitement.

But when he opened the garden doors and stepped one foot out onto the deck, the sound of Christy's laughter, mixed with Jim Holloway's, echoed across the yard and stopped him in his tracks. He spotted them immediately, in the back corner, under the small arbor of trumpet vines. She was leaning toward Jim in a decidedly coquettish pose. She laughed again and rocked her hips with a delighted little twist that made the fluted hem of her floral skirt sway. Holloway pointed at something on the ground and, together, they squatted down to look at it. They had their backs to him, bending over while Holloway talked and Christy nodded. Again her musical laugh rang out.

Sam stepped all the way out and pulled the door closed behind him. Meggie was nowhere in sight. He felt annoyed with himself for not noticing Meggie's absence first thing, and he was annoyed with his so-called nanny for flirting with the hired help when she should have been watching out for his daughter at all times. He headed across the yard with determined strides.

Christy and Jim moved closer together, their heads bent, their thighs touching as they continued to peer down at something.

Seeing them that way, Sam felt a jolt of what could only be jealousy. It made him quicken his steps across the freshly mown grass. He told himself he was determined to find out where the hell his daughter was, in the middle of the day, at lunchtime, while his nanny was flirting with the sprinkler guy, but a low little corner of his heart continued to darken with undeniable envy.

As he got closer he heard Christy's resonant laugh again, and when they looked up at each other he overheard Jim saying, "So. What do you say? Would you have dinner with me tonight?"

"Sure," Sam's nanny answered. Way too fast, way too eagerly.

"Christy," Sam barked. "Where is Megan?"

Christy maintained her childlike squatting pose, clutching her skirt around her knees, leaning trustingly toward Jim Holloway as she turned in the direction of Sam's voice. She smiled up at him. Innocent, distracted, as if he were an afterthought. "With Gayle," she said as if he should know that.

"Oh." Sam dragged his hand through his hair. "Right." His mother had returned from her month in Belize only a few days ago, and Gayle had decided to take Meggie shopping for clothes at Woodland Hills first thing. The child had gained enough weight to outgrow practically everything she'd brought from California.

"Look what Jim found." Christy pointed at something curled in the dirt. "It's a baby gecko. Jim thinks he must be somebody's pet. He must have gotten lost, separated from his family, during the tornado. It's a miracle the poor thing survived this long. Jim said they only eat soft-shell crickets."

"He was under that big rock we moved for the line," Holloway elaborated.

"Isn't he cute?" Christy added. "Meggie will love this!"

Sam walked around and looked past their shoulders at the small lizard, with brown spots, bulging eyes and an infantile round head. "Yeah," he said, although he could have cared less. He was thinking about Jim Holloway asking Christy on a date just now...and her easy answer.

Holloway stood, and damned if he didn't offer Christy his hand and assist her to her feet. What was Holloway doing touching Sam's nanny that way? The two hardly knew each other. Jim Holloway, Sam decided, had let his aggressive nature stray way out of the bounds of good business.

"How's it going today, Sam?" Holloway said, friendly and confident as ever. All smiles. Well, who wouldn't be smiling if they were holding Christy Lane's hand?

But Sam certainly didn't feel like smiling. He frowned, pointedly, and said, "Fine. How's my pipe work coming?" He wanted to remind the man why he was in Sam's backyard—to work for *him,* Sam Solomon, owner of Solomon Architectural Masterpieces, a major source of Holloway's income. Sam straightened his posture, suddenly feeling mean spirited and peevish for thinking like this. Holloway was hardworking and utterly reliable. But he was supposed to be laying pipe, not charming the household nanny.

Jim Holloway kept smiling—at Christy. His eyes flicked away from her only a second when he said to Sam, "I've made some changes. So—" he returned his adoring gaze to Christy "—is it a date, then?"

Christy smiled and shrugged. "Why not? I just have a few more clothes to fold and then I get off early—I do get off early today, don't I, Sam?"

Sam felt as if he'd been socked in the chest. A *date?* They were making this date right in front of him as if he were some kind of eunuch! After that kiss, didn't Christy realize he'd like to ask her out himself except for… Her boyfriend. Whatever happened to Christy's boyfriend, the sweet, sweet cop? Or didn't he care if his girlfriend went out with another guy? No guy was that *sweet.* So what was the deal here?

"Sam?" Christy was giving him an expectant smile, as if she was waiting for him to say something.

He realized she'd asked him a question; he just didn't know what it was. "Huh?"

"I get off early today, right?"

"Yes. Yes, of course." He ran a frustrated hand through his hair. *Sheesh.* He was standing here, acting like some kind of gut-punched jerk.

"Your mom said she wanted you to come over for dinner. She and Meggie are going to call Andrea this evening."

"Huh? Oh. Right."

Christy smiled up at Jim Holloway. "I guess I can go."

"Great! I'll call you as soon as I get home," Jim said.

"Okay. Bye." Christy waggled her fingers, like a genuine, honest-to-goodness flirt as she walked off in the direction of the house, giving both men plenty of time to observe her curvy backside undulating in the filmy skirt, as it swayed with each careful step over the trench of dirt in the grass.

Sam barely heard Holloway's technical explanation of how he'd put in some extra sprinkler heads to accommodate the crepe myrtles along the driveway.

''So, I figure, even if it costs you an extra elbow joint, you'd want those bushes to get sprayed, too. A smaller head under each one saves water. No sense in watering your driveway.''

''Huh?'' Sam said again. He hadn't said *huh* this much since Mrs. Dougherty's English class in high school. Actually, right now, his raging emotions made him feel like he *was* sixteen all over again. What was it about this woman that upset his equilibrium this way?

''I said, putting a smaller head under each one is the way to go. Don't you think? Hey. Are you okay?''

Apropos to absolutely nothing, Sam blurted, ''Did you just ask my nanny out on a date?'' He wasn't successful in keeping the ire out of his voice.

Jim looked taken aback. As if a few of Sam's marbles had plunked out on the lawn or something. ''Well, yeah. I asked her out. She's a very attractive young woman.''

''She's not that young, and she's got a boyfriend.'' Sam wished to hell he could control his mouth, but he just couldn't seem to stop himself.

Jim frowned. ''Boyfriend? You mean that cop? She told me about him. They broke up.''

''She told *you* that?'' Sam felt unexplainedly miffed that she hadn't told *him* that.

''Yeah. I guess they'd been dating a while and when he didn't want to get serious, she decided it was time to move on. She told me she wants a home and family someday, and at her age she doesn't have time for a dead-end relationship.''

''She *told* you that?'' Sam repeated.

''Yep. That girl sure knows her own mind. Christy Lane is a remarkable woman.'' Jim gazed off toward the house where she'd gone.

Sam narrowed his gaze at Jim Holloway. Truth was, they didn't come any nicer than this guy. He was the kind of nice guy Christy Lane would probably want to date. The kind of guy who'd want a home and family some day, too. Had Holloway even *told* her that already? The contractor had been coming to Sam's house intermittently for exactly four days now, and already he and Christy Lane were yakking about stuff like *home* and *family.*

A weird sense of panic assailed Sam. A feeling far more threatening than when the tornado had swooped down upon them. At least on that night, he'd had Christy safe in his arms. That blessed, blissful night when he'd held her safe in his arms— Blessed? Blissful? *What the hell?* Sam blinked. Why was he thinking like this? He told himself he'd been under too much strain lately, too many bad things had happened, leaving him needy, vulnerable. Naturally, he would start seeking comfort from the nearest source—Christy Lane.

But he'd let it all go too far, at least in his mind. He'd convinced himself that their kiss, and now this crazy persistent urge to hold her again, actually meant something. It didn't mean anything beyond his vulnerability. She wasn't his type at all. His feelings would settle down once he got used to the novelty of having this strange—and he meant that literally—woman in his house.

BUT SAM'S FEELINGS FOR Christy Lane didn't settle down. They only got more stirred up. He was distracted by more and more intrusive thoughts that evening. And more dreams that night.

After Christy left, his mother called and said she wanted to take Meggie out for dinner.

"I'll pass," Sam said.

"Are you all right?" his mother said.

"I've had a long day."

"We're going to call Andrea when we get back from the restaurant."

"That's fine."

"They can talk as long as they want," Gayle assured him. "In fact, why don't you let Meggie stay the night with me."

He sighed heavily. "That's a good idea. I've had a lot on my mind lately. It wouldn't hurt me to stay home and clear my head."

Or brood.

He did make a halfhearted attempt to work on the house. A little plastering. A little staining on the repaired woodwork. No good. He ended up giving in to his bad mood, nursing a rum and cola, and watching something stupid on TV.

He woke up in his black leather chair soaked in a hot sweat, the victim of another vivid dream. About a storm again, but this one seemed to rack his body instead of his house. In the midst of it he'd grabbed for Christy Lane. She was wearing the shapeless lilac sweatsuit—which melted right off in his hands—and nothing underneath. Her hair was wild; her mouth, too.

He swiped the sweat from his forehead, amazed to see it.

The air-conditioning still wasn't cutting it. He thrust himself up out of the chair and paced to the window, like a panther in a cage. How in the *hell* was he going to live with this woman right under his nose all summer? Secretly lusting after her night and day? But he couldn't let her go now. Meggie was attached to her. Meggie needed Christy Lane. That's what he told himself, *Meggie* needed her.

CHAPTER EIGHT

SAM HAD GONE UPSTAIRS that night and had dreamed about making love to the woman yet again. This one was a sort of possessive, fierce dream in which he'd yanked her out of Holloway's hands and carried her upstairs to his own bedroom.

As far as he knew, Christy went on her little date with Jim Holloway, but Sam couldn't ask her about it the following day without the risk of betraying his crazy feelings.

They were standing in his kitchen around suppertime when, out of the blue, Christy said, "You know, that thing with Jim was only a date," as if she could read his mind or something.

Boy, he hoped not.

He'd been loosening his tie, leafing through the mail, but not really seeing any of it because he was thinking about that damn weird dream for the tenth time. It had been like the other one, so vivid it felt as though it had left an impression on his body. He'd woken up in another hot sweat with a painful erection. The woman from that haunting dream was now standing at his kitchen island, calmly slicing strawberries, looking as innocent as a nun in a snow-white apron, except that it had Kiss the Cook stenciled in red across her bust.

Kiss the cook. She wouldn't wear that apron around here if she knew what he'd been dreaming about last night. She'd just said something to him. ''Pardon?'' he tossed the mail on the counter, frowning.

''I said it was only a date.'' Christy was looking at him curiously.

''What was only...'' Sam wagged his head as if he didn't know what she was talking about, but of course he did. ''What was only a date?''

''That thing with Jim Holloway last night. It was only a dinner date. I could tell you weren't too happy about it when he asked me out.''

''What do you mean? That's none of my business.''

''True. It's just that I might be going on a lot of first dates now that I've broken up with Kyle, and I just want you to know that doesn't mean I won't have my mind on Meggie. This is just how I do it. I go on a lot of dates at first, until I find a guy I like.'' She smiled as if it were all so very simple. Sort of like shopping, like those stupid Wal-Mart shopping sprees she was getting Meggie hooked on.

She was certainly confident about filling her date calendar. But then—he sneaked a quick look at her face, then her figure—that confidence was completely justified. Under the apron she was wearing a lace-trimmed white camisole top that hugged her curves. Was it his imagination, or was Christy Lane dressing a little sexier these days?

"Why in the world should I care about *your* social life?" Sam realized he sounded as cantankerous as he felt. His bad mood was merely the residue from the dream, which was not her fault. He was mad at himself for acting like a horny animal...in the dream, at least. The reality was, he wasn't about to get involved with this woman, kiss or no kiss, dream or no dream. She simply was not his type. She was too expressive, too...flamboyant.

Christy seemed a little hurt by his grumpiness. "Well, I guess you shouldn't. It's just that you just acted a little...I don't know...peeved or something when Jim and I were with you out in the yard. I thought you might be concerned that I was making a date while I was at work. But when Meggie is here, I want you to know that I am always completely focused on her. I just want you to know that even though my social life is going to be a little busier for a while, it won't interfere with my work in the least. Meggie is still my number-one priority." She scooped the strawberries into a little glass bowl.

Meggie. Sam's irritation vanished. Again, he felt torn apart. Here was this woman, telling him his daughter was her number-one priority, when Meggie should be *his* number-one priority. What was the matter with him? It wasn't that he didn't trust Christy to take good care of Meggie, it was just that there had been a lot of men trailing in and out of the house because of the repairs: carpenters, electricians, drywallers, painters. All of them looked at Christy with hungry glances, as if they'd like to have *her* for their afternoon snack, and for some reason that situation bothered Sam no end. She was *his* nanny, wasn't she? What were these guys looking at?

He'd seen enough of her feminine ways around men to convince him that Christy Lane could have all the dates she wanted. And how could Christy, now apparently available, not respond to all that male attention?

But he forced himself to be reasonable, to focus on Meggie instead of his churned-up feelings about Christy Lane. "Don't worry about it. I trust you completely. Your private life is none of my concern." Or so he told himself.

Even so, over the next two weeks Sam started hanging around his house longer in the mornings, dropping in at odd moments during the day to see how the work was progressing, coming home early enough to check on the men before they left for the day, pushing to get the job done faster.

Christy often took Meggie over to Gayle's to get away from the noise and mess of the construction. One day Sam found a note on the counter: *Come to Gayle's for lunch and see your daughter swim!*

As he drove to his mother's his skepticism about his daughter's swimming resurfaced. Getting out of his truck he heard Meggie's squealing, echoing off the back wall of his mother's massive house.

He stepped around the corner and saw Christy and Meggie up to their necks in the pool, under a patch of dappled shade.

"Now, try again," he heard Christy say.

He hung back to watch as Christy tilted Meggie onto her back. Meggie was giggling nervously, stiffening her limbs and fighting Christy.

"Rela-a-ax," Christy crooned. "Now, wiggle your fins like Mr. Charlie."

Meggie extended her arms at her sides, waving them gently, and started to flutter her skinny legs.

"Good," Christy encouraged, and started to ease away from the child. "Now you're floating."

"Don't let me go!" Meggie's plea was high-pitched but gleeful.

"You're float-teeng," Christy sang out as she released Meggie entirely.

Meggie looked at the sky, and with a big smile on her face, stayed afloat alone.

"Wow, Meggie," Sam said from the side of the pool.

Startled, Meggie lost her concentration and sank, flailing and coming up sputtering as Christy jerked her back to the surface.

"It's okay! It's okay!" Christy said as she held the crying child up.

"Dad-dee!" Meggie whined as if the whole thing were Sam's fault.

He squatted down at the edge of the pool, but Meggie splashed water at his suit. "Meggie, stop it!" he said.

"Meggie—" Christy began.

"I want my nonnie!" Meggie screamed.

Gayle emerged from the patio door, frowning at the sound of Meggie's crying.

Christy brought the child to the ladder and Meggie climbed up.

Sam tried to intercept his crying daughter as she cut a path to her grandmother, but Meggie charged around him.

Gayle snatched a towel off a patio chair, wrapped it around Meggie, and led her into the house.

Christy pulled herself from the pool. "I don't know what got into her." She grabbed a towel and dabbed at her hair.

Sam took in the tantalizing sight of Christy in the bathing suit, then forced himself to look toward the house. "It doesn't take much to upset Meggie these days. Are you sure this swimming isn't too much to ask of her?"

"She's coming along very well," Christy defended. "All children have some fear when they first get into deeper water. It's important for her to learn to swim."

"Why?"

"For safety, of course. Just like for any other child. And it helps her have a more normal life, to feel connected to the larger world. Can't you see that?"

"But..." Sam still wasn't convinced that Meggie was up to the physical challenges of swimming. "I can see that it frustrates her."

"That's just part of learning," Christy said with a smile.

Sam knew she was right. "Well, if you think it's okay..."

"I do, Sam." Christy gave him a gentle smile.

"You'll just have to deal with the fact that your child is growing up."

Sam couldn't help smiling back.

THE WORK ON SAM'S HOUSE stopped for the Fourth of July weekend. Losing a whole day, Sam felt thwarted yet again. But he knew many of the craftsmen needed a break. Ever since the tornado, crews had been working nonstop all over his part of town.

The crews out at Moonlight Grove also were taking the long weekend off, so Sam found himself at loose ends, with no plans for the holiday. Normally, with Meggie back in California by the Fourth, he'd take some hottie out to the lake to water-ski, or he'd attend a barbecue with his single crowd in Tulsa.

But this year Meggie needed him. The week before the Fourth he started to make definite plans. He checked the papers for events a child might like. The Fourth Fest in Woodward Park looked promising. Face painting and the like. Maybe he could get KFC and make it a picnic, or grill outside. He'd buy the stuff for a barbecue.

The Wednesday before the Fourth he decided to take a calculated risk and ask Christy if she'd like to come along for the holiday. Grill outside, take Meggie to Woodward Park, then see the fireworks. He'd make it sound like the whole idea was for Meggie's benefit. That way, it wasn't exactly a date, what with Meggie involved. But even with Meggie as a cover, he still felt nervous, asking Christy to do something with him in her free time.

He even waited for the right moment, while Meggie was taking her afternoon nap.

But she said no.

She had plans, she said, and left it at that.

Sam wondered who the lucky guy was this time.

ALREADY, AT TEN O'CLOCK in the morning, heat swam up off the sidewalks. Christy lifted the plastic vase holding the red carnation off the car seat, straightening the baby's breath and the little flag. The arrangement looked sad, wilted in the close July air. Well, no one would notice. Christy had no illusions about the fact that she performed these little holiday rituals for her own benefit. She slowly walked the flights of stairs and once inside her apartment, Christy placed the vase beside the picture of her mother on the piano.

She had been so tempted when Sam asked her to come over for a cookout on the Fourth. But she wanted Sam to focus on Meggie for a day. When Christy was around, she noticed, Sam had a habit of talking to her instead of to his child. It would be so good for them to be alone together all day.

But it was going to be a lonely holiday, the first one in a long time without Kyle. The breakup had hurt them both, but what else could she do? The instant Sam had kissed her on the night of the tornado, she knew Kyle only had half her heart. And more than anything, she wanted a man she could love with all of her heart. There was probably a song in there somewhere.

She sighed, shifting the little flower arrangement. Funny how she missed Mama more on holidays. Maybe later she'd go over to her sister Kate's and watch fireworks with her family.

In the meantime, she had her songs to write. If Christy had learned anything, it was how to use her blues.

She sat down on the bench and plunked a few notes. When nothing special came she looked up at her mother's picture with a heavy heart.

"Maybe I should give up writing these stupid little songs," she said to her mother's unmoving face. "I don't know," she mumbled, and plucked at the keys. "The new job pays well—and it's more fun than I thought it would be. But it's complicated." Her hands stilled. What was she doing talking to her mother as if she could answer? *If she only could.*

She stared at the uncompleted bars on the sheet music before her and her hands started traveling over the keys again.

"It's just that Sam's so handsome. Whenever he's around I—" She censored herself, wondering if she was losing her mind, talking to a picture this way.

From the photograph, her mother smiled out, all of eighteen years old, oblivious to Christy's problems.

"You believe in love, don't you, Mama?" Christy said aloud and tapped out a few more notes. "Well, I believe in love, too. And, I think I love...Sam."

Christy stopped playing, stunned by what she'd just admitted out loud.

The picture smiled on patiently. As a young woman

Wanda Lane had been as pretty as Christy herself. Christy played some more, the notes sounding sad to her ear. When a new thought struck her, she looked back up at the picture.

Her fingers began to pick up speed and Christy began to sing along with the music. ''What would Mama say if she knew about you? What would my Mama tell me to do?''

Her mind drifted off into images of how Sam grew up attending parties and playing varsity sports and going skiing. While Christy's childhood had consisted of taking care of the other kids while her poor mother worked endless shifts at the Piggly Wiggly. ''Taking care of the kids prepared me to be a really good nanny,'' she said, starting to talk out loud again as she continued to play. ''And you wore your poor little fingers to the bone working for us, I know that.''

''Oh, Mama. When I look at Sam's life, and then at mine, I can never see us together. Not really. Not as equals.''

Abruptly, she stopped playing and lowered her head, recognizing real fear in her voice. She covered her stinging eyes with a shaky palm. ''I am all mixed up, Mama. I broke up with Kyle. I just couldn't keep seeing him after I kissed Sam. Kyle was nice. But he wasn't Sam. Somewhere in the back of my mind, I think I knew that all along. And now I'm trying to date other guys. Nice guys that I have a lot in common with. But none of them are Sam, either. He's the one I want.''

"I guess he's in my heart, and that's where he'll stay. He's in my heart, forever and a day."

She lowered her palm, snatched up the pencil from the piano tray, and sketched those words onto the sheet music. Then she wrote *He's The One I Want* at the top of the sheet.

Christy looked at the words for a long time before she stood and walked to the apartment's lone window. She pressed her forehead against the picture window, which was filmy on the outside and already warming with July heat.

"He's the one I want," she whispered.

CHRISTY FINISHED WRITING her song, but wasn't all that satisfied with the result. When afternoon rolled around and the piece still refused to gel, she went over to her sister and brother-in-law's house. The cookout there was in full swing. Hot dogs on the grill. Ice cream maker churning. Kids running around everywhere.

Kate was the baby of Christy's family—four years younger than Christy—but had already settled down. She and her husband Joey had two kids and were working on a third, filling up that rambling ranch house, Christy teased them, and drove a couple of spanking clean minivans. Their home was a place where Joey trimmed the hedges with military precision and Kate kept the two freezers in the garage full to bursting.

When Kate and Christy went to the kitchen to get

the salads Kate had prepared in advance, Kate asked her sister how the new job was going.

"Oh," Christy sighed. "It's complicated. I was just thinking about it today while I was trying to get some work done."

"A new song? Hey. Any word from Mary Jane about that other song?"

"No. She's got it with some agent in California."

"Cool! That must mean they're going to do something with it!"

Christy, mixing salad dressing, just shrugged. "I guess."

"Hey. What's the matter with you?"

"Oh, Kate!" Christy stopped stirring. "I think I'm falling in love with my boss."

"Really?" Kate stared at her sister. "What about Kyle?"

"I broke up with him. It didn't seem right to keep going with him when I can't think about anybody but Sam Solomon."

"Sam Solomon?" Kate's jaw dropped as she stared even harder. "The big football star from Central High?"

"Yep."

"You're working for him?"

"Yes. And it's killing me. I had a hopeless crush on him back in high school, and now it's ten times worse. He actually kissed me and—"

"He kissed you!"

"Yes, after the tornado."

"That is sexual harassment."

"No it wasn't. I wanted him to kiss me, but even though we're attracted to each other, I can't see how we could ever have a real relationship. We're way too different."

"You can say that again. As I recall, the Solomons have all kinds of money. Besides, didn't he get married?"

"They're divorced."

When Kate just shook her head and wouldn't comment, Christy continued.

"I can imagine that you're thinking I should quit my job, if I'm that miserable about this man. But I can't do that. Like I told you, it's complicated. The little girl, she needs me so. She's a special needs child. When I started with her she was a real brat. Nobody had ever told her no or taught her how to obey rules, like Mama did with us. Right away I started in, teaching her how to behave and showing her that there was a time and place for everything."

"You remember Mama a whole lot better than I do," Kate said. Christy's sister had a hard, practical edge to her personality, a way of compensating for their rough childhood, Christy supposed.

"Yeah, I guess I do."

"*You* were my Mama." Kate smiled at Christy, then picked up the potato salad. "Come on." They took the salads outside.

When they got to the picnic table, Kate said, "Anyway, what about this little girl?"

"Well, you should see her now. She's settled down so much and she's learning to do all kinds of fun things. She swims right into my arms now, gives me a big hug, and then flings herself off to swim the other way. But her little life is so uncertain. Her mother's sick—"

"You kids get off that balcony!" her sister bellowed. "You were saying, her mother's sick?"

"Yes. Cancer. Meggie could be left without a mother, the way we were."

Kate nodded. "It happens. But she'll survive. It sounds to me like you're getting too attached to this child, and what's worse, to the daddy—" her sister favored Christy with one of her no-nonsense looks "—and you'd better watch that. You'd better get yourself out of this deal."

"I know you're right. I just can't leave little Meggie," Christy said this last part in a remote voice, as if she was talking more to herself than to her sister. "Not right now."

AT WOODWARD PARK, MEGGIE got cotton candy in her hair, let a dog drink from her cola and had a fit because Sam wouldn't let her get into the fountain. Apart from that, Sam's Fourth of July with Meggie was fabulous. He had never had so much fun with his daughter.

Everywhere they went she found something to delight her—a puppy, a flower, balloons. She squealed with every burst of fireworks in the night sky, and when he tucked her in that night the smudges of the small flag painted on her cheek were still there. He looked down at her in awe and wondered why he hadn't made more of an effort to have days like this with his child. He promised himself that he would. Just as soon as his house was fixed, just as soon as Moonlight Grove was back on track.

IN MID-JULY, NEAR THE END of the fifth week of repairs, Sam parked his car in front of Mrs. Southard's again, behind the perennial line of pickups, and noticed Christy out in the drive talking to the young, trim carpenter. She leaned up against the cab of the truck where he had one muscled arm braced above her in a stance that left no doubt about his intentions. Earlier that morning, Sam had heard her offering this guy a cup of coffee—coffee from *Sam's* pantry. Unlike quiet, responsible Jim Holloway, this guy posed a different threat. He had all the markings of a male on the make. He was about Christy's age, tall and brawny. Brawny and *hairy*. The guy wore muscle shirts that did nothing to hide either of those features. He was friendly and jovial. Laughing like an idiot every time he was around Christy...like right now.

When Sam walked past, both of them smiled at him. The guy gave him a two-fingered salute. "All done for the day, Mr. Solomon. Christy's bow-window idea is looking real good."

"Great," Sam muttered, and kept moving. That single word had come out churlish and he hadn't favored them with a reciprocal smile when he said it.

"Meggie's asleep!" Christy called after him. He could hear a smile in her voice.

Gee. They sounded like they were having such a

good time. They'd been talking a lot lately and had even cooked up this idea, Christy and the carpenter, for a window, built of three tall casements canted into a bow overlooking the backyard terraces. *He* was the architect and it was *his* house, but now Christy Lane was getting all creative with the carpenter. Trouble was, it was a great idea. Trouble was, he was starting to appreciate a lot of her great ideas. Christy was the most upbeat, creative person he'd ever met. He liked that in a woman. Apparently, so did the carpenter.

"I apologize for all the disruption around here lately," he told Christy at lunchtime the next day.

"Oh, it's okay. Meggie and I are on the go so much now that we hardly notice the men. We go swimming over at Gayle's almost every afternoon. And we have softball practice every other day now, you know."

Sam nodded. "Even so, I don't want you to worry about anything having to do with the work or answering the workers' questions, or...anything like that."

Christy tilted her head. "You do like the window idea, don't you?"

"Yes, very much," he said truthfully. "I just don't want you distracted by dealing with the workers." He had wanted to add, *Or by making them coffee, or flirting with them.*

But, of course, he bit his tongue. Instead, he told her to page him and he'd come home and handle whatever came up immediately, which was not the smart way to handle his other business, considering the pressures mounting out at Moonlight Grove. The cost of the project was climbing and every day seemed to bring a new disaster. Sam was torn by his competing priorities. When he'd hired Christy, he'd thought she would solve all his problems. Instead, she had added one more distraction to his life.

He thought about telling Christy that talking to the workmen was not a good example for Meggie. Weren't they trying to teach the child to be cautious around strangers? He thought about telling her that he preferred that she not accept dates while she was on duty. He thought about telling her a lot of childish things, but he didn't. Even thinking such thoughts made him feel mean and small. This wasn't Christy's fault. It was the men who were coming on to Christy—that was plain to see. They were all, even the married ones, constantly opening doors for her, grabbing her elbow to make sure she didn't trip over construction materials, winking at her when they walked by, laughing too loud at her little jokes—stuff like that. And now a couple of them had evidently worked up the nerve to ask her out.

Mean and small—that's what he was. The truth was he wanted Christy Lane, with her soothing hands and musical voice and sunny smiles and homey cooking, to be waiting in the kitchen when he got home. Waiting for *him.* In *his* kitchen. Not standing out at the curb talking to some tanned gorilla of a construction worker, giggling up at him and twirling a blond curl around her index finger.

The truth was, he wanted to ask her out on a date himself. Which is precisely what he intended to do.

CHAPTER NINE

SAM DECIDED TO GRAB HIS CHANCE the very next day at lunchtime. That morning the carpenter had arrived early, wearing enough aftershave to flatten a horse and bearing a cappuccino from the 7-Eleven for Christy.

Sam decided he'd better make his move before that guy got his paws on her.

But as soon as he came through the dining room and saw Christy standing in front of the fridge with Meggie, patiently arranging the colored plastic numbers in order, he felt his insides tightening up. Was this wise—dating his child's nanny?

Well, they weren't dating yet. He hadn't asked.

So ask, his aggressive side urged.

Not in front of Meggie! his cautious side warned.

Okay, maybe later. And just one date. Off the premises.

One date, to get the woman out of his system. Then he'd never ask her out again, because undoubtedly, they wouldn't really click. They were, after all, totally wrong for each other. He was an urban Tulsa button-down preppy, and she was a country-and-western down-home girl.

He had to keep his head about him. Had to think about why Christy was on his mind so much. *I feel this way because she is so good with Meggie. I feel this way because she has turned my house into a home. Of course I'm attracted to her—she's warm, open and beautiful. And then there was that kiss…*

Just one date.

Gorilla Man, the carpenter, poked his head in the door just then. "Christy?" he said brightly.

"Mike!" she said just as brightly and stood up. Only then did she notice Sam through the double doors. "Oh, hi, Sam."

"Hello, Mr. Solomon," the carpenter said.

Sam hated the way some of these young craftsmen treated him like he was an old man. This guy wasn't that young…maybe twenty-five. "Hi, Mike. What's up?"

"Daddy!" Meggie launched herself into Sam's arms.

"Hi, sweetheart." Sam hugged his daughter to his waist and kissed her fluffy hair.

"I'm headed out for lunch," Mike the Gorilla explained, "and I thought I'd see if I could pick up a little something for Christy and Meggie."

Meggie was clinging to Sam. "Dad-dee! I'm so glad you drived home for lunch wif me."

"On second thought—" Suddenly the gorilla seemed to be assessing the situation with dawning shrewdness. "As long as Mr. Solomon's here, maybe he wouldn't mind if you took a lunch break for once.'' He raised his black bushy eyebrows at Christy and smiled.

''Oh.'' Christy turned to Sam. ''Would that be okay, Sam? I could fix some sandwiches before I leave, or maybe you and Meggie would like to go out to eat together.''

''IckDonald's!'' Meggie shouted, hanging on to Sam's wrist. Sam was astounded at the child's continual ability to pounce on any opportunity to eat at McDonald's. Even if he could talk her into trying somewhere new, Sam dreaded taking Meggie out to a restaurant although his mother managed to take Meggie out a few times without major incident. Even at a fast-food joint like McDonald's and outing could all too quickly turn into a public fiasco. But when he looked into his daughter's glowing blue eyes, his heart melted. ''Will you promise to be good?''

''I will be so-o-o good. I been bein' real good a lot lately, ain't I, Christy?''

''You've been very, very good,' Christy said with a smile.

''Great!'' The gorilla smacked his hairy paws together. ''I know a great little Mexican place right around the corner. They have a nice, shady outdoor patio.''

''Sounds wonderful!'' Christy grabbed her big red tote. ''I'll be back in an hour, Sam.''

Stunned, Sam could only nod as he watched them take off, while his heart sank into the same jealous quagmire he'd experienced when Jim Holloway had asked Christy out.

Meggie jerked on Sam's wrist. "Pick me up, Daddy. I hungry."

"Okay, sweetie." Sam swung her onto his hip, then rubbed her thin back lightly, the strokes working to soothe and comfort himself as much as his child. As light as she was, Meggie was getting too large for him to carry around with her legs dangling around his knees like this, but even so he carried her over to the large window in the dining room. He didn't make her get down while he watched Christy and the carpenter make their way down the walk.

The carpenter had his big palm spread against Christy's back. They reached his truck, which was nice, clean enough for a work truck. He opened the door for her, held her hand while she climbed into the high seat, and even tucked her long denim skirt up out of the way before carefully closing the door. Sam thought, *Oh, please. Cut the Sir Galahad crap.* But his heart tightened as he watched the carpenter swing into the driver's seat, start the truck and throw his arm across the seat back, nearly touching Christy's soft hair. They backed out of the driveway and there was then nothing more to see.

Sam knew about that great little Mexican restaurant, too. Best chicken enchiladas in Tulsa. In fact, that was where he'd planned to take Christy on *their* first date. How in the hell had the carpenter ended up taking her there instead?

"HOW WOULD YOU FEEL ABOUT going out with *me* sometime?" Sam got right to the point the minute

Christy walked back into the kitchen from her lunch with the carpenter.

Meggie looked up from the table where she had been coloring. The child was apparently reading this scene loud and clear, but Sam couldn't stop himself. He wasn't going to sit idly by, hedging around and waiting for the precise moment while Christy Lane dated goons that weren't good enough for her. Not when he, Sam, was already falling in love with her.

In *love* with her? He thought that he'd been over this already. So when had he decided that? *How* had he decided that? He hadn't even slept with the woman, had only kissed her once, for crying out loud. Man, this whole situation was driving him crazy.

Christy was looking at him as if he'd spoken to her in Swahili. "Go out with you?" she repeated, while she shot him a warning look, tilting her head in Meggie's direction. But Meggie had resumed her coloring, humming pleasantly while she scribbled on the drawings Sam had sketched for her after they got back from McDonald's.

"I mean, now that you and the cop are no longer an item, I was thinking maybe the two of us could do something together some evening. You know, just go out together and have a nice dinner or something."

"Take her to IckDonald's, Daddy," Meggie advised without looking up from her drawings. *Good girl, Meggie,* Sam thought. His daughter, at least, was not fazed by this turn of events. Sam was so relieved he actually chuckled out loud.

"It's not funny!" Meggie's face threatened to break into a pout.

"Oh, Daddy's not laughing at you, pumpkin." He walked over and swept back the child's soft curls with a gentle palm. "I actually think that's a pretty good idea. How about it, Christy, will you go to McDonald's with me tonight?"

Christy stared down at the child, then at Sam. He waited.

"I...UH." CHRISTY LOOKED at Meggie again, making an effort to arrange her face into a reassuring smile. She couldn't believe this. Sam Solomon, the object of her high school adoration—no, her *employer*—was finally asking her on a real date. Even if it was to McDonald's, and she wasn't in a position to accept. How ironic. "I...uh. I can't."

"Why not?" Sam asked.

"Why not?" Meggie echoed.

Christy pointed at the big black kitchen clock on the wall above Sam's desk. "Meggie, look at the time. Better go get the little Choo-Choo and start picking up so we won't be late to softball practice."

Meggie shot off to the living room.

"Sam..." Christy turned on him the minute Meggie was gone. "What are you doing? Asking me out like that? In front of Meggie?"

"Meggie is basically a three-year-old," Sam argued, sensibly, he thought. "She has no idea what's what."

"Despite her disabilities, Meggie is not exactly a

three-year-old. She's a complex child who is rapidly making friends with a baseball team full of sophisticated ten-year-olds. Believe me, those girls *do* know what's what. What do you think is going to happen when Meggie tells her friends about this? When she tells them that her father is dating her nanny?"

Sam couldn't imagine that it mattered what Meggie's softball team thought. They were just little girls. "Look," he blurted, "if you don't want to go out with me, all you have to do is just say so. Don't use Meggie or her friends as some kind of excuse. You certainly didn't have any qualms about making a date with Gorilla Man right in front of her."

"Gorilla Man?"

Sam wanted to slap his own mouth. "I mean," he muttered, "the carpenter."

"Michael?"

"*Yes.* I meant *Mike Smith.*" Sam dragged a frustrated hand through his hair. This conversation was going badly. "All I meant to say was—" he scrambled to redeem the situation "—what do we care what a bunch of little kids think? As long as you're doing all this dating lately, why not go out with me?" The more he talked, the lamer he sounded.

"It goes deeper than that, and you know it. This is a confusing and scary time for Meggie. Under the circumstances—" Christy turned away "—I don't think dating you is a good idea." She stared out the window above the kitchen sink.

He stepped around beside her. She glanced at him once, and Sam felt his vitals tighten at the sight of those alert blue eyes. Man, this woman had a powerful effect on him—too powerful. Right in the middle of this mess, this confusion, this oppressive sadness over Andrea's illness, he found himself starting to feel alive again, maybe even falling in love again. He'd never wanted anyone so badly in all his life. She wasn't anything like the women he normally dated, the ones he kept at a careful distance. But for some reason, there seemed to be no keeping this woman at a distance.

She grabbed a sponge from the sink and started to scrub at the counter, though the granite was perfectly clean. Something about her determined rhythm told him she was upset. But why? He was pretty sure she had feelings for him, too. No one kissed like *that* unless they had some strong feelings of attraction.

"You're only complicating things," she said.

He leaned around the curtain of hair so he could see her expression. Sure enough, her mouth was a tight little rosebud of resistance. God, he wanted to kiss that mouth again. He really did. "Complicating things? Why?"

"Because I'm Meggie's nanny, and because she needs me."

"So?"

"So we can't start dating. What would that be like for Meggie? I mean what if we…"

"If we what? End up being attracted to each other?" He was thinking of the kiss again, of the fact that there was no denying the intensity of it. He would bet she was remembering it, too. Her cheeks were starting to look like ripe twin peaches. "I'm already attracted to you, Christy. It's a fact. There is no *if.* And unless I'm completely delusional here, I think you might be attracted to me, too."

"Our feelings are not the point. Like I said, under the circumstances—"

"Under *what* circumstances?" He wanted to get to the bottom of this. If she was going to give him some crap about the impropriety of dating one's boss…

"What would happen if it *didn't* work out between us? If we get involved, Meggie will know. And then if we break up, how will I keep working for you? I mean—"

"You mean we can't get to know each other like ordinary people?"

"We're *not* ordinary people. This is not an ordinary situation. In case you've forgotten—" again, Christy started scrubbing with a determined rhythm that told him she meant what she was about to say "—your ex-wife is seriously ill. Your child, who's already struggling against serious challenges, needs us."

"But what about us? What about you and me? You're here in my house every single day. Every single day I see you. I hear you…singing, talking so sweetly to Meggie. Every day I—" He started to say, *Every day I smell you,* because for him, that was by far her most elusive, most attractive quality, but he had the good sense to stop himself. "We've gotten to know each other, every day. I'm attracted to you. And if you're attracted to me, what would it hurt to go out?"

"It's not a good idea, that's all." She kept scrubbing, and Sam felt there was more to this than she was telling him. She was giving him all kinds of rational-sounding excuses, but he sensed that she was afraid of something. But what?

"This is about that kiss the night of the storm, isn't it?" The sponge halted and Sam felt a beat of warning skitter across his chest. He shouldn't have kissed her like that. He shouldn't have kissed her *in this house,* even if they had both been badly shaken that night.

He'd known it the minute he'd held her. He'd told himself he was comforting her, and, at first, he'd meant to, but with the first taste of her lips he'd been driven beyond reason. Since then, that kiss had worked like a drug in his blood. And now, right now, he wanted more. She could sense that, and she was afraid he'd take advantage of her because she worked for him.

She turned her face up to him. Her mouth had dropped open into a soft O. "You promised not to mention that," she breathed in accusation.

He had promised. He'd said that he would act as if it had never happened. And yet, less than a month later, he was acting like, feeling like, everything hinged upon that one impulsive act, as if everything started and ended with that kiss. And it did, somehow. Or rather, it started and ended with her, with Christy Lane, who was looking at him now as if he was some kind of depraved monster just because he'd taken the next logical step and asked her to dinner.

"I'm sorry," he said, wishing she would stop staring at him like that. "I did promise not to mention it again. It's just that..." He dropped off, feeling frustrated in the face of his own need for her. But as he looked into her eyes, that need only became stronger, driving him as he leaned forward, angling his face over hers.

She did not turn her face away. But she breathed, "Stop," as if she knew exactly what he intended to do.

"Do you mean that?" he said, leaning closer, breathing directly against her partially opened mouth. "Because I will stop if that's what you really want."

He leaned in closer and sealed his lips over hers. The jolt and the impact of her mouth felt the same as it had the first time. No woman had ever had this effect on him. It was a heady sensation. It was as if he'd never been alive until now, until he'd found Christy Lane. She threw her arms up around his neck and in one fluid motion their faces angled, turned, as their seeking mouths drank in more and their bodies fit to each other like matching pieces of a living puzzle.

He brought his hand up and cupped the back of her head in a possessive way that made her tighten her arms around his neck. A great wave of joy informed him that she must feel the same thing for him as he did for her. *Desire.*

Out in the living room Meggie made a high "choo-choo" sound and they broke apart.

"You see?" Christy said, clearly out of breath. "We can't do this in your house."

''Okay. We won't. That's why I'm asking you out on a date.''

''What would that solve?'' But there was a new note of uncertainty in her voice and she cast her gaze downward.

''It would clear the air,'' he pressed. ''I haven't been able to think straight since we kissed.'' He turned away and raked his hands through his hair. ''Despite everything else I've got to worry about—Meggie, Andrea's illness, the trouble at Moonlight Grove—I find myself thinking about that damned kiss way too often.''

''Well, that's why we shouldn't have done it,'' Christy said softly, sensibly, from behind him.

He turned around again and studied her, trying to find the lie in her face. Her lips were still puffy and wet from his assault and her cheeks looked flushed, beating with life. Her words were saying they shouldn't have done it, but her body was saying something else.

''Why don't you go out with me so we can find out whether we should have done it or not.''

She dropped her gaze again.

''Why not?'' he persisted. ''You're dating these other guys....'' He trailed off, wondering if his passions were getting the better of him. Right now he was practically throbbing with desire for her. ''Look. We're adults. We can keep our relationship out of this house, away from Meggie if we want to. Just one date.''

''Okay.'' She heaved such a heavy sigh that Sam

thought she might as well be agreeing to a prison sentence. ''But it can't distract you from spending time with Meggie.''

''It won't. We can go out late, if you want, after her bedtime.''

''Okay. One date. As long as Meggie doesn't know.''

CHAPTER TEN

IT WAS NEAR HER BEDTIME when Sam dropped Meggie at Gayle's elegant old home in the historic Maple Ridge area of Tulsa.

"I'll be out pretty late," he told his mother.

"That's fine. Meggie can stay overnight." Gayle's eyes twinkled and Sam wondered if his mother had some idea of what was going on between him and Christy. He hoped not.

Sam picked up Christy and one look at her took his breath away. For their first date she'd chosen a simple black halter dress. She'd pulled her blond hair back into a loose ponytail, bound with a stunning turquoise clip that matched an unusual choker at her throat.

Sam took her to the Polo Grill, where their dinner—delicious, elegant and most definitely romantic—got off to a wonderful, easy start. Over drinks and appetizers they discussed Meggie, her amazing progress at swimming and Sam's plans to take her out to Moonlight Grove with him soon. And Sam was not surprised that he and Christy discovered plenty of things to talk about besides Meggie. He felt as if he could talk to this woman about anything.

He was amazed to learn that Christy was on the verge of selling a country-and-western song she had sent to Nashville.

''Mary Jane Haggerty is interested in it.''

''You're kidding.''

''No. It's just a simple ballad. But I do think her voice is right for it.''

''That's so cool! What's the song about?'' Sam was interested, excited, by this facet of her. From the start it had been obvious that she loved music, but he'd never guessed she was an aspiring songwriter. He suddenly flashed back to the sophisticated instruments he'd seen in her apartment. He hadn't imagined there was any commercial side to Christy's musicality and hadn't thought about the sacrifices she might have made for the sake of her art. He also hadn't thought about the fact that this explained her checkered, and somewhat mediocre, employment history.

''Oh, I'd rather not say what it's about.'' She smiled that contagious smile of hers. ''I'd rather you were driving along one day, minding your own business—'' she leaned back as if taking a lazy drive and her voice took on a dreamy lilt ''—just listening to the radio, and then…'' She sat forward with her palms splayed at him, fingers spread, ''Suddenly you hear it! And you think, oh, my gosh, that's Christy Lane's song!''

He chuckled. She certainly had a way of delighting him. ''But I don't listen to country-and-western stations,'' he explained apologetically. Because he could see this was very important to her—it was her art—

but he thought it was equally important to be honest about their likes and dislikes, their differences and similarities. He couldn't imagine being dishonest with her, especially because she was taking care of such an important part of Sam's life—Meggie. They had to be able to trust each other, to be open, on so many different levels.

"You're kidding. You live in Oklahoma, and you never listen to country-and-western music?"

He raised his hands in a helpless gesture. "Sorry. Call me culturally challenged."

"I didn't know it was physically possible not to listen to country-and-western music in Oklahoma," she teased. Then she flapped a hand at him. "It's okay. This song'll be a crossover." Her tone was completely confident.

"A crossover?"

"The kind that will get picked up by pop-rock stations, easy listening, the whole spectrum." She sighed. "At least I'm hoping so."

"Me, too. But if you won't tell me the title, how will I know it's the song you wrote?" He was finding himself caught up in this dream of hers, imagining actually hearing a song written by Christy Lane on the radio.

"Oh, the title, once you hear the title—and the words—that will pretty much tell you." She smiled again. "I like to think no one else could have written it."

"You're kidding," Sam repeated, but he could tell she wasn't playing a game with him. She'd actually written a song that was actually being considered by Mary Jane Haggerty. Sam felt himself becoming increasingly intrigued, enlivened with an excitement that he hadn't felt in a long time.

"I hope it actually happens for you," he said sincerely. "I truly wish you luck with this, Christy."

"Why, thank you." She looked down, her pretty face demure. "There's always some luck involved, for sure, but mostly it's about hard work. I'm not afraid of that."

No, Sam thought, she certainly wasn't. He'd seen how hard she could work around his house. Christy Lane was a woman who threw her whole self, heart and soul, into everything she did. He was starting to realize that behind that perpetually smiling face was a fierce determination, a fire in her belly, similar to the drive he felt about his own work. The two of them were alike in many ways. Maybe that was part of the attraction.

"I admire people who work hard."

"I know you do. You work pretty hard yourself. Which reminds me…"

"Yes?"

"I've been meaning to bring this up with you."

"What?"

"It's about Meggie. She needs you, Sam. She needs more of your time, especially now. And, well, she has a softball game this Saturday."

Sam tensed up, feeling trapped between responsibility and guilt, as he often felt when Meggie was in his care. He could never figure out a way to reconcile

Meggie's needs with his work even under the best of circumstances, but now…Sam bit his lip. ''I'm afraid I'll have to see if Mom can take her.''

''Gayle told me she wouldn't be able to make it. She has to be at a photography showing.''

''Then can you take her? I'll pay you overtime.''

''Sam, she needs *you.*''

He sighed. ''I can't just drop my responsibilities out at Moonlight Grove.''

''She's had two games already and you've missed them both.''

''This project is at a critical place, Christy. We're due to start pouring the concrete again this Friday, and we can't stop until it's done. I can't change that.''

''Things are at a critical place for Meggie right now, too.''

When he merely shook his head, Christy sighed. ''Okay. I'll take her.'' She took a sip of her wine and changed the subject. ''Tell me what's going on with Meggie's mother, if you don't mind. I do care.''

He gazed across the candlelight into her gentle blue eyes. That was the thing he liked about her, loved about her—she did care. More than anyone he'd met in a very long time. This woman cared in a way that lowered Sam's defenses and melted his heart.

''It's not good.'' His forked scraped and chimed on his plate as he pushed the food around, unable to take a bite.

''You mean the clinical trial?''

''Yes.''

''What will happen?''

"Andrea says that they'll try again in a few months, but I think she's just being brave. I think...it may only be a matter of time now."

A long silence passed while Christy's gaze traveled up to a brass wall sconce. In the candlelight Sam thought he saws tears welling in her eyes. Then she lowered her head and touched her folded hands to her lips in a praying pose. "Poor little Meggie," she finally whispered.

"Yes."

The waiter came to pour more wine, but Christy shook her head and Sam waved him away. "Let's get out of here," he offered. "Would you like to go for a walk?"

SAM SLOWLY DROVE TO Woodward Park, which was nearby. There were other couples strolling around the ornamental gardens in the moonlight, and as he went around to her side of the Suburban and helped her out of the door, Sam imagined he and Christy must look similar to them. A young couple about to stroll under the huge trees and along the terraced rose beds. Holding hands and...falling in love.

Instead, they were going to be discussing his tragic circumstances and Andrea's illness and what to do about it. Discussing how to support his mentally challenged daughter through this crisis. He wished instead that he could simply make small talk with Christy, the way he imagined those other couples were doing. He wished he could touch her hair, so soft looking in the moonlight, sit with her on a secluded bench somewhere and kiss her once again.

But this was Christy, who already knew more about his life than any of the other women he had dated. She broached the heavy subject of Andrea's illness immediately.

"What, exactly, will happen to Andrea now that this clinical trial has failed?"

"They will give her some more chemo and wait and see if new tumors occur."

"And if they do?"

"More surgery. More chemotherapy. Everything I've found on the Internet indicates that at her stage this new vaccine therapy was her best hope. And now it's failed. I don't know," Sam added as they climbed a moonlit hill toward the rose gardens. "I keep hoping her doctors will find a way to eradicate the disease."

The roses were in peak blooming period, and the lighter-colored varieties floated in the moonlight like hundreds of ghost flowers. The place was redolent with the roses' feminine scents—fruit, spices, honey—and as they strolled the paths, close but never touching, Sam's ache for Christy grew. They stopped once—Christy inclined her head to the sound of a guitar strumming somewhere in the distance—and behind her the ethereal white blooms of a blooming bush fluttered in the moonlight. Sam thought he might actually kiss her then, but Christy continued with her ruminating about Andrea. "What can we do to help her?"

"I think about that all the time."

They pondered the problem in silence as they continued over the rock pathways, past benches and over footbridges. Christy returned Sam's glances as they walked. In the moonlight, he couldn't make out her features distinctly, but he could sense her compassion.

They stopped in an area where the winding stone paths meandered beside the rippling waters of a man-made watercourse, designed to give the effect of a falling chain of small pools and streams, when in actuality it was fed by the city water supply. The pools were swollen and the "creeks" were running faster on this night because of this summer's persistent storms.

"I'm still sending her child support, of course," Sam said, "even though Meggie's here with me now. And I try to talk to her on the phone frequently and give her support that way."

"It seems to me the main thing she needs is time with Meggie," Christy said softly. "I have an idea. The last game of Meggie's softball season is on August 10—"

"Oh, man," Sam groaned, "that's the weekend the investors are coming out."

"We can talk about that later." Christy went on. "That would be also about the time Andrea finishes up her next treatment. That might be a good time for Meggie to go out to California for a visit before she has to come back here to start school."

"But what would that do to Meggie? Seeing Andrea like that? Is it selfish of me to want to shield my daughter from all of this?'' He had stopped on a raised stone pathway that curved through glowing beds of periwinkles and impatiens.

In the mixed illumination of the moon and the park lights, Christy spotted a rock outcropping that jutted out over a gurgling pool of water. ''Let's sit down over there,'' she suggested.

They picked their way around the flower beds, and when they got to the ledge they lowered themselves onto the stone, close together with their legs stretched forth on the honeycombed limestone, still warm from the day's sun.

''You're not selfish,'' Christy began when they were settled. ''You're human, and you wish this weren't happening. But if Meggie doesn't go back to California soon, it sounds like it could get too late.''

He glanced over his shoulder, where her hand was touching him. When she slid it away he sighed and pulled a piece of tall grass out of the nearby brush and stripped it between his fingers. ''I just wish I could wave a magic wand and give Andrea's life back to her.''

''But you can't. And now we have to do the best we can. Andrea needs to see her daughter somehow. And I think Meggie needs to see her mother as much as Andrea needs to see her.''

''I know,'' Sam conceded. ''You're right. But I can't figure out how to do that. I can't just stick the child on a plane and send her back to her mother for a visit. Andrea can't handle her alone anymore. And I get the impression that my former in-laws are overwhelmed by all of this—they're older and Andrea's dad's not well himself—and I can't take time off from Moonlight Grove right now. The place is a disaster." He sighed and braced his hands behind him. "We're having to change the drainage completely. Some of the manholes we're dropping are huge, and with the ground so wet, we're having trouble digging the holes. It seems as if as soon as I get one part of my life under control, another part goes haywire. It's like I'm on a roller coaster and I can't get off. I don't know how I'll ever be able to take care of Meggie full-time."

Moments passed with only the sound of the rippling water below.

Finally Christy offered quietly, "Why don't I help by taking Meggie to California?"

"You'd do that?"

"For Meggie I would. And…for you."

He smiled. "I'm amazed at your generosity."

"It's not totally unselfish. Mary Jane has set me up with a talent agent out in California. I'd welcome the opportunity to meet with him in person."

"Nevertheless, I'm very grateful." He felt so close to her right now. "Could I hold your hand?" he asked.

They laced their fingers and Sam's heart sped up as he rubbed his thumb over hers. All of the feelings they hadn't yet spoken coursed between them in this simple bond.

"I keep thinking…" His voice broke, then he continued. "I keep wondering if all the grief from our divorce didn't contribute to Andrea getting sick. You know, maybe it weakened her immune system or something."

"Oh, Sam. Don't do that to yourself." Christy squeezed his hand.

"Why do I always end up spilling my guts to you like this?" Sam asked. "I mean, sometimes I feel like I've known you all of my life or something."

"Actually..." Christy hesitated. "Actually, you may have known me for longer than you think...from a distance. Maybe you don't remember, but we went to the same high school."

"We did?" For a moment he was genuinely surprised, but then he shrugged off this news. "Central High was a huge school, wasn't it?"

"Yeah. It's okay that you don't remember me. You wouldn't have noticed me in a million years."

"I can hardly believe that." His gaze swept over her face, her mouth. He looked down at their linked fingers, frowning. "We didn't ever have a class together, did we?"

"No. We were on different planets. You were popular and I was shy. You were the tall, handsome football hero, and I was the short, geeky musician, who didn't know how to fix her frizzy hair, how to act, how to dress." She emitted a self-deprecating little laugh.

Sam smiled to himself, thinking that Christy, sometimes, still didn't know how to dress. But he was also thinking how little that mattered now, when he'd seen the tender-hearted woman beneath those offbeat clothes. A woman he was falling in love with.

"I remember once, out in the school parking lot, some big guys were pushing around this new kid. I think he was new to the country and he couldn't even understand the names they were calling him. You trotted over and made them stop, ran them off. I'll never forget it. Do you remember that?"

He squinted up at the stray strands of her hair, shimmering like a halo in the dim moonlight. "Vaguely," he said. He was trying hard to remember *her* from high school, but honestly couldn't. It seemed impossible that he hadn't noticed her. She was the most stunning creature he had ever seen. "Your hair's not frizzy," he said, because he wasn't ready to tell her what he was really thinking. "It's lush and very pretty. I really love your hair," he said honestly. The truth was, he liked everything about her. "It's unique."

Christy reached up to self-consciously pat the massive pony tail that belled out from her neck. "Well, it's the same old hair I've had since high school. In fact, lately I've been thinking about cutting it. Long, curly hair seems kind of—" she hunched her shoulders "—I don't know...juvenile or something."

"No! Don't ever change it. In fact, don't ever, ever change anything about yourself." Keeping a firm grip on her, his free hand tilted her chin up so he could take in her features.

As she looked into Sam's eyes—eyes that sent every one of her nerve endings singing—Christy thought how amazing it was that her feelings for Sam Solomon had never gone away. What a wondrous thing desire was. And she definitely had it for Sam Solomon. Always had.

But she couldn't help remembering that while she had secretly loved him, he'd married another woman, and looking at Sam a moment ago as he spoke of his ex-wife's illness, Christy had to wonder what he was really feeling now. The tragic damage to their child had torn them apart, but what if they still loved each other despite the divorce? She couldn't go one step further with this man until she knew the answer to that one.

She turned away from the magnetic intensity of his gaze and said, "I know it's hard, watching someone you care about going through all this pain and suffering." She drew a huge breath, then said in a rush, "Do you…do you still love her?"

"No." He frowned down at her. "If I still loved Andrea, I'd be with her right now instead of sitting in this park with you."

"Oh." His blunt answer stunned Christy. And thrilled her. There was actually hope. But still, she needed reassurance. "Why *are* you sitting in this park with me?"

"I think you know why." Sam tried to force a light laugh, but the sound came out husky, as if his breathing were suddenly tight.

He curled his fingers under hers, gripping her small ones in a double "C." Christy looked down at their hands, cupped together like two bass clefs. The physical chemistry between them was so strong. It was going to be a challenge to keep it constrained. But she knew she would. She always let the men she dated know, as soon as possible, that for her there would be no sex without a firm, exclusive commitment. She found that most men could accept that. Most even admired it. Sam Solomon wasn't going to be any exception to her rule. This was the time to test—and set—the boundaries.

Sam was thinking about the fact that he'd told himself he was going to just go out with her this once, just to get her out of his system. But it hadn't worked out that way, not at all. The more time he spent with her, the more time he wanted to spend with her.

They passed a moment in silence as the water made the wet sounds of a rainy summer below them. She merely sat there, looking at him with her eyes wide, as if waiting for him to make the next move. Her mouth looked soft and full, her lips unconsciously parted, unconsciously inviting. He let his gaze fall to that open, shimmering mouth.

He reached out and cupped the back of her neck, pulling her head toward him, studying her eyes, her reaction, as he brought his mouth closer and closer to hers. Right before his lips reached hers, he stopped, giving her time to say no.

Her breath was hot, sweet. Her mouth like a luscious fruit that he wanted to devour. But aware that for her this was some kind of test, he kept control and let their breath mingle for one more instant before his lips touched hers. It was more like a taste than a kiss, for he was truly ravenous for her and knew that soon his willpower would shatter.

Sam, who'd done so much partying in the Tulsa singles scene that he was thoroughly sick of it, was amazed that a mere touching of lips would have such import for him. But it did. His heart thudded a drumbeat in his chest. How many women had he bedded, only to feel hollow afterward? Even with Andrea, the sex had often felt like…just sex. One of life's fine pleasures.

But with Christy things were different.

It wasn't just that Christy was exciting—that was too insipid a word for it. It was that one kiss, just one kiss with Christy Lane, felt momentous. It felt like a *decision.*

With extreme control, he traced his lips over hers, slowly, almost reverently, as if to communicate the wonder building in him. She moaned and he opened his eyes so that he could watch hers closing with the weight of emotion. Her fingers tightened inside his. His heart pounded harder with the knowledge that she was as affected by, as terrified by, this moment as he. She, too, must feel the gravity of what they were doing.

As her mouth opened wider to him, he could no longer suppress the urge to crush her to him, to possess her. He released her fingers and pressed his strong hands around her ribs. She responded by twisting her body into his so that they were pressed fully chest to chest. Heart to heart.

There was no fear, no clinging together in sorrow,

no storm outside to explain away their fierce reaction this time. They were locked together, surrounded by the earthy smells of the moonlit park, two beings made for each other. As their bodies molded and fit and the kiss deepened and grew more passionate, Sam thought how they would have no excuses with which to dismiss their passion later.

She moaned again and they only took enough time for a quick breath before he slanted his head the other way and fastened his mouth over hers again. This time their joining was almost savage. Their tongues danced, their heads moved and they quickly found the thrilling fit that would lead them, time and again, straight to passion.

"Christy," he breathed against her mouth when the kiss ended. "Don't think I'm crazy, okay? But I think I'm falling in love with you."

Christy drew her head back in sheer wonder. Surely this was a dream. Sam Solomon was saying that he was falling in love with her. But no, it was real. She ran her palms over the muscles in his forearms, his sun-bleached hairs coarse under her sensitive fingers. He was solid, real, under her hands. "Oh, God. When did you realize that?"

Sam ran his hands up her sides, around her back. "I think it was the night you made chili for me at your place. I wanted to touch you so badly. Like this." He pressed his hands at her waist. "I wanted to stay right there with you and pretend that was our place. That Meggie was our little girl, eating macaroni and cheese in front of the TV and that you were making my dinner in our kitchen. That later, we'd go into that pink bedroom of yours, and..." He released a shaky breath.

His eyes studied her face while his hands kept up their insistent pressure. "Oh, Christy. To tell you the truth, I think I actually started to love you the minute I saw you sitting at my piano, that first time we met."

As Christy studied his sincere eyes, she could only think how she'd been in love with Sam Solomon for years. Carrying a torch as they say. Never able to get her high school hero out of her mind. And now, because of some poor woman's misfortune, because a tornado had swept through town, Sam Solomon was holding her and telling her he was falling in love with her.

"What about you?" His eyes looked so open and vulnerable that she had to look down. Even as she did, he did not lose his nerve. "Are you starting to have feelings for me?" he asked. "Or is that just wishful thinking on my part? Christy, I have to know." He pulled her to him and murmured near her ear. "This is driving me crazy."

She closed her eyes as the sound of the rushing water filled the silence, its rhythmic pulsing counting off the beats of this moment that Christy Lane never dreamed could happen. All this time she'd tried to get him out of her system. All this time she'd told herself he was only a high school crush, a teenage fantasy that she sometimes wrote songs about. All this time she'd dated man after man, trying to find true love, but true love never came because she could never get

Sam Solomon out of her heart. And now here he was, holding her, waiting for the answer to a question that had never even been a question for her.

"Yes," she breathed, then disciplined herself to keep her words careful, "I have feelings for you."

He released a pent-up breath and squeezed her so tight she almost felt her bones give. "Wow. When did you realize that?" He backed his face up and the look of boyish wonder on his strong, handsome face moved her as nothing else in her life ever had.

But Christy's heart thrummed a counter-warning, stopping her from being as open as Sam. Why couldn't she just tell him she'd had a thing about him ever since high school? Because he was one of Tulsa's most eligible bachelors and she was afraid he'd feel trapped, as if she'd manipulated this whole nanny thing from the start? Because bringing up the past would highlight the vast differences in their backgrounds? Or was it simply because she was afraid that—her heart beat harder at this thought—afraid that he was clinging to her because she'd become some kind of anchor, a safe place in the recent storms of his life. She had this long-cherished notion that true love could never exist without honesty. And she had kept all of her relationships totally honest. And all of her relationships had ended, too. Just like the most recent one with Kyle. Was there such a thing as too much honesty?

While she wrestled with these tortured thoughts his eyes beseeched her.

"When did you first realize you had feelings for me?" he repeated.

She looked down, afraid he might read the truth in her eyes. "I...I don't know. I...I guess it was watching you with Meggie, it...it touched me, you know?" That much was true.

But he mistook the meaning of her lowered gaze. "Christy," he whispered, and kissed her brow. "You don't have to be shy with me. I think you are beautiful. So, so beautiful."

He wrapped his arms fully around her and angled his face under hers as he pressed a tender, moist kiss to her lips. When her lips opened, he took his chance and assaulted her mouth again, tipping her head back as he threaded his long fingers up into her hair, loosening her ponytail from its moorings.

"Sam..." She pushed away, making a business of tucking in the ends of her unraveling hair, when she was actually struggling to sort out her confused feelings.

"Here." He reached up, stilling her hands, then guiding her fingers away. "Let me." But instead of anchoring the stray strands of the ponytail, he unsnapped the colorful clip and pulled it free, fanning her long curls over her shoulders.

Christy's hands fluttered up in a gesture of modesty. "Sam—"

"Shh. Let me." He took his time touching, weaving his fingers through her tresses.

Christy was helpless to resist his touch. With his hands still threaded in her hair, he briefly clasped the back of her neck again, this time massaging as if in the grip of some intention, some urge, that he was holding back. As she looked at his face, she found herself unable to recall her doubts of only a moment ago. His hands, his eyes, his mouth were obliterating her worries about his first marriage, about her high school crush, about everything but *him*, this moment. "Sam..." She tried to fight this tumult of feeling.

"I've been dying to touch you like this," he whispered.

Christy felt her passion, and his, threatening to escape its bounds. She whispered, "This is going too fast. You'd better take me home, Sam." She tried to say it calmly and sensibly, though her pulse was thundering, betraying her with a shaky voice.

Sam backed his face away from hers. Christy Lane, he had no doubt, was an honest, simple, gentle woman. Not some sophisticated, manipulative socialite. He was pretty sure that for her sex wasn't a form of recreation. He knew he'd have to win her over before she'd let him prove, in the deepest way he knew of, how much he cared for her.

While he looked in her eyes, he said the very words he'd told himself he wouldn't. "Okay. I understand. I'll take you home. But first, would you promise to go out on another date with me?"

CHAPTER ELEVEN

ANOTHER DATE BECAME TWO, then three. Four. Five. Too many to count. Movies. Dinners. More long walks.

Christy stopped accepting dates with Jim or Mike. Jim backed off like a gentleman, but Mike continued to pressure her. He even made an issue of Christy's rebuffs in front of Meggie one day.

"Are you dating the boss or something?"

Christy felt her cheeks flame as she checked Meggie's reaction.

"Who's the boss?" Meggie said, all innocence.

"Nobody," Christy answered, and shot the carpenter a censuring look.

The next day, Sam found another carpenter.

In the meantime, Gayle seemed happy to baby-sit—surprisingly, without asking questions—while Sam took Christy to the Kitchens à la Tulsa architectural tour. She took him to an outdoor jazz festival. He took her on a nature hike through Redbud Valley. She took him on a picnic under the cottonwoods and willows in the riverside park near her apartment. Together, they finally took Meggie to Moonlight Grove, where under their supervision, Meggie explored while

Christy sadly examined the damage and the massive cleanup work in progress.

"It is a mess," Christy had to agree.

"Doesn't look much like a fancy resort now, does it?"

"But it will. I can see how this will be a beautiful, peaceful place, like a living Thomas Kinkade painting. It will attract people in droves."

"I'm beginning to wonder."

"What are those things?" Trying to distract him from his discouragement, Christy pointed at three huge concrete structures, shaped like bells.

"Those are the manholes. Some people call them cisterns. I've got to get them in the ground before Mr. Yoshida returns in August."

"On the tenth?"

"Yes," Sam said ruefully, "the day of Meggie's last ball game." They'd been avoiding this conversation.

"Isn't there some way to work it out?"

"I'll try to make it up to her," Sam promised.

But the weeks before Meggie's last softball game passed in a blur.

When Sam continued to miss the games, Christy felt obligated to help him see how important the team had become to his daughter.

"Meggie's last ball game is tomorrow," she reminded him as he hurried out the door that Friday morning.

"Damn!" Sam snapped his fingers.

"You still can't make it?"

"I told you, Yoshida and the investors are flying in to evaluate the situation at Moonlight Grove."

"But you haven't made one single game and this is her last one!"

"These investors aren't just a bunch of downtown bankers." Sam's voice grew testy while he searched for his keys. "They're flying in from *Japan,* Christy. Try to understand. This project has been in the works for years."

"So has Meggie," Christy said quietly. She reached past his shoulder, plucked his keys out of Meggie's arts-and-crafts litter on the kitchen desk and handed them to him.

Sam snatched the keys. He wasn't sure if he was irritated with Christy or with himself. He loved Christy, but this baseball thing had become a sore point between them. He had thought the whole idea was ill advised from the start, and now Christy was making him feel guilty for not participating in this pretense. He sighed. Meggie was never going to play in a real game, but Christy had proceeded to take Meggie to practice on schedule and Sam had supported that. It had seemed like a convenient way to keep Meggie and Christy out of the place as much as possible during the house repair work.

But Christy had refused to see that that's about as far as it went. "It's not like she's ever going to actually play in a game, Christy." He forced his voice to be reasonable.

"She might."

"She hasn't yet, has she?"

"No, but she could. You never know. The coach is a really nice person. She's been encouraging Meggie a lot. And the other girls have been really patient with her. She could be ready to play any time now. You should at least come to the game and show your support. Sometimes a person just has to show up."

"And sit on the sidelines and watch all the normal little girls play?"

Christy stifled a gasp and bit her lip.

"I'm sorry," Sam said immediately. He came toward her with his hands out. "I shouldn't have said that."

But Christy turned away. She didn't want him to touch her at this moment, though some part of her understood Sam's poor attitude. In fact, she understood Sam better than he understood himself. Gayle had told her some things about his childhood, how his father was. And Christy could only imagine how it must hurt a former superathlete to see his own child so incapacitated. But no matter how much Meggie's problems hurt him, Christy expected Sam to do better than this. Couldn't he see that Meggie had to be accepted the way she was, loved the way she was? Couldn't he see that escaping into his work, because it was less painful than watching his daughter struggle to play a simple game of baseball, was wrong? Wrong for him, wrong for her.

Sam waited for her to speak, but when she wouldn't he finally said, "You just don't understand, Christy. A man's work has got to come first."

Still, she wouldn't look at him. She couldn't. She

wanted to point out that he sounded like his father. But who was she to be telling him such things?

After another moment of silence she heard his heels rapping on the hardwood floor as he passed through the dining room, then she heard the lonely sounding click of the front door as it closed behind a man choosing work over love.

And that night, for the first time, Christy broke their date, using a lame excuse. But the truth was she didn't have the heart to sit across the table at some fine, intimate restaurant and look into the eyes of a handsome man who was too blind to see that he was doing the same thing to his child that had been done to him.

MEGGIE WOKE UP RIDICULOUSLY early on the morning of her last softball game. Christy was thankful that she had arrived extra early and was already in the kitchen, preparing a hearty breakfast for the child.

"Where's Daddy?" Meggie bounced down the stairs and snatched a crisp piece of bacon.

"He had to go, honey. He had to work."

Sam's leave-taking an hour before had been filled with the tension created by his guilt and Christy's disappointment. He'd come down the stairs just as Christy was unlocking the back door. "Good morning," he said, unsmiling.

Her heart fell when she saw that he was wearing a suit, because that meant he was determined to go ahead with his big meeting. She wanted to be angry with him for that. But why did he have to look so incredibly handsome!

Lately, she'd gotten used to seeing him every morning in polo shirts, cargo shorts and hiking boots—his standard uniform for the hot, dirty work out at Moonlight Grove—so that the sight of him in the tailored dress suit made her almost breathless. The taupe gabardine fabric complemented his flaxen hair. The box-pleat trousers emphasized his flat abdomen. The collar of his snow-white shirt with a dark tie cinching it set off his tanned skin.

"You're here early," he said.

"I want to be sure Meggie eats a decent breakfast."

Christy swung her big red shoulder bag up onto the counter. She had everything she'd need for the game stashed in there: water, sunscreen, her camera. She wondered if Sam would have thought about any of those things.

"Christy, please don't be angry at me because I can't get behind this baseball thing. I just don't want Meggie—and you—to be disappointed by unrealistic expectations."

Maybe not, Christy thought, but didn't say, *but you also don't want to accept your daughter for who she really is.*

THE DAY WAS PERFECT, sunny, the kind of summer day made expressly for baseball.

Christy parked her little Contour alongside the Lexuses and Land Rovers driven by the parents of Tulsa's upscale Woodward Park area.

When Meggie spotted the hot-pink jerseys of her

teammates she flew across the expanse of green grass and collided with them in a hopping jumble of girlish hugs. As Christy passed by the little cluster, she saw one of the bigger girls cheerfully thumping Meggie on the back. ''You ready to beat those Stars today, Meggie girl?'' the child said sweetly.

Christy smiled and continued toward the dugout, lugging her lawn chair. The bleachers were often packed, and would be especially so for this final game between the Woodward Angels and the Broken Bow Stars. These teams had played each other several times earlier in the summer and all the girls knew about Meggie—that she was special, that she wasn't really expected to do anything athletic or even particularly coordinated.

Sam was probably right. There was no way the coach was going to let Meggie play. Not today, of all days.

Despite her down mood, Christy pasted on a warm smile as she greeted the mothers of Meggie's teammates. Many of the mothers, and both of the coaches, too, knew that Meggie's mother was dying of cancer, and they had been kind. Christy was mindful of the fact that on most teams a child with Meggie's disabilities would not be included. She was also mindful of the fact that it was through the aegis of Gayle that Meggie was able to ''play'' at all.

She spotted Gayle in the distance, near the dugout. Christy and Gayle both preferred to sit there so they could help the coach manage Meggie if the child got too excited.

Gayle, looking chic as always in matching pineapple-print shirt and shorts, had her hand on the back of a lawn chair talking to another grandmother-age woman. It was Lou Allen, Amy Pearson's mother. When Christy had worked as Amy's nanny, Lou had always acted as if her grandchildren were little gods, superior to all other children. She wondered if Gayle had to suffer the woman's misplaced pity because of Meggie.

"Sam's not coming?" Gayle asked as soon as Christy was within earshot.

"No." Christy didn't elaborate and proceeded to unfold her lawn chair.

"Hi, Christy," Lou Allen cooed, "how are you liking your job at Sam's?"

"Just fine." Christy really wasn't in the mood for Lou Allen's self-serving brand of chitchat, which was sure to follow even the most polite inquiry.

Lou turned on Sam's mother. "I will never forgive you for stealing Christy away from us, Gayle. Amy has been forced to rely upon Cloretta Waddle for child care this summer. That woman certainly has no talent for bringing out the potential of gifted children, the way Christy does."

Here it comes, Christy thought, glad that her sunglasses kept Lou Allen from seeing that she rolled her eyes.

"Why, Little Joshua was actually beginning to master Chopin under Christy's tutelage. I don't know where we'll ever find another piano teacher like her."

"Oh, look, Lou," Gayle said in an effort to deflect

the woman from her bragging. "I think I see Bradley and Amy." She shaded her eyes, squinting toward the bleachers. "Better get up there. It's almost time for the game to start."

"Yes! I'd better run! My granddaughter Kaitlyn will undoubtedly be first up to bat!" The other woman turned and waved as she headed toward the bleachers.

Gayle shook her head when Lou was gone. "I suppose in Lou's opinion, a talented nanny like you is wasting her time with a child like Meggie."

"Well, I'm not." Christy plopped down in the lawn chair. "Meggie likes to sing and draw and have fun just like any other child. And she likes to play baseball."

"I couldn't agree more." Gayle sat down beside her. "Where is my son?"

"A meeting," Christy answered tiredly. Her disappointment in Sam made her weary. It was as if she was an inflatable woman and someone had let the air out of her. "With Japanese investors."

Christy could feel Gayle studying her profile. "Over the years I have tried and tried to get Sam more involved with Meggie. I thought if anybody could accomplish that feat, you might." Gayle stared out at the baseball diamond. "You would think Sam would realize that he is making the same mistake his father made," the older woman said.

Christy turned to her, suddenly interested. "I was thinking the same thing, kind of. About how Sam wants Meggie to be a certain way. How he wants her all contained in a tidy little padded box stamped Disabled. How he can't just let her try something even if it's..."

"Pointless?" Gayle supplied. "That's what Sam's father always called Sam's obsession with surroundings, with color, with..."

"Beauty?" Christy supplied.

"I was going to say 'design.' But Sam's father, I'm afraid, really did think beauty was pointless as well. He told Sam that a 'designer,'" Gayle made quote marks in the air with her fingers, "could never make real money like someone in law or oil or banking."

"And Sam has spent his life proving otherwise."

"Yes. And the irony is, he's about to succeed at it, in a big way, only now his father is dead."

Christy suddenly had a clearer picture of why the Moonlight Grove project was such an obsession with Sam. For the millionth time she wondered how she could ever help this family achieve real peace.

"The game's starting," Gayle said.

And then they watched. By the top of the eighth inning the Angels were losing by six runs. During a lull in play, Meggie came spilling out of the dugout, running breathlessly to Gayle and Christy in their lawn chairs. "Coach says I gits to play!" The child was fairly squealing with delight.

Christy shot a smile of gratitude to the young coach.

"Then go back and get ready!" Gayle said excitedly.

Meggie shot off. But she wasn't sent in immediately.

Then in the bottom of the eighth, Meggie's team scored two runs.

In the top of the ninth the other team quickly suffered three outs, and Meggie's team was up to bat again in the bottom half.

The crowd in the bleachers grew tense, repeatedly standing up and sitting down, yelling more than they had at any other game.

Gayle's face suddenly paled as she looked off toward the parking lot. "I don't believe it," she said.

Christy swiveled her head to look in that direction.

Coming across the field with long-legged strides was Sam. He was wearing sunglasses and had removed his tie, ditched his suit jacket and rolled up the sleeves of his white shirt. His cell phone and pager were clipped to his belt, and his digital camera swung from a strap around his neck. To Christy he looked like an apparition. Tall and tanned and trim, with his golden hair shining in the sun.

Meggie spotted him and came plowing out of the dugout again. The child's body slammed into him and Christy could hear Sam's laughter all the way across the field as he swung her off her feet.

They hugged and then Christy heard Meggie say, "I gots to go play!" at the top of her lungs. She ran back to the dugout, thin legs kicking up like a gangly foal's.

Sam sauntered up as Christy and Gayle stood.

Sam gave his mother a cursory hug. "Hi, Mom."

"Hi, yourself," Gayle said, unable to wipe the look of utter surprise off her face.

"You came." Christy smiled into Sam's eyes.

"I'm sorry I didn't make it sooner." His blue eyes studied Christy's with a depth of feeling she had never seen in any other man. There was no one like Sam Solomon, never would be anyone like him.

"And what about the Japanese?" Christy asked softly.

"I presided over the business meeting at the offices, but then I let my partner, Josh, escort them out to Moonlight Grove. You were right. Some things are more important than work."

Sam's mother nodded approval and smiled.

"Meggie said she gets to play?" Sam questioned, looking off toward the dugout.

"The coach told her that when they were behind by six runs, and it didn't matter," Christy explained. "But now the picture has changed."

Gayle and Christy sat down and Sam squatted on his haunches beside Christy's lawn chair. The Angels hit another home run and the crowd in the bleachers went wild.

Now behind by three runs, two of the Angels scored base hits. It was the bottom of the ninth inning and the Angels had only one out and runners on first and second.

"The game is so close, I'm afraid the coach isn't going to let Meggie play," Gayle observed sadly.

"But every other girl has been up to bat at least once," Christy said, though she didn't feel much hope, either. ''Maybe the coach will give her a chance.''

Sam and Christy looked back at Meggie, who gave them a charming little thumbs-up from the dugout. Dispirited, the couple looked into each other's eyes. She was thinking that her stubborn optimism had forced this situation, and now Meggie was going to be crushed. He was thinking that he'd give anything to be proved wrong and see Meggie out on that field.

Then, Christy was astonished to see Meggie loping out of the dugout toward the plate like a wild pony. Her airy blond curls puffed from under her batting helmet like pulled cotton candy. With her thin arms, she could barely hold up the bat. She smiled at the pitcher, then at the trio of adults who had risen to their feet over by the dugout, two of them holding their breath, one of them snapping away with his digital camera.

Looking bewildered at Meggie's appearance at the plate, the young pitcher swiveled her head toward her own coach for guidance. Christy saw the Stars' coach make a silent signal and in her grateful heart, she blessed that woman.

The pitcher lobbed a very soft ball to Meggie. Meggie took a clumsy, futile swing. The volunteer ump said ''strike'' quietly. The whole field fell as silent as a church.

Again, the pitcher gave Meggie an easy target, and again she swung the bat crookedly and missed. ''Strike,'' the ump said again.

With the kind of prescient sense that comes over

people of goodwill at such moments, Meggie's young teammates clotted together behind the batting cage. The Stars spontaneously joined them. The Angels' best batter, the strong girl who had thumped Meggie on the back earlier, conferred with the Angel's coach, then with the umpire. Then she stepped up, positioned herself behind Meggie, and helped the thinner child to hold the bat up, straight and high.

This time the pitcher didn't question, she stepped close and, smiling sweetly, sent Meggie a soft, easy pitch. Meggie and the stronger girl behind her swung at the ball, sending a grounder back.

The other two Angels ran home while the pitcher picked the ball up, and instead of flinging it straight to the first baseman and putting Meggie out, she cocked her wrist and threw it in a long, high arc to right field. As the ball flew far, far beyond the reach of the first baseman, the dumbstruck crowd in the bleachers got to their feet.

Meggie stood like everyone else, watching the ball make its arc. From behind the batter's cage the Angels started yelling, "Run, Meggie! Run to first!" The muscular star batter gave Meggie a gentle push, urging her to first base.

As she ran, everyone, the whole crowd, took up the cry, Sam the loudest of all. "Run, Meggie! Run!" But Christy could only cover her mouth with tense fingers and fight back tears as she watched Meggie, awkward but overjoyed, make it to first base.

Now the game was tied, with Meggie standing on first.

The strong hitter who'd helped Meggie stepped up to bat and this time the pitcher showed no mercy. One strike. Two. But then the big batter whacked the ball over the fence. The game was won.

Again everyone started yelling, "Run, Meggie, run!" The other girls were waving her home like mad. Meggie took off, smiling, but then she got confused. At second base, the opposing shortstop gently took one of Meggie's hands and ran along side her to third. They stopped so Meggie could tap third with her thin little foot, and then they ran, curls and ponytail bouncing, all the way home. The star hitter trotted in behind them, but it was Meggie who had actually scored the winning point.

All the little girls had flooded out onto the field, shouting, "Yay, Meg-gee! Yay, Meg-gee!" as they crowed around her, jumping and screaming as if she were the prize athlete of the game. Meggie accepted their jostling hugs, her face lit up like the sun.

Elated, Sam and Christy grabbed each other and hugged tightly. Without thinking, Sam swept Christy off her feet, swung her around and planted an emotional kiss on her neck.

Christy felt like her heart might burst with happiness. Later, she would always say that on that day, the Stars were truly stars, and the Angels truly were angels.

CHAPTER TWELVE

IMMEDIATELY AFTER THE GAME, Sam took both teams out for ice cream at a nearby Braum's to celebrate. Meggie refused to remove her ball cap in the restaurant. She sat crowded into a booth with six other little girls, eating her ice cream and giggling even when it was obvious she didn't understand the jokes. When she squealed a little too loudly, one mild look from Christy was all it took to settle her down.

Sam's heart swelled when he looked at his daughter. And it expanded even more when he looked at Christy, sitting beside him. All the earlier tension between them had evaporated in the afterglow of Meggie's victory and the wonderful gift her teammates had given her. Sam looked at the giggling girls around Meggie—he could learn from these kids. And if not for Christy, he thought, he might have missed it all. He understood now, as he never had before, that some moments in life were too precious to miss. And that those moments couldn't necessarily be planned. It was exactly as Christy had said, "Sometimes you have to just show up."

Three years ago, at the time of his divorce, he could never have imagined that he would ever again feel as happy as he did at this moment.

Lou Allen came up to the booth that Gayle and Sam and Christy shared across the aisle from Meggie. "I swear," she said without preamble, "I never saw anything like that game, did you?"

"It was wonderful, wasn't it?" Gayle gushed.

Sam leaned back, looking up at the woman and pressing his shoulder into Christy's as he did so.

Lou Allen peered down at their pose, which smacked of familiarity, and blinked twice. Then she pasted on a mawkish smile. "You certainly look happy, Sam."

Sam seemed unruffled by the woman's nosy attitude. He swung his arm up, resting it on the back of the seat, not touching Christy but conveying a certain intimacy none the less. "Lou, do you know Christy Lane?"

"Oh, yes. I know Christy. She used to be my grandchildren's nanny, before you Solomons stole her." She pursed her lips, meaning to look cute and teasing. "Something tells me that we're going to have to work very hard to win her back." Again the woman eyed Sam and Christy's nearness.

"Too late, Mrs. Allen. I love taking care of Meggie." Christy smiled at the woman, but she didn't add any comments about missing the Pearson children or any other such polite sentiments. She didn't miss those kids. They had been awful to her. She wondered if Lou Allen could possibly grasp that Meggie—wonderful, innocent, unpredictable, affectionate Meggie—was preferable to snotty youngsters like the Pearsons.

Christy had already promised to go across town to her niece's birthday party that afternoon, so Sam and Gayle took Meggie home.

Sam did some yardwork while Gayle cooked an early dinner. Later, they all watched a home video. A baseball story. Sam stopped the tape often to answer Meggie's perpetual questions.

That night Sam tucked Meggie in. "I was proud of you today, sweetheart."

"You mean when I hitted the ball and runned?"

"Yes, when you hit the ball and ran."

"I wish Mommy had seed me."

Sam's heart ached for his child. "I took lots of pictures for Mommy," he said softly. "You can show them to her next time you see her."

"When's that, Daddy?"

"Soon, sweetie. Soon."

"Okay." Meggie gave a big yawn. "I tired, Daddy."

"Time for my little softball player to get some sleep." He pulled her blanket up under her chin.

"I love you, Daddy."

He bent and kissed her hair. "Daddy loves you, too, sweetheart. Just the way you are."

"Good night."

"Good night, Meggie."

Meggie was practically asleep before he closed the door.

"Mom, could you possibly stay here with Meggie tonight?" Sam asked Gayle as soon as he came down the stairs into the kitchen. She was loading the dishwasher, though Sam hadn't asked her to.

"Where are you going?"

"To Christy's."

"Christy's?"

"I want to thank her for...for today."

Gayle stopped rinsing the dishes and studied her son. "Is something up between you two?"

"What do you mean?"

"I saw how you swept her off her feet at the ball game."

"That was certainly a special moment, wasn't it?"

Sam's effort to deflect her question didn't work.

"Sam. I'm not blind. I saw you kiss her neck."

"So? That is none of your business, Mother."

"Perhaps not, but you might consider that I wasn't the only one who saw it. You might consider Christy's reputation."

"Her repu— Mom." His voice grew impatient. "This is the twenty-first century. And Christy is a grown woman."

"She is also your nanny, your *employee.*"

"I would never do anything to hurt Christy, or her *reputation,*" he said impatiently. "Now, can you stay here with Meggie or not?"

SAM BOUNDED UP THE TWO FLIGHTS of stairs to Christy's apartment, taking two steps at a time. On the way, it occurred to him that he might have called her on his cell phone before coming by.

No.

Unromantic.

They'd already seen to all the awkward, unromantic details. He smiled to himself and quickened his steps, remembering how natural it had been for Christy, such a stickler about health and hygiene, to insist that they both get tested before any intimacy took place.

He was determined to make this first time special. Tonight, he wanted to see the surprise on her face, the delight, when she answered her door.

He finally reached her apartment, full of anticipation.

"Sam!" she said when she answered his quiet knock. Her expression said that, sure enough, she was surprised. She was already wearing her pajamas—short blue cotton ones printed with clouds and sheep—and a pair of house shoes made to look like bunny rabbits. "My gosh." She pressed a palm to her bosom. "I was just thinking about you. How did you know I was hoping you'd come?"

Before he could answer, she threw herself at him, almost knocking the flowers he had hidden behind his back to the concrete, kissing him lushly.

She jerked her head back. "Hey. What have you got behind your back?"

"Let's go inside." He danced her backward through the door.

He whipped the roses around as he kicked the door shut.

"Oh, Sam, they're beautiful. And red is my favorite color." Her voice grew hushed as she leaned away from him, only far enough to accept the dozen long-stemmed roses, wrapped loosely in green florist paper. "What's the occasion?" She buried her nose in one of the freshly opened buds.

"It's the first night we'll make love I hope."

Christy's head snapped up from the roses. Her cheeks flamed as red as the blooms. Sam stared at her, thinking how he loved her so. He studied her face, wanting to imprint each detail in his memory for all time.

"I love you," he breathed. "There's no one for me but you. Please say yes."

She fixed wide, serious eyes on him above the flowers. She drew a long, ragged breath and released it. "Yes."

His expression, he figured, looked as solemn as a judge's. But for him this was a most solemn occasion. "I love you so much it hurts. I've never loved anyone like this."

"Oh, Sam." Her lips parted and her breath came short. "I love you, too."

Between them, the roses got crushed. After they'd kissed he removed the flowers from her hands and stepped over to lay them aside on her little oak table.

"I want to put them in some water," she protested.

"Okay. But hurry."

While she arranged the flowers in a cheap glass vase he stood behind her, his hands riding her hips impatiently.

When she said, "There," indicating that she was

done, he whirled her around, grabbed the back of her neck and pressed his mouth to hers.

"Christy," he whispered while gently nipping her lips. "I couldn't stand it this morning when I thought you were disappointed in me."

She pushed back from his chest. "That isn't why you came to Meggie's game?"

"No! I came for Meggie's sake. I'm glad I was there. I wouldn't have missed that for the world. But I wouldn't have seen the light in the first place without you. That's part of the reason I want us to be together. I'm a better person when I'm with you."

"Oh, Sam. I've never felt this way, either."

Her admission filled him with a burst of gladness that had to find release. He grabbed her and kissed her again.

While they kissed he felt a shiver of anticipation course through her and it was exactly the reaction he wanted. They couldn't hide their true feelings from each other. Their bodies betrayed them. He wrapped her in his arms—tight.

When they were done, she pressed her forehead to his chest.

Above her head he closed his eyes and tipped his face up to the ceiling in a silent, joyous hosanna. "I won't disappoint you."

"Oh, Sam. That could never happen. If only you knew..." She broke off, short of telling him something that he felt certain he wanted to hear.

"If only I knew what?"

"Nothing. First, I have to go to the bathroom."

He smiled. "I'll wait."

As Sam stood waiting at the threshold of Christy's pink cocoon of a bedroom, he felt whole, complete, *right.*

The bed was a mass of white lacy linens, rumpled, unmade. One of the little white lamps was on low, casting a cozy, golden haze in the small space. The window shade was pulled all the way down. A cookbook lay pressed open on her bedside table.

When he heard the bathroom door open, he turned to face her. She had brushed her hair and kicked off her house shoes. He opened his arms and she padded to him in a rush, wrapping her arms around his waist and burying her face in his neck.

"You're sure about this?" He ran a gentle hand up and down her slender back.

"I've never been more sure about anything in my entire life. But I have to tell you something first."

"What?" Glad of heart, he snuggled her against him, happier than he had ever been in his life.

"Back when we went to the same high school? I had the worst crush on you. In fact, I carried a torch for you for years. I've even dreamed about you. A lot. Right there in that bed."

Keeping her pressed firmly against him, Sam turned his head, looking at the messy bed. He smiled against her hair. "From the looks of that thing those must have pretty wild dreams."

Christy chuckled. "Are you making fun of me when I'm trying to tell you my deepest, darkest secret?"

"*That's* your deepest, darkest secret?" Sam leaned back at the waist and made a wry face at her. "We'll have to work on that one."

She faked a slap at his shoulder. "I mean it. It was hard for me to confess that to you."

"Why?"

"Because I've been in your house all this time, every day. I was afraid you'd think I had the hots for you from day one."

"Didn't you?"

She blushed. "Sort of."

He kissed her temple, then the corner of her mouth. "Okay, if it'll make you feel better, I've got a confession to make, too."

He tipped her chin up so that she would look into his eyes. His face became serious and his blue eyes grew hooded with desire. "I've been dreaming about making love to you, too."

"You have?"

"Ever since the storm."

"Oh, my," she breathed.

"But, Christy, this—" he lowered his head and breathed into her soft, barely open mouth "—is no dream."

They fit their mouths in a promise of growing passion as he kissed her again.

He gathered her up into his arms, swung his shoulders into the room and carried her to the bed. He tenderly laid her in the nest of sheets, then stood above her, unbuttoning the white shirt he'd worn to work that morning, all the while observing her with hooded, smoldering eyes. As Christy watched him jerk the tails of the shirt free from his waistband, then peel it over his massive shoulders, her mouth went dry. She realized she'd never seen Sam bare-chested.

Being blond, he had spare chest hair, only a small dusting—surprisingly dark—down the center between two perfectly honed pectoral muscles. His skin was tanned and smooth and his nipples were small, dark as raisins. His flat abdomen was etched with muscles, tapering to a hollow that urged her eyes to seek lower. Sam's face was movie-star stunning, but Christy could never have imagined that the rest of him would be this beautiful as well.

He was unbuckling his belt, unzipping his trousers. "Are you nervous?" His deep voice made her jerk and shift her eyes up from the bulge that had fascinated her.

She looked into his eyes and shook her head no. But she was.

"Don't be. Remember that I love you."

Again she nodded.

He yanked the trousers free with a snap and tossed them aside, revealing gentlemanly snow-white cotton briefs.

Christy had lain on her side all this time, stock still, clutching a pillow to her front, legs curled up, with knees stacked one on top of the other.

He leaned over the bed and took hold of her ankles, pulling her toward him. He rubbed his strong thumbs into the tender spots behind her ankle bones, then slowly massaged his thumbs downward, around, and into the arches of her feet. This caused her to relax a fraction, and he pulled her legs straight, flipping her onto her back.

As he ran his palms up the outsides of her thighs, Christy felt small and fragile in his hands.

He wedged her legs open with one knee and breathed her name reverently, ''Christy,'' before he lowered his full length upon her, pressing his fully aroused body into the vee of her legs.

He lay still upon her for a moment, looking into her eyes with his heart pounding against her breasts, and she expected him to kiss her then, but instead he simply allowed their breaths to mingle. ''I love you,'' he said again.

''I love you, too,'' she tried to echo, but no sound came out. Her throat was dry and her own heart had set to quaking. She was about to find out what it was like to make love to Sam Solomon and her whole being seemed suspended, about to tumble over the brink of some ethereal precipice. Once she took the leap, nothing would be the same, ever again.

''Kiss me,'' he commanded, and lowered his mouth over hers.

The kisses they'd shared heretofore had promised passion, begged for fulfillment. Now, at last, fulfillment would come. They would allow this kiss to spiral into all that a kiss was ever meant to be...and it quickly did.

Moist heat and open mouths and the urgency of tongues that couldn't get enough overcame any shyness Christy felt. She moaned deep in her throat and he groaned into her mouth in answer.

When his hands pressed upward beneath her pajama top and his strong palms closed over the lush, intimate parts of her that he'd been denied for so long, Christy sucked in a sharp breath and arched into him. With a pounding heart and fevered longing driving her, she tumbled over that precipice. Willingly. Joyfully.

From that point on Sam had his way with her, totally, and in turn she drew from him a response so fierce she would have been frightened if it had not been her long-familiar, long-dreamed-of Sam doing these things with her.

When it was over, she finally found her voice, though it sounded breathy and weak from spent passion. "Sam. You were wrong. I think maybe this is a dream."

The hours of that night, their first full night together, passed in a haze of pleasure. Their tastes, their smells, mingled into the scent of life as they made love again, then slept, then made love again in the tiny room, until at last dawn broke into their dream world.

"Are we going to make love like this all the time now?" she asked as the cool blue morning light emphasized the contours of Sam's muscular back and legs. He was putting his clothes on.

He turned his head and regarded her seriously. "Absolutely," he said softly. "If that's what you want."

"Then we'll have to find a way to come back here." Christy twisted, pulling her pink sheets up over her chest. "We certainly can't do this at your house."

He stopped buckling his belt and bent a knee to the mattress, causing her body to tip toward him. He twisted his torso, covering her, flattening a palm on either side of her head as he balanced there. He studied her eyes, then brought his face closer to hers, and while continuing to look into her eyes, he drew the sheet down, exposing her breasts. Slowly, he lowered his head, and then all she could see was the line of one tanned shoulder and the blades of her ceiling fan high above, taking shape in the gray light of dawn.

But she could *feel.* Oh, she could feel his hot breath skimming her flesh and then the pressure of his strong mouth as he wet her and suckled her and bit at her with newfound familiarity.

When he was done, when she was left gripping the sheets at her sides, breathing hard, quivering, he rose up and kissed her lips lightly again. "No," he said huskily, "I guess we can't go there and do this."

"No. We could never do this in your house," Christy whispered. "Never, ever," she finished in a deeper hush, "in your house."

CHAPTER THIRTEEN

SAM HATED TO LEAVE CHRISTY, but Sunday or not, he knew he had some makeup work to do with the Japanese investors. He felt bad about the way he'd left, practically before the sun had come up, but he needed to get to his office early. He rushed home, bypassed his mother in the kitchen with a quick "Gotta hurry" and jumped into the shower.

When he came downstairs fifteen minutes later in a business suit, all freshly shaved, Gayle scowled at him.

"I hope you know what you are doing, being out all night."

"And I hope you're not about to comment on my personal life."

"Christy—"

Sam snapped his fingers. "Speaking of Christy, she has the day off. Mom I hate to ask, but..."

Gayle's scowl only deepened, but then she said, "Ask."

He gave his mother a quick peck on the cheek. "How would you feel about taking your granddaughter to church?"

"And where are you going, all dressed up on a Sunday morning?"

"Mr. Yoshida's still in town. I'd like to connect with him once more before he leaves. Seriously, Mom, can you take Meggie all day?"

"I hope you know what you are doing," Gayle repeated.

"I'm doing the best I can!" Sam dashed out the door.

THE NEXT WEEK flew by in an exhausting whirl for Sam. Mr. Yoshida wanted to scale back the original design of Moonlight Grove, leaving part of the original town under the flood waters created by the storm. He felt it was just too expensive to start over in that area. Sam had to scramble to convince Yoshida's people that the restoration of the charming old rock structures was the key to his vision. He offered to redesign other parts of the resort in order to keep the old town area as planned. They wanted to see the new designs, and some excavation work at the site when they made a return visit in three weeks. Three weeks!

In the midst of this stress he worried continually about Meggie, and his heart longed to be with Christy constantly. How frustrating, how painful, to have finally discovered the meaning of true love and not be able to spend time with the object of that love. Every fiber of his being yearned to touch her, to gaze at her, yet it felt like they hardly saw each other.

Christy did her usual miraculous work, cheerfully preparing Meggie physically and emotionally for the coming trip to California. They had made the plane reservations for one week hence, when Andrea would be finished with her latest round of chemotherapy.

"You are a wonder," he whispered to Christy's sleeping form late one night when he came dragging in from a long session of drafting on the computer CADD program at his office.

She was curled up under the coverlet on his couch, and to him, she was the most beautiful thing he'd ever seen. It was 1:00 a.m. and he felt as if he was using her, having her stay with his child so late. And yet, the work needed to be done, in record time, no less. Yoshida had clearly been unhappy the day Sam had abandoned the investors and gone to Meggie's game. His partner hadn't done a great job of explaining Sam's new plan, so Sam's position had weakened. If he couldn't show the investors that the project could come in under budget and still salvage the old town, all was lost, at least in Sam's mind.

He looked down at Christy again. He didn't know what he would have done without her these last few weeks. Right now she looked too beautiful for words. Her hair fanned over the black leather of the couch like rivulets of white water. Her face, free of makeup and in complete repose, was like an angel's.

He knelt next to the couch and kissed her lightly.

Her eyes fluttered open. "Sam."

His heart thrummed to hear her say his name like that.

"Hi, baby doll. Sorry I'm so late."

"It's okay." She started to sit up.

He pressed her shoulders back. "Don't get up. I

like you like that.'' He kissed her again, this time not so lightly.

Her body responded immediately, and when he felt her movements toward him, he slipped his hand under the blanket. She was wearing a loose T-shirt and he slipped his hands over the thin fabric. With his hands on her breasts, she twisted off the couch and they wrapped around each other on the floor, murmuring.

Sam pulled her thighs up around his hips. ''I love you,'' he vowed, pressing into her to prove it.

''Whatcha doing?''

At the sound of Meggie's singsong voice in the dark, Sam and Christy lurched apart as if they'd been electrocuted.

''Meggie,'' Christy breathed.

Sam jumped to his feet. ''It's way past a certain little girl's bedtime.''

''What you doing?'' Meggie repeated.

''We were just playing,'' Sam hedged. ''Just...wrestling around.'' He took Meggie's shoulder and turned her around.

''*Whatever,*'' Meggie said with feigned disgust as her daddy aimed her back toward the stairs.

''Whatever?'' Sam asked Christy with amusement when he came back into the room.

''It's her new all-purpose word.'' Christy was sitting on the couch, huddled miserably under the coverlet. ''She learned it from the girls on the softball team.'' But Christy was not amused. She was worried. ''Oh, Sam, what are we going to do? She *saw* us like that.''

"It's okay." He sat down next to her and brushed her hair back from her face, consoling. "Meggie won't even remember any of this in the morning."

THE NEXT DAY WHEN SAM, Christy and Gayle explained to Meggie that she was going to California to see her mother, the child angrily crossed her arms over her chest and said, "I don't wanna go to Cal-for-na!"

"But Christy's going with—" Sam started.

"Whatever!" Meggie screamed. And before they could even ask what was wrong, she ran up the stairs, slammed the door to her room and started in with the loud verbalizing that they hadn't heard in weeks. "I not going!" she yelled from behind the door. "I never going!"

The three adults looked at each other, dismayed. They hadn't been prepared for this regressive behavior.

"Maybe she hasn't grasped that softball is over now," Gayle suggested. "Maybe the trouble is she thinks we're taking her away from her new little friends."

"Maybe she's forgotten about Andrea," Sam said worriedly.

"Maybe she didn't hear you when you tried to explain that Christy was going along, that it won't be as scary as her last plane ride."

"Well, she's going and that's that," Sam said.

"Perhaps it would help if I take Meggie shopping

to pick out a few special items for the trip,'' Gayle mused.

''Oh, fine,'' Sam said sarcastically. ''Take her out for a fast food lunch afterward while you're at it. Spoil her rotten.''

''You've been so preoccupied with Moonlight Grove that you haven't found time to take your daughter *anywhere* lately.''

With that, Sam headed up the stairs to talk to Meggie.

Christy had said nothing. She feared there was more to this outburst than Sam and Gayle could guess. She feared that Meggie, in her simple-minded way, had decided that the scene last night meant that Sam and Christy were getting married or something, and that Meggie was being sent off to California as a result. Trouble was, *Sam and Christy* hadn't decided anything yet.

CHAPTER FOURTEEN

THE ORANGE COUNTY AIRPORT was not as bad as Christy anticipated, certainly it had to be a better choice than L.A. International. Meggie clutched Christy's hand and was surprisingly well behaved, which made Christy wonder if the child sensed her nanny's insecurity in this overwhelming place.

Andrea's parents, Lorna and Bud Haynes, were waiting there.

"Meggie!" they cried from a distance of twenty feet, and with that, Meggie wrenched free from Christy's hand and rushed into their arms. Christy was relieved to see that Meggie remembered her grandparents.

"You've grown so much!" both her grandparents exclaimed as they hugged the child.

The Haynes were nice people, typical California retirees with a little extra weight on their middles, an immaculate white Lincoln Continental and a generous, welcoming attitude. But they both seemed very tired.

Andrea's father appeared short of breath as he hefted their luggage into the trunk, but he refused to let Christy help. Meggie suddenly became shy with her grandparents, clinging to Christy and acting withdrawn on the confusing freeway ride to Huntington Beach.

As soon as Meggie saw Andrea, who was sitting on a garden bench in her parents' courtyard-style entryway, the little girl came to life. "Mommy! Mommy!" she cried, and flung her skinny body into the woman's even skinnier one.

"Oh, my!" The mother had instant tears in her eyes as she tried to arrange the gangly child on her lap. "Look at you, Meggie. Look how big you've gotten!"

"Christy!" Meggie exclaimed, glancing over her shoulder with a look of pride. "This is my *mommy.*"

Christy walked over and placed a soothing palm on Meggie's back, creating a tenuous connection through the child to the obviously ill woman on the bench. "Hi. I'm Christy, Meggie's nanny. We've spoken on the phone." She smiled into the saddest gray eyes she had ever seen.

Andrea eyed Christy's outfit—a bell-sleeved bohemian blouse and patchwork denim skirt—with a glance that was slightly patronizing, but her greeting was genuinely warm as she touched Christy's arm. "It's nice to meet you at last. It sounds like you've been taking excellent care of my Meggie. Sam's told me a lot about you."

"I hope some of it was good," Christy replied with the standard quip.

Andrea smiled weakly and Christy dismissed the woman's haughty assessment of her clothes. Some people simply valued appearances more than others. Even as a convalescent, she noticed, Andrea was carefully dressed in a sleek knit outfit.

To greet her daughter, Meggie's mother had donned a chic scarf that wrapped around her skull and had applied careful makeup, complete with false eyelashes. But the ravages of her disease were plainly visible. The veins in her cyanotic hands stood out like road maps and she was so thin she looked as if she might break if she moved too fast. Instantly, Christy wished that before she'd left Tulsa, she'd been considerate enough to look at a picture of the woman before disease had destroyed her looks.

But there were plenty of pictures inside the comfortable home of Andrea's parents. Andrea, their only child, and Meggie, their only grandchild, were both captured at every age, in every pose, on every wall and tabletop and on the mantel. Andrea had been a beautiful child, like Meggie. And a very, very beautiful woman. In every photo she was stylishly dressed, immaculately groomed.

The Hayneses ordered in some Chinese food. Andrea picked at hers, while the Hayneses limited themselves to moderate-size portions. But after struggling with Meggie all day, Christy was starving. She *ate.*

Meggie didn't. Not a bite. She pouted at the plate in front of her and whined for McDonald's.

"I could take her." Andrea started to rise from the table, her arms trembling from the effort of pushing herself up.

''No, no dear,'' her mother admonished, ''I can go.''

Bud had started up from his chair. ''I'll go. I should have thought of it on the way home from the airport.''

Christy read the signs so clearly—Andrea was in no shape to drive anywhere, and Bud and Lorna, exhausted from their long trip over the freeways to the airport, were in no mood to fight the traffic again.

But like the others, Christy wanted Meggie to have her comfort food. ''If you'll give me directions and trust me to drive that beautiful car of yours, I'd be happy to take her.''

In the days that followed, the Hayneses came to rely upon Christy in a thousand such small ways. She began to cook tasty treats in the kitchen, ran their errands, watered plants. She even pitched in with the laundry. She did not, in short, act like a guest in a household that was laboring under the burden of a grave illness. Instead, she was like an infusion of sudden strength into this beleaguered family. Her daily presence seemed to cheer Andrea, in particular. The two women talked endlessly about Meggie—her needs, her progress, her emotional state.

To conserve Andrea's energy, Christy tended to Meggie as she always had, supervising her baths and fixing her hair, reinforcing the child's efforts at brushing her teeth and other hygiene habits. Beyond that, she tried to stay out of the way so that mother and child could have one-on-one time. When Sam called to talk to Meggie every night at bedtime, Christy talked to him, but only briefly and in a circumspect, friendly way, reporting on Meggie and the beautiful California weather and the like. And she would always leave the room when Andrea took the phone, respecting their privacy.

As she did everywhere she went, Christy found she could help best by establishing little pleasantries that fit into the Hayneses' routine. For one thing, she made muffins, gourmet coffee and fresh-squeezed orange juice for the family every morning. Then she usually went out for her run. Andrea, who suffered from early-morning insomnia, seemed to especially enjoy coming down the stairs and finding fresh food waiting.

"It smells good in here," Andrea said quietly one morning at the end of the first week. It was sunrise, the only time of day when Andrea seemed to have any energy at all, and she had come into the kitchen for breakfast. She hadn't put on her headscarf yet, and she was wearing what looked to be one of her mother's afghans. It hung off her thin frame like a pair of loud draperies. "But you don't have to cook for us."

"I don't mind." Christy turned and smiled. "I enjoy cooking. Besides, Sam is paying me well. I feel like I need to do something to earn that money. Can I get you some coffee?"

"And a muffin?" Andrea smiled back as she sank into a chair at the table. "Those ones with the walnuts are delicious."

Christy took a plate out of the cupboard, buttered a muffin and added a fork and napkin.

"Well, I'd better go for my run before Meggie wakes up." She set the food in front of Andrea.

Andrea was staring out the wide glass doors to the Hayneses' backyard. The look on her face could only be described as resigned. Or was it peaceful? "Would you mind joining me out on the patio instead?" she said. Her voice was trancelike, as if her thoughts were elsewhere. "It looks so peaceful out there this morning. And I need to tell you something."

The patio, covered by a white arbor, had the homey feel of a place that had been well loved and well-tended for many years. Out in the yard there were close-hugging palms, a lemon tree, beds of sun-loving flowers. Down a short bank of steps, an aging swimming pool glittered pink in the reflection of the morning sun. Christy and Meggie had already had hours of fun splashing in that pool.

Christy opened the heavy door for Andrea, then carried out a tray with the muffins and juice and two coffees. The women sat down at a redwood table below a dark green umbrella.

"It's so beautiful here, especially in the morning," Christy commented.

Andrea sighed. "Yes, it is." The woman definitely had a distant, wistful aspect about her that concerned Christy.

"Did you grow up in California?" Christy tried to draw Andrea away from whatever thoughts were troubling her.

"No, but my parents did. I grew up in Tulsa. My father worked for Boeing. But they always wanted to return to Huntington Beach. They came back here when Daddy retired. I came out after I divorced Sam."

At the mention of Sam, they both became uncomfortable and covered it by sipping their coffee.

"How did you and Sam meet?" Andrea asked, her voice suddenly a touch wary.

"How did we meet?" For some reason, Christy thought Andrea was asking her about high school, but that couldn't be. Sam would never have mentioned Christy as a high school acquaintance—after all, he'd confessed that he didn't even remember her after she told him the truth.

"Do you mean, how did I come to work for him?"

"I suppose. If that's how it started."

That last remark confused Christy. Was Andrea trying to check her background, her qualifications, as Meggie's nanny? If so, it was a bit late for that.

"Gayle Solomon came to me one night at Wal-Mart and asked me to call her. When I did she explained that her granddaughter would be coming to Tulsa soon and would need a nanny."

"Gayle?"

"Yes."

"So good old Gayle has got her fingers in this," Andrea mused. "I should have realized she was playing matchmaker again. The way she talked about you—"

Matchmaker. That word gave Christy pause. "*Gayle* talked to you about me?" she clarified.

"Well, of course. We're still friends." Andrea's

voice, even this early in the morning, sounded tired and dry. *''Wal-Mart?''* She made a face, pronouncing the word with evident disdain. ''Why on earth would Gayle go to *Wal-Mart* to find a nanny for Meggie?''

''Wal-Mart was my night job. In the daytime I was Amy Pearson's nanny. Gayle knows Amy's mom, Lou.''

''Aah.'' Andrea's face lit with recognition. ''So you worked for Amy.''

''Didn't Sam tell you all of this?''

''No. Sam never tells me much of anything. All he does is send money and nurse his guilt.''

But Christy clearly remembered that Sam had said he told Andrea all about her. And Andrea had said as much herself, on their first day in California. Why was Andrea asking all these questions now?

And to Christy, Andrea's last remark about Sam's money and his guilt had seemed unkind, perhaps even ungrateful. Hadn't Sam told her that he tried to occasionally talk to Andrea and boost her spirits? So who was being dishonest, Sam or Andrea?

Again the two women took sips of coffee while the comfort level of the conversation plummeted.

''You're much more to Sam than Meggie's nanny, aren't you?'' Andrea said as she placed her cup back on its saucer with a shaky hand.

Christy couldn't keep her jaw from dropping. She stared at the woman, unable to come up with a tactful response while her cheeks grew hot. She closed her mouth and bit her lip and turned her eyes to the pool, away from the sad gray ones regarding her with an eerie calmness.

"Meggie said she saw you and Sam...*wrestling.*" At that word, Christy thought she could hear a faintly sarcastic note in the woman's voice. And sure enough, when she looked at her, Andrea was wearing a wan smile.

Looking down at her faded jogging shorts, Christy shaded her eyes. Her fingers trembled as she spoke. "Andrea, believe me, I don't want to hurt anybody."

With weak movements, Andrea leaned forward, as if to urge confidentiality. "Are you in love with Sam?" she asked softly.

"We didn't mean for this to happen." Christy looked at her solemnly.

As if that was all the answer she needed, Andrea twisted her head, pressed her eyelids closed for a second, then opened them and studied Christy with quiet resignation. "You know, I was surprised when I saw you. For some reason, I expected a nanny to look...I don't know...plain. Frumpy. But you dress...well, it's certainly unique, the way you dress."

Again, Christy looked down at her faded navy jogging shorts and unadorned white T-shirt. Sometimes she did dress plain and frumpy. But sometimes she dressed like the free-spirited songwriter she was. What did it matter how she dressed as long as Meggie got good care?

Andrea rubbed her fingers lightly over the sparse hairs on her scalp and stared out at the palm trees, the manicured lawn. ''Do you know what it feels like to know that you are going to die?''

Christy bit her lip, struggling to find words of comfort. ''Andrea, for Meggie's sake, you can't give up.''

''For Meggie's sake?'' Andrea skewered Christy with eyes that flashed, for one instant, as cold as steel. ''Surely you realize that's all I can think about these days. What will happen to Meggie.'' Then her gray eyes softened and pooled with tears. ''Meggie is not like other children. She is so vulnerable!''

Christy got out of her chair and dropped to one knee to the concrete beside Andrea.

''I love Meggie,'' she said sincerely, clutching the arm of Andrea's patio chair. ''And I would never do anything to make your child feel insecure, or to make her think that I was taking her father away from her or anything like that, if that's what you're worried about.''

Andrea stared at Christy with the strangest mixture of gratitude and resentment in her eyes. Then she turned her face away. ''You seem like a nice woman. A very kind woman. And I believe Meggie loves you, too. It's not Meggie I'm worried about, it's you.'' The gray eyes swerved back, spearing Christy.

''Me?''

''Yes. I don't know how involved you are with Sam, how serious your relationship is, but...''

''Andrea...'' Christy stood and walked to the edge of the patio, keeping her back to the woman. ''I'm sorry, but I—'' she folded her arms across her middle

"—but my relationship with Sam is really none of your business."

"Maybe not. But think. Has it crossed your mind that it would be very comforting for me to think that there would be someone to care for Meggie after I'm gone, someone to buffer her and protect her in her life with Sam?"

Christy turned to face her, astonished. "To buffer her life? You make it sound like Sam is a bad man."

"He is."

Now Christy was appalled. How dare this woman talk about Sam this way? "How can you say that?" she accused.

"I can say it because I was married to Sam. I can tell you from personal experience that Sam is a self-centered workaholic, just like his father, who will never change. If he has to choose between his work and his child, his child will always lose. And if he has to choose between his work and you, *you* will always lose."

"That's absurd! Only recently, he left a meeting with some important Japanese investors to come and see Meggie play in a ball game."

"Crumbs. He will give you crumbs like that. Especially if he senses that you are growing tired of his neglect. He'll do something dramatic to make you think he cares, to lure you back in. But before long he'll slip back into the same old habits. Work, work, work."

Christy sank into a chair, horrified that this woman

had so accurately described exactly what had happened on the day of Meggie's last ball game.

It was true that Christy had witnessed Sam putting in long hours since she'd come to work at his house. But wasn't that just because of the tornado? Because the stakes were so high out at Moonlight Grove? What would life be like with Sam under normal circumstances? Would she be left alone to care for his handicapped child? To sit in a lawn chair at ball games beside his mother? Reheating his meals and rubbing his back when he was exhausted? And being there for him, late at night, when he wanted to come to her with his passions? Were the awful things this woman was saying about Sam true? Even so, what could possibly be motivating her to tell Christy these things?

These questions rushed through Christy's mind, building to a crescendo like a brooding symphony. *Sam.* All of her life she'd worshipped him from afar. Was that hero worship blinding her to the kind of man he truly was? Was he the kind of man who would neglect his family?

"I know you think I'm awful for saying these things," Andrea continued in her dry, weak voice. "I'm only telling you this because I don't want to see another woman hurt the way I was. And Gayle Solomon will only make things worse. She is a consummate meddler. I actually think she pushed Sam to marry me. And now you tell me she had you all picked out—even went to the *Wal-Mart* store to find you." Andrea halted, overcome with a coughing fit.

Christy stepped over and handed Andrea her juice glass and a napkin.

''Thank you.'' Andrea sipped, pressed the napkin to her lips, then sighed. ''A few days ago, when Meggie told me that she'd seen you like that with Sam, well, for a while I thought about keeping this warning to myself.'' Andrea stopped again, catching her breath. ''But I just can't. I like you, Christy. You've been good to Meggie. But Sam Solomon is a handsome, charming, selfish man, and if you get involved with him, he will only break your heart.''

Still in shock, still one beat behind, Christy whispered, ''You're wrong.''

''I wish I were, but I don't want you to end up like me. Alone and bitter. When you started helping us around here, being so efficient and kind, I saw how it was. I thought, this is so easy for Sam. He knows he's going to have full custody of Meggie soon, and he's found himself a woman to step in and make it easy for him.''

Abruptly Christy stood. ''Please, Andrea. Stop. I know you're very ill, and I don't want to upset you, but you've crossed over a line here. My relationship with Sam is strictly between Sam and me. If you speak to me this way again, I'll have to go back to Oklahoma immediately, and you'll have to ask one of your parents to return Meggie to Tulsa.''

Christy walked to the sliding glass door opened it, and went inside. When she slid the door closed she refused to look back at Andrea. She wondered if the woman even had the strength to open the door by herself. Compassion forced her to go back to the master bedroom and tap on the door.

Lorna answered, clutching a powder-blue quilted robe against her chest.

"Mrs. Haynes, I hate to wake you up so early, but—"

"Is Andrea okay?" The anxious look on the woman's face reminded Christy that this poor lady was coping with the pain of having a seriously ill daughter.

"Yes, she's fine. She's out on the patio. We, uh…I can't go back out there, and I was wondering if you could go to her. I think the door might be a bit heavy for her to manage."

"Of course. Are you okay, Christy? You look a little pale."

"I don't feel well. If you don't mind, I think I'll go to my room until Meggie gets up—"

But right then they heard a frightened scream. It came from Andrea, out on the patio. Then they heard Meggie's voice, too, yelling, "Mom-meee!"

Both women rushed through the large house toward the screaming and shouting. When they got to the patio, Andrea was standing, clutching the ugly afghan to her throat. "Look!" She pointed.

High above the arbor, Meggie had inched out onto the sloping roof below a large dormer.

"Meggie!" Christy rushed forward. "What are you doing up there?"

"I going on a 'splore," Meggie called out, breathlessly.

"Go back!" Christy yelled, but Meggie had clearly gotten too far out on the steep roof to climb back to the dormer.

Meggie slipped and slid over the edge, hanging from a rickety trellis, her feet dangling twenty feet above the small plot of grass that sloped sharply into the pool.

"Meggie!" Christy yelled. "Hold on!"

"I falling!" Meggie answered. Her little face was twisted with fear.

Christy had never acted so fast. Without having to think about it, she dragged a small parson's table over to the side near some latticework. She stood on the table, got a foothold on the lattice and shimmied up to the top. She crawled up on the beams and navigated across the arbor like a tightrope walker, then she stretched her body toward Meggie's legs at the other end, her hands just short of the child's feet. She gripped a post with one hand, her fingers like vices and said, "You must come down toward me, sweetie. I won't let you fall."

"I ascared!"

"I know, but you have to come down, Meggie. There's no place else to go. Christy is here, sweetie."

Meggie did as she was told, and Christy was able to wrap her hand firmly around a thin calf, then get a grip on Meggie's waist and pull her onto the top of the arbor with her. Below and behind her, Christy heard Andrea give a stifled cry. Clutching Meggie to her, she walked the beams again and lowered the child to the parson's table and her grandmother's outstretched arms.

Andrea rushed forward and grabbed her child. "Meggie! What were you doing out there like that?"

"I was going on a 'splore!" Meggie sounded defensive, but also like she might cry.

Guilt sluiced through Christy. *A 'splore.* Now that Meggie was familiar with this concept, she would need constant supervision, even more than before.

Meggie did start to cry, and her grandmother and mother whisked her off into the house, leaving Christy alone on the patio with her guilt.

Later, upstairs in the small guest room, Christy carefully packed her bags. She wanted to be ready to leave, to fly immediately back to Sam, if Andrea said another word against him. How dare that woman, seriously ill or not, sow seeds of doubt into her budding relationship with Sam! She would hate to leave Meggie like this. The incident on the patio had only highlighted how much the child needed a strong, alert adult to watch over her.

She would hate to miss her big appointment with the agent, Nathaniel Sadelle, the day after tomorrow. On the phone he had hinted that they were going to discuss something important.

But her first priority was the man she loved. And if there was one thing Christy was sure of in this entire mess, it was this: she loved Sam Solomon.

She would leave if she had to. She zipped her carry-on bag with fierce conviction, but even as she did it, she could feel the seeds of doubt burrowing into the recesses of her mind.

CHAPTER FIFTEEN

CHRISTY DISCOVERED THAT WHEN the seeds of doubt take root, it can be very difficult to eradicate them.

Throughout the remainder of her visit in Los Angeles, she could not shake off the accusations Andrea had made against Sam. Two days later when she went to have her all-important appointment with the agent Nathaniel Sadelle, the unanswerable, circular questions still plagued her, stronger than ever.

Was Sam using her to solve his problem with Meggie?

Was he a selfish workaholic?

Mr. Sadelle's offices were on the tenth floor of an old art deco office building on Santa Monica's beautiful Ocean Park Boulevard. Christy got on the quaint, narrow elevator and counted the floors as she watched them clip past an ornate metal grille set in the top of the polished wood paneling.

In Sadelle's reception area a young woman took her name and said to please wait.

Christy then perched on a narrow vinyl bench and arranged her bandanna-print rayon skirt over her red Roper boots. She touched her vintage stone necklace, studded leather belt and embroidered denim jacket as if they were talismans. She hoped she looked like the kind of person who could write songs that people loved.

In no time, Mr. Sadelle came out to the waiting room to greet her himself. "Christy Lane!" he boomed as he crossed the room in three long strides. "We're so glad you've come!"

"Mr. Sadelle?" He was wearing a lavender polo shirt and shiny black workout pants with a white stripe down the side.

Christie, feeling suddenly overdressed, tried not to wince.

"At your service." He shook her hand, then ushered her into his office and closed the door. The large window behind the desk had a view of the ocean, though on this August morning there was enough brownish smog to blur the scene. Still, even on a hazy morning, the whole room seemed as bright as the southern California sunshine. The pieces of furniture were various primary colors, even Sadelle's desk, which was cobalt blue. The carpet was lemon yellow, the drapes tomato red. Christy had never been in an office quite like it.

"Are you enjoying Los Angeles?" Sadelle asked, aiming his hand at a bright green leather chair.

She sat down, a bit overwhelmed by the cachet of the place, hardly able to believe she was actually here, talking to *her* agent. "Santa Monica is really nice."

Sadelle was not what she had expected an agent in the music business to look like. He was, in fact, a homely looking little man, with deeply etched features, crooked wire-rimmed glasses and little tufts of gray hair sticking out behind his ears.

"Yes. We like it here. Now..." Facing her, Sadelle propped his bottom against his desk and crossed his arms over his little potbelly. "Let's get right down to business. We took your CD to Ayer Properties—a couple of guys who put records together for MCA—and they think it's quite good. Miss Haggerty already liked the song, as you know, and it was just a matter of convincing the producers that it would be a perfect replacement." He smiled. "That's my job."

"Replacement?" Christy echoed. She didn't understand.

"Yes. A replacement for the song that got pulled. We think your song would be great for the movie."

"The movie?" Christy blinked. She had been a little overwhelmed, trying to follow the machinations of the entertainment industry, but that word came through loud and clear.

"Yes." Sadelle pumped his bushy eyebrows, obviously excited. "The *movie.* It happened so fast that when we found out you were coming to California, we decided it would be simply marvelous to wait and let you know the deal in person. Ms. Lane, Shining Star Productions wants your song as the title song for a new romantic comedy. Ms. Haggerty has been contracted to sing the soundtrack, slated for release in 2004. The story's already in the works."

Christy's mouth fell open and for a moment she actually had to gulp for breath. "My...my song," she squeaked, "is going to be on a movie soundtrack?"

Nathaniel Sadelle nodded. His craggy face looked like it was about to crack, he was grinning so hard. "It should earn you some lunch money."

"Oh, my gosh!" Christy pressed her palms to her cheeks. "I didn't realize Mary Jane wanted the song for a movie!" She looked around Sadelle's vivid office, while in her mind, her whole world opened up. Gifts for her family. A new car. Actually *saving* for once instead of always scrimping.

Sadelle clapped his hands and rubbed them together with glee, acting almost as excited as Christy felt. "This is the part of my job that I love! I hardly ever get to tell composers the good news in person." He gave her another satisfied smile, then marched around his desk and sat down, ready to seal the deal.

"Now, we'll be sending you a contract in about two weeks. The guys in production want to hear Mary Jane's rendition of it before they give final approval. But of course, she'll do a good job—she always does. However, you know what they say in this business—it's not the voice, it's the song. And this song has everything it takes to be a hit. Memorable lyrics, lilting melody. That is one hell of a song, Miss Lane. I hope you plan to write some more of the same."

"I do." Christy breathed. "I most assuredly do."

"Good. We'll be in touch. I wish I had time for lunch—nothing gives me more pleasure than hanging out with my artists, but you know how this business is." He looked at his watch.

Christy didn't have a clue about "this business." All she knew was her dreams were coming true. All of her life her songs had poured out of her and now someone, somewhere was going to be moved by one.

"Mr. Sadelle—"

"Call me Nate. I'm your agent now."

"Nate, could I hug you?"

WHEN CHRISTY STEPPED OUT of Nathaniel Sadelle's office building into the bright midmorning sunshine, she found herself floating down the Santa Monica sidewalk like one who had been reborn. Everything looked fresh, beautiful, as she contemplated her future…a future as a songwriter.

She wanted to sing and shout and hug people. Knowing Bud would not be back to pick her up for at least another hour, she found a pay phone, took out the calling card Sam had bought for her and dialed his office. The secretary said that he was tied up out at the Moonlight Grove site, but that Christy could call his cell phone if this was an emergency. No, Christy told the woman, it could wait. But having to wait to share her excitement deflated Christy just the teensiest bit, and she wondered again if life with Sam would be as Andrea had warned, with Christy and her concerns always coming in second to Sam's work.

Forced to walk and think, she headed up to the Promenade where upscale stores hawking expensive silk T-shirts were interspersed with cozy coffee shops, where people sat working at laptops and talking on cell phones. The ambience of the area lifted her spirits. She could tell by looking that these were all creative people—like her. Among such people, Christy felt in her element. Even her *clothes* felt right here. Two young men with backpacks slung over their shoulders passed on either side of her, all smiles. Did her face look different now that she'd finally sold one of her songs? Did she have a glow about her? Surely she did.

The ocean breezes had swept the smog away, and the colors of the lush vegetation glowed brightly in the strong Pacific sunshine. Flowers—a bird of paradise, some oleander, even the fading lower fronds of the palm trees seemed, to Christy, bursting with life. At the corner she stopped to listen to a couple of street musicians playing flute and guitar. They were surprisingly talented. She smiled and felt even more strongly in her element in this place, almost as if she'd come home.

She resisted the urge to hug herself and dance in a circle right there on the sidewalk. She could thrive out here, living on this beautiful ocean. But then her smile faltered, grew troubled. No. She couldn't live out here, not without Sam, not without Meggie. They had become like her family. She could never be happy in a place so far away from them.

But she didn't know if Sam felt the same way about her. He said he loved her, but what did that mean…to Sam?

Her doubts about her relationship crept in like smoggy clouds over the horizon, threatening to overshadow this miraculous day in Santa Monica.

But even as her doubts grew in the days ahead, Christy firmly refused to discuss them with Andrea.

Andrea did not bring up the issue of Sam again, either, apparently taking Christy's threat about leaving seriously. It seemed she valued the continuity of Meggie's care more than anything. As the visit drew to a close, Andrea grew more quiet, more pensive. And Christy, ever soft-hearted, put aside their differences about Sam for more weighty matters.

On the last day, out on the patio, with the California sunshine radiating all around them, Andrea said, "You will take care of her, won't you?"

"Of course, for as long as I can," Christy replied with tears in her eyes.

"Do you think my little girl will remember me?"

Christy clasped Andrea's thin hand tightly in her own. "She will if I have anything to say about it." Fearing that this would be the last time she'd see Andrea Haynes Solomon, Christy added, "I will never let her forget you, Andrea. Never."

MUCH TO CHRISTY'S disappointment, it was Gayle, not Sam, who picked up her and Meggie at the airport.

"Oh, you both look wonderful!" Gayle exclaimed as she hugged Meggie to her side.

"Nonnie! Don't mess up my hair!" Meggie pulled away.

"Oh, it looks so pretty." Gayle lightly touched the neat French braid trailing down Meggie's back.

"Christy fixed it."

"Where's Sam?" Christy couldn't help asking. It was seven o'clock in the evening. They'd flown into

Tulsa, taking the extra leg down from St. Louis, thus avoiding the time-consuming trip to Oklahoma City. Christy had thought Sam would surely be through at the office in time to pick them up himself.

"He's up at Moonlight Grove. He wants to take advantage of the long daylight hours while he can."

"I see."

Gayle eyed Christy but didn't comment on her crestfallen look. Instead she chirped at Meggie, "Are you hungry, sweetheart?"

"Could we go to McDonald's?"

"Oh, *Mick*-Donald's, is it?" Behind Meggie's head, Gayle gave Christy a wide, approving smile at the child's improved pronunciation.

"Can we?" Meggie persisted.

"I suppose. Is that okay with you, Christy?"

"Would you drop me off at my apartment first? I'm really very tired."

ONCE SHE HAD HAULED her luggage upstairs, Christy did her best to console herself with the comforts of home. She put Kathy Mattea's "Walking Away a Winner" on the CD player, turned it up nice and loud, made herself a grilled cheese sandwich and some tomato soup, and poured a big glass of ginger ale. After she finished that, she ran a steamy bubble bath and lit her tiny bathroom with scented candles.

She sank down under the line of the soothing water and told herself she had no right to feel so down. After all, she'd finally sold a song and it was going to be used in the soundtrack of a *movie*, no less. She should be celebrating, not moping. Who knows? She might actually make enough money to move out of this cramped apartment and get a place where she could set up a real music studio.

Strangely, it was that thought that brought the tears. Because she realized she didn't want to move anywhere except to Sam Solomon's house. She realized she'd already imagined herself composing songs on his grand piano, making a studio of his wasted spare room. She'd already seen herself in his kitchen putting on a pot of soup, then going back to curl up in the bow window she had designed, dreaming up lyrics while she looked out over the snowy backyard. She'd already seen herself kissing Meggie good-night, with Sam looking on lovingly, then the two of them going off to his massive bed.

Oh, she'd gotten her hopes up, all right.

Well, just get them back down, she told herself, and swiped bubbles across her tear-streaked cheeks. Your hopes aren't going anywhere until you find out where that man really stands.

Although she had the urge to jump out of the tub, throw on some jeans and roar over to his house right that minute, demanding to know his intentions, her wisdom won out. She put on her threadbare lavender sweats and crawled into her pink-and-white bed instead. There would be time enough to talk to Sam when she reported for work the next day.

"Everything looks brighter in the morning," her mama had always told her.

And so, Christy made herself wait for the morning light.

CHAPTER SIXTEEN

BUT THE MORNING BROUGHT only gathering storm clouds, and at Sam's house, the disheartening sight of the man in a tense rush to get to work.

"Sam." Her voice stopped him with his hand on the doorknob. "We need to talk." She stood at a distance from him, in the dining room, gazing calmly at him through the double doors.

He turned, frowned, stood in the tight-shouldered pose of a male already on the defense. "Can't it wait? I'm in a hurry."

"It can, but not for long."

Something in Christy's tone made Sam release the doorknob. "What's wrong?" he said as an unnamed dread tightened in his throat. He should have picked them up at the airport, he thought. He should have gone over and made love to her last night instead of working late at the office. Here she'd been gone almost three weeks and he wasn't even acting as if he'd missed her.

And he had missed her. Oh, yes. He had missed the hell out of her. The only reason he hadn't called her more out in California was out of consideration for Bud and Lorna...and Andrea, of course. If he had allowed himself to have the long, intimate conversations with Christy that he had craved, the three of them would have eventually guessed that he and Christy were in love. And Sam couldn't see any reason to make Andrea's ordeal any harder on her than it already was.

"Tell me what's wrong," he repeated, taking a step toward Christy. "I can see that something's troubling you. Is it about Meggie?" He pushed down his dread with the hope that maybe Christy just wanted to have another of her heart-to-hearts about him not spending enough time with his daughter. And he would spend more time with Meggie. He really would. Just as soon as this damned project was finished.

"It's not about Meggie. It's about us."

"What about us?" With any other woman, this conversation, this "we need to talk about us" bit, would have been Sam's exit cue. But this was Christy, whom he loved so fiercely that he could hardly find the words to express it.

"I need to know where I stand with you, Sam."

"Where you stand with me? I'm crazy about you, that's where you stand with me."

"Are you?"

"Yes!" He tossed down his briefcase and crossed the dining room and went around the table, reaching out to her. He had to touch her. But when his hand grazed her arm, she turned away. He thought he knew what the problem was. "Baby, please. I'm sorry I didn't come and get you last night. We worked so late out there. We're having trouble with a cistern.

The sides keep threatening to cave on us. We have to get it concreted in before the rains start in September."

"Do you think we have a future together, Sam?"

Sudden fear closed around his heart as Sam remembered his conversation with Jim Holloway. *That girl sure knows her own mind,* Holloway had said that as he described how Christy had broken up with that cop because he wasn't the marrying kind.

It would be so easy to tell her something facile that would soothe her insecurities. But Sam didn't operate like that. "I don't know," he said honestly. "I'd like to think so, but it's too soon to tell, don't you think?"

"Why did you get involved with me, Sam?"

"What do mean? I told you, I'm attracted to you—more than I ever have been to any other woman. Isn't that enough?"

"No, it isn't. I need more than a physical relationship."

Sam took two steps across the small space and grabbed Christy, pulling her body to his as if she were a rag doll. By God, he would kiss this woman until her ears rang. If she thought what he felt for her was purely physical…

When they were both nearly breathless from the kiss, he growled, "This goes a lot deeper than a physical relationship and you know it."

Christy touched trembling fingers to her stinging lips. "How do I know that if we don't talk about where we're headed?"

He raked his hands through his hair, pulling his

scalp tight. "What do you want from me, Christy? Do we have to have our whole lives mapped out after a four-month relationship? That's not the normal course of things is it?"

"Our situation isn't like other relationships."

"How's that? You're a woman. I'm a man. We're in love."

"We have Meggie to consider."

"Meggie? What has Meggie got to do with us?"

"Everything. Her mother is dying, Sam. So am I just a mother substitute for Meggie?"

"No! I love you!"

"Are you sure?"

He gave his hair one more swipe. "What on earth has caused you to suddenly start thinking like this? Why are you questioning our relationship all of a sudden? Unless it's because—" He stopped himself. "Did something happen out in California?"

"No." But Christy was a very poor liar. "Yes. But I don't want to talk about it."

Sam, radiating frustration by now, threw his hands up and gave a mirthless sputter of laughter. "Okay, Christy! You obviously called me back in here to talk about this thing, and now you don't wanna talk about it. So, what do you suggest? Sign language?"

"Don't be ugly, Sam."

He turned on his heel, stepped around the table and snatched up his briefcase. "I've gotta get to work." He headed for the door.

"I guess she was right, after all."

That stopped him.

''Who was right?'' But he had a feeling he already knew.

''We're having a crisis, and you're avoiding it by running off to work like you always do.''

''What did Andrea tell you?'' He *knew* that was the trouble.

''Actually, she told me the same thing you once did. That you had a bad habit of avoiding life's problems by escaping into your work. She seems very bitter about what happened during your marriage.''

''Is that what you think I'm doing here? Escaping? Good Lord, woman. A tornado ripped through this area three months ago, and it damn near destroyed the project I've dreamed about my whole life.''

''I know that, Sam. It just feels as if that's all you think about. And if that's the way it's going to be...I just...I just don't want to get into some dead-end relationship.''

''Dead-end relationship? We've barely *started* our relationship. How can you be worrying about dead ends?''

''I don't know.'' She looked down, clearly confused. He wanted to hold her, to reassure her, but at the same time these doubts of hers hurt him, cut him to the quick.

''How can you doubt our love this way?''

''Because Andrea...I don't know, Sam. She'd been talking to Gayle about me, and she sounded so sure...I don't know. It's not that I listened to the things she said about you. I didn't. I told her I'd leave California if she said one more word.'' Christy drew an unsteady breath. ''But she just got me thinking that maybe the basis of this relationship isn't as sound as it should be. I got to thinking this whole thing is...wrong. She even seems to think your mother somehow arranged to get us together.''

It was a good thing Andrea was out in California where Sam couldn't get his hands on her right this minute, because if he could, he might just shake her teeth out.

And his mother. What was she doing talking to Andrea about Christy? Was there no limit to his mother's meddling? He could understand it—having a child die the way Lila had would make anybody a little...obsessed with her surviving children. But in Sam's case his mother seemed to have no boundaries. It was unhealthy. But maybe it was partly his fault. His brothers had gone on with their lives, while he'd remained dependent on his mother for help with Meggie. Nevertheless, it was time to put an end to Gayle's interference, once and for all. But first he had to make sure Christy understood how much he loved her—for herself.

''Christy,'' he pleaded, ''please, listen to me.'' He stepped around the table again to face her. Carefully he took each of her hands in his own. ''This is...we'll work this out, okay? I'm not going to repeat the mistakes of my first marriage. This is just a bad time for me.'' She looked up into his eyes—hers were so beautiful—and he could tell she was really listening to him. ''I didn't fall in love with you because I need somebody to take care of my daughter.'' He squeezed her hands tighter. "I didn't fall in love with you so I'd have a housekeeper. I didn't fall in love with you so I could run around and neglect you. That's not my plan. Understand?"

Christy nodded, saying nothing, but he could read a residue of doubt in her eyes.

"And I sure as hell didn't fall in love with you because my mother arranged it. She's always meddling like that. It's been her way ever since...well, you just leave my mother to me."

SAM FELT LIKE A TIGER in a trap. He had no choice but to drive directly to the office and make nice with the Japanese investors, but where he really wanted to be was across town, at his mother's house. He couldn't do anything about Andrea, but he could straighten out his mother once and for all.

Fortunately, Mr. Yoshida liked his liquor. After indulging in a three-martini lunch his jet lag kicked in and the elderly gentleman was ready for a nap.

"It is good to see the storm," Mr. Yoshida announced as the first drops of rain pocked the windshield while Sam was driving him across Tulsa to his hotel room. "My driver will take me later to Moonlight Grove so that I can see for myself how this new cistern works."

"I'll be out there later," Sam told him, "after the storm clears."

Sam dropped Mr. Yoshida at the Adam's Mark hotel and decided to take this opportunity to go to Maple Ridge.

The rain was cascading down the brick steps as Sam jogged up to his mother's front door.

"Sam! What are you doing here? You're soaked!" Gayle pulled him inside.

She had hardly closed the door behind him when he began. "Mom, have you been talking to Andrea about me and Christy?"

Gayle blinked twice, but as always, she maintained her composure. "The subject of Christy has come up a time or two. Let's go in and sit down."

Gayle seated herself on her plush couch, but Sam paced in front of the fireplace. Gayle had never seen him so agitated. She wondered if the pressures of the last few months had finally overwhelmed her son's strong constitution.

"You had no right to discuss Christy with Andrea," he said.

"I was only trying to reassure Andrea that Meggie is in the care of a really nice person," Gayle defended herself. "I certainly didn't reveal anything...personal about the two of you."

"Well, somehow Andrea found out that Christy and I have become...involved."

"Not from me."

"Fine. The point is, Andrea told Christy what a sorry you-know-what I am. Told her I'm a workaholic, that I was planning to shove Meggie off on her, all kinds of crap."

"Oh, my." Gayle pressed her fingers to her lips. "What did Christy do?"

"Christy told her she'd leave California if Andrea said one more word against me."

Gayle gave a satisfied nod. "I always knew Christy had spunk. Even back when she was little—"

The stunned look on Sam's face made Gayle stop. He took one giant menacing step toward Gayle, his height and bulk dwarfing his petite mother.

"When she was little," he repeated. Gayle felt a tremor of dread at his too-calm tone. "When she was little? You know Christy? I mean, you knew her before she came to work for me." The way he stated it as a fact caused the dread in Gayle to increase tenfold.

She started to say, Of course I knew her! How else would I have found her for you? But what was the point in playing games and stalling the inevitable revelations. "Yes."

"How?"

"She...I...I first noticed her when I did charitable work for the Junior League. Later, we helped Christy pursue her musical gifts with scholarships."

Sam allowed a heartbeat of silence to pass, but Gayle didn't reveal more. Maybe, she thought, she wouldn't have to tell the whole story.

But her son gave her a shrewd look. "Why do I get the feeling there's more to it than that?"

With growing uneasiness, Gayle sensed that Sam was looking straight into her guilty heart. But why should she feel guilty? She had done nothing wrong! It was just that now Sam had fallen in love with Christy, and when he found out the truth, he would think she, Gayle, had manipulated the whole relationship. Which was not true at all. When she had thought of Christy Lane a few months ago, she had been thinking only of Meggie. Her motive had been to hire Christy, with her simple goodness, and make her grandchild's life happier. Of course, she'd always assumed that Christy would undoubtedly grow into a pretty girl—just like Lila would have—but how could she have known that Christy had become, in fact, stunningly beautiful? How could she have known that Sam would lose his heart to her?

Until Christy moved into Sam's house, Gayle had only seen her on very rare occasions, recently only in her baggy Wal-Mart vest, with all the goofy buttons weighing it down, over an equally baggy denim dress. Her hair had been drawn back at her nape, and she wore little or no makeup. That version of Christy did not look anything like the sleek beauties Sam normally pursued, certainly nothing like Andrea. The whole thing had begun so innocently. But how could she make Sam see all of this? If only she hadn't pushed the relationship with Andrea all those years ago. But there had been a baby involved, and Andrea had seemed like a quality person. She had only wanted her son to be happy. Couldn't he see that?

Testily, he said, "*Mother,* answer me," in that drawn-out overly patient voice he sometimes used on her.

"Yes, it goes a bit deeper than high school scholarships, deeper even than pure benevolent interests."

"Benevolent interests? Mother, speak English."

"Sam, you mustn't think my involvement with Christy had anything to do with you. It didn't."

"Then I think you'd better explain it to me."

Gayle held her breath. She had never allowed herself to discuss Lila with her sons. She had always felt it was her duty to protect them from the full impact, the great pain of that loss. Edward had been the only one to fully share her pain. But now Edward was gone and she had grown tired of keeping this painful place sealed off in her heart. Lila was real. A lovely daughter. She was their sister. Lila wasn't merely the sister-who-died. She was *their* sister, the one who happened to have died. With a burst of air, she said, "Christy looks like Lila."

Sam reacted to the name with a jolt. He hadn't, in fact, heard his dead sister's name spoken aloud in several years. *"Lila?"*

"Yes."

"But Lila died when she was practically a baby. I was only five years old."

"Yes." While her mind struggled to form an explanation, Gayle couldn't seem to get out more than that single word. Again, she reminded herself that she had done nothing wrong. She had helped Christy Lane, a deprived young girl who sorely needed it. If that assuaged her own grief, why should she feel guilty? Oh, how had this situation ever gotten so complicated?

"How can you possibly know that Christy and Lila resemble each other?" Sam pressed. "Lila was only three when she died."

"Actually, I...I met Christy when she was just slightly older than three. She was five, just entering kindergarten."

Sam frowned, blinked twice, as if he couldn't process this. "Kindergarten?"

"Yes. Shortly after Lila died, I went to Christy's house. To deliver coats to the children for the Shared Warmth program."

Gayle had turned her face away while admitting this. She didn't want Sam to see the pain in her eyes. "Their little house was so wretched, Sam. They were poorly dressed, underfed. And this tiny blond child, the oldest, answered the door, not the mother. The mother was sick. Apparently the mother was always sick. That child looked so much like Lila it took my breath away!"

"Kindergarten," Sam repeated absently. "Then I would have been in kindergarten, too. Right after Lila died."

"Yes." Gayle bit her lip to keep from crying over the bitter memories. It was all so long ago—over twenty years. "At the time I was trying to stay busy with my charitable activities to keep from going insane. Your father...well, that doesn't matter."

"My father was gone all the time...working. I know that as well as anybody, Mom."

"Christy...I don't know. She was special." Gayle released a light, sad laugh. "But I guess I don't have to tell you that."

"Or Meggie," Sam said quietly.

Gayle grew somber, remembering. When Sam and

Andrea had announced that they were having a baby girl, Gayle's hopes had soared. Maybe the pain was over now. Maybe a new life…but then Meggie was damaged, so very damaged. And then the divorce. So wrenching. It seemed life had brought her poor Sam nothing but pain. But with Christy's arrival, Gayle had felt hope again, the same strange, irrational hope she had felt every time she'd been around that precious child.

Sam couldn't begin to understand Gayle's long-buried pain. He'd only been a small child himself when Lila had died. He was concerned only with what was happening now, and rightly so. He stepped around to confront his mother.

"You have known Christy all of her life?" He said this so accusingly that Gayle blinked as if struck.

"Yes. Her father had abandoned the family. Four little children. I had to help."

"But what really drew you to the Lanes was not their need. It was Christy. Being around her comforted you. It was like watching over Lila."

"Don't make it sound like I was using her or something. I always loved Christy for herself."

Sam's expression abruptly changed, as if an idea was dawning. "You're just like the rest of us. Christy eased your pain, made you feel whole, and you saw your chance to maybe get her into this family, through me."

"No!" How cruel of him to accuse her of manipulating him that way. She had to make him understand. She had never intended for anyone to discover all the things she'd done for Christy over the years. Those were things she had done for herself, a way to heal her own heart after losing Lila. It was that simple. At least at the time it had seemed that simple. ''I love Christy for herself,'' she repeated with vehemence. ''I wasn't *using* her to make myself feel bett—''

''Of course you were!''

''No! I was genuinely trying to help her.''

''In any case, Christy became your special project after Lila died. What else did you do for her—or would it be more accurate to say what did you do *to* her?''

Gayle shot her son a hurt look. He made her generosity sound almost evil. ''I merely helped her from afar. She is a wonderful child, Sam!''

''She's not a child and neither am I!'' Sam rammed a hand through his hair and turned away from his mother.

His frustration with Gayle was positively palpable. *Why was Sam making such a big deal out of this?* Gayle fretted. Didn't he trust his own feelings for Christy? Had Gayle really been such a terrible busybody?

''Why didn't you tell me all of this before?'' Sam demanded.

Gayle didn't know what to say. She hadn't told him she knew Christy long ago because she didn't think it mattered.

''You don't have to answer that.'' Sam thrust up a palm. ''I think I know why you didn't want me to know that you'd been helping Christy all of her life. Same old song, huh, Mom? Same old meddling. Trying to arrange everything so everybody's all peaceful and happy. So now you're matchmaking for me and getting Christy for yourself in the bargain.'' He'd reached his conclusion, and in Gayle's mind it was all wrong.

''No!''

''You figured you'd maneuver Christy into my house and, like magic, we'd fall in love—''

''No! I was only thinking of Meggie!''

''Oh, that was the best part of the whole deal, wasn't it? You knew Christy so well. You'd been watching her all of her life. You saw how she took care of her younger siblings. How she held her family together when her mom got sicker and sicker. You knew how good and kind she is. You knew she would accept Meggie, even love her. You were counting on her gentleness, her softheartedness, to save Meggie, to save *me.*'' Sam stared at her. ''How could you, Mom? Didn't you think about Christy? What about her feelings? It's time you stopped arranging people's lives, Mother.''

''Good heavens! I had nothing to do with your relationship. Do you think I have the power to make two people fall in love?''

Sam squinted at his mother. No, she hadn't made him fall in love with Christy. He'd done that entirely on his own. From the moment he'd seen her playing that piano, a part of him had known that Christy—quirky, artistic, softhearted Christy—was the only woman for him. "Of course I fell in love with Christy on my own. But admit it. You were playing matchmaker again."

"Maybe somewhere in the back of my mind I did know you and Christy would make a wonderful match. But so what? Is that a crime? I haven't been over at your house night and day, playing fairy godmother. I went away to Central America for a month, for heaven's sake. I hadn't decided what you two would do, what you would say to each other. How you would react to life's stresses. *That's* what made you fall in love, seeing each other day after day, seeing who you really were, working as a team to help Meggie...*and* to help Andrea."

"Andrea. Don't remind me. She very nearly poisoned our relationship before it even got started."

Sam stomped to the foyer. Gayle followed him, saying, "Try to be more understanding of Andrea, Sam. She's so very ill. She's probably not even thinking straight."

Ever so slightly, his shoulders slumped, as if some terrible admission had defeated him. "You still love Andrea, don't you, Mom?"

"Of course. And if you're honest, you'll admit that you do, too."

"No." He faced her squarely. "I don't love Andrea, Mom. I'm not sure I ever did. Not the way you wanted me to. Not the way I love Christy." He jerked the door open.

"Where are you going?"

"I am going to find Christy."

"Oh, Sam. What are you going to tell her?"

"I'm going to tell her that you've been playing dolls with her all these years."

Now Gayle's hurt turned to anger. "How dare you talk to me that way! After all I've done for you, for Meggie." But even as she upbraided him, Gayle held her hands forward, palms up, pleading. "Don't be angry with me, Sam. I only wanted to make your life easier."

Sam hung his head, stood for a minute with eyes closed. Then he spoke in a low, final-sounding voice. "Mother, I am thirty-one years old. I have a *life.* Whether it's easy or not, it's *my* life and I have the right to live it *my* way. From now on, I want you to stay out of it."

He stomped out the door before Gayle could stop him. As she watched his muscular form sprint down the terraced sidewalk toward his Suburban, tears stung at her eyes. What *had* she done?

She only wanted Sam's happiness. She only wanted to see him with the woman who was right for him...and right for Meggie. Fear gripped her. What would Christy say when Sam told her about all of this? What would she *do?*

CHAPTER SEVENTEEN

ON THE DRIVE FROM HIS mother's mansion on Madison Street to his own house, Sam had time to calm down. At each stoplight he felt the ire draining from him like air seeping from a tire. Lightning flickered and thunder rumbled in the distance as the storm moved on to Moonlight Grove. By the time he got to his own front porch he had made up his mind.

It didn't matter what his mother had done. It didn't matter what Andrea said about him. What mattered was Christy. And Meggie. What mattered was becoming a family. He knew what he wanted now. He would put an end to all these doubts by asking Christy to marry him. Now. Tonight. The sooner the better. And then he would get down to the lifelong business of taking care of Meggie and the woman he loved. It was all so clear to him now.

He unlocked the door and walked toward the sound of Christy's voice, somewhere down the stairs. In the laundry room?

She was singing with Meggie again. It was a song he didn't recognize. Something about an angel. The sound of their voices pulled at him, actually had a physical effect on him. He stopped at the top of the basement stairs, listening to the lovely song, feeling grateful, again, for Christy's ways. He knew she had kept Meggie from being afraid while the thunderstorm passed.

What was he going to say to convince Christy of the depth of his love? What would he say to convince her that they belonged together for life? Apprehension tightened his gut as he wondered if Christy had any inkling of his mother's meddling in her life? He hoped she'd be able to see that none of that mattered now. What mattered was being together.

"Christy."

"Oh!" Christy jumped, startled at the sound of Sam's voice. She was on the landing carrying up a laundry basket full of Meggie's folded clothes. "Sam!" she cried. "I didn't hear you come in. What are you doing home this time of day?"

Meggie was on the step above Christy, pressing a skewed stack of folded washcloths between her little hands.

"I should have called out." He stood looking at them solemnly. "Hi, Meggie."

"Hi, Daddy." Meggie cut around Christy and trotted over to Sam. "Lookit what I done!" She held the washcloths out.

"That's good, sweetheart." He gave the washcloths an approving glance before returning his solemn gaze to Christy.

Ever intuitive, Christy tilted her head and said, "Sam, is something the matter?"

''Don't you have speech therapy, sweetie?'' He glanced at Meggie, then at his watch.

''Nuh-uh. I gots it tomorrow.''

''Oh.''

''Come with us while we put these clothes away,'' Christy suggested.

As Sam followed them up the stairs he took his cell phone out of his jacket and punched a number. This wasn't a conversation he wanted to have in front of Meggie.

As Christy climbed the stairs she heard him say, ''Mom, if you get this message, call me. I need you to come and pick up Meggie. Plan on keeping her until after dinner.''

It seemed to Christy that Sam was leaving an awfully brusque message with his mother. What in the world was the matter with him? She balanced the laundry basket against her hip and studied his face as she rounded the corner into Meggie's room. His lips were pressed in a tight line and the dimples beside his mouth looked deep-etched, grim. Was he angry? At her? Was he going to break up with her or something because she'd pressured him about their relationship?

''We need to talk,'' he said, when Meggie skipped off to the linen closet with the washcloths.

''About what?''

''About us.''

Christy's heart constricted with dread. ''Okay. Let me put another load of clothes on and I'll make us some tea.''

"No. No tea. And no laundry." He took the laundry basket from her and set it on Meggie's bed. He looked her up and down pensively, and she wondered what he could be thinking. Today she was wearing a crisply laundered wide-striped shirt belted over a full denim skirt. Passably subdued, she supposed. Except that her belt was odd. A turquoise-and-carnelian buckled thing that she found at a flea market. Well, it didn't matter. Nothing did, if Sam was breaking up with her.

He turned and eyed the traveling storm clouds outside the window. "Unfortunately, I've got to get out to Moonlight Grove soon. Mr. Yoshida is meeting me out there to inspect the new deeper manhole. He wants to see how it will hold up after this storm." He sighed. "I hope it solved our drainage problem. He's so edgy about every little detail now. I feel like he's been breathing down my neck all the way from Kyoto—"

He stopped ruminating about his business and gave her a look that was full of some emotion that Christy didn't understand. "I was thinking we could talk on the way there. I've got something important to say and I don't want to put it off." He studied her outfit again. "The wind's up. You might need a jacket."

Meggie came bouncing into the room and Sam said, "Get a jacket, Meggie, we're taking you to Nonnie's house."

"Yay! Nonnie's!" Meggie bounded over to her closet.

THEY REACHED GAYLE'S HOUSE, where Sam jogged up the wet brick walk, rang the doorbell, waited, then pounded on the door. After a while he gave up and climbed back in the Suburban. He glanced out the windshield in frustration at his mother's darkened parlor window.

"She doesn't answer. She was here just a while ago." He checked his watch. "I can't take a chance on missing Mr. Yoshida. Meggie will have to go with us."

"Where we going?" Meggie piped.

"Moonlight Grove," Christy answered.

"I don't wanna go to the Moon-night Grobe," Meggie grumbled from the back seat. "It's *boring* out there."

"Don't you want to see all the new work Daddy has done?" Christy gave the child a bright smile. "We can go exploring around all the new buildings and stuff."

"A 'splore!" Meggie seized upon that idea.

The drive across Tulsa took almost an hour because of the weather and the rush-hour traffic. When they reached Moonlight Grove it was almost sundown.

There was no sign of Mr. Yoshida's limo, although they could see tire tracks in the newly graveled road, indicating that someone had been out at the site after the rain. The thunderstorm had moved on, and the sun had punctured a hole in a vast bank of slate-blue clouds, gilding Broken Arrow Lake with crimson brilliance.

"Let's sit up there so I can watch the road." Sam

pointed at the outcropping of rock that jutted out over the lake. ''He couldn't have come and gone already.''

They climbed the rough stairway made of flat boulders. At the top, they stood quietly for a moment, each holding one of Meggie's hands, looking at the construction below and the lake beyond.

''Let's sit down.''

''No!'' Meggie jerked their hands upward as they sat. ''You said I can go on a 'splore.'' She had been happy while they were climbing the rocks, but at the top she had immediately grown restless.

''We could keep an eye on her from up here,'' Christy suggested.

''Okay. You can only go up and down the steps and out as far as that little footbridge.'' He pointed to the arched sandstone footbridge that would form the focal point of the entertainment square. ''But stay where Daddy can see you.''

Meggie, excited to have even this small bit of freedom, bounded off.

''This is where it all started,'' Sam said as he grasped Christy's fingers and guided her to a level spot where they could sit and watch Meggie. ''This is where I was when I got the call from Andrea. When she told me about her cancer. It was even at about this time of day.''

''I see,'' Christy said, but she didn't, not really. Sam was acting so strange. She wondered if it was just because he was remembering all that had happened in the past few months.

"Sam." She took his hand. "Everything will be okay. We'll do all we can to help Andrea."

She started to lower herself to the rock, but he pulled upward on her hand. "Wait." He stripped off his jacket. "Sit on this." He spread the jacket on the ledge, then took her by the hand again and pulled her down with him. "Let me hold you." He settled her into the vee of his legs and wrapped his arms across her front. Surely he wasn't planning to break it off if he was holding her this way.

Reassured, Christy leaned back into his chest, feeling his deep sigh. "Sam, are you okay?"

"Yes. I'm better than I've ever been."

The way he said it caused her to glance up, checking his expression. He was looking at the sun, which by now was very low on the horizon, with some great emotion filling his eyes. Despite what he said, she could tell there was something terribly serious on his mind. Her chest tightened as she wondered what it was. "You said you needed to talk to me about something."

"I don't want one more day of tension or misunderstanding between us. I couldn't stand that." He turned his head and looked down at Meggie on the terraces below. "And I don't want one more moment of insecurity for Meggie."

They watched the child as she hopped from stone to stone like a happy little billy goat.

"Do you love me?" he said as he continued to look out over the partially restored ruins and the lake beyond. The expression on his face worried Christy. He looked so vulnerable. Had she hurt him by raising all those doubts earlier?

She turned her face toward the lake. "Sam, I love you more than anything in the whole world."

"Are you sure?"

She twisted around to look into his face again, but his eyes remained fixed in the distance.

"How can you possibly doubt that?" She leaned back slightly so she could better study his profile.

"Because..." He stopped himself short, then finally looked down at her.

"Because?" she encouraged, holding his gaze. "Because I talked to you about what Andrea said? I told you, I didn't believe her. I just needed to hear you say that the same thing wasn't going to happen to us."

"It won't."

"Then what's wrong? I can tell that something is really bothering you. That's why you brought me out here. You can tell me, whatever it is. You can tell me anything. Anything. There shouldn't be any secrets between us."

"My mother...she can be kind of manipulative, you know."

"She means well."

"I wonder."

"Sam. What is this about?" Christy didn't understand where he was going with this. "Did you explain to your mother how you feel? Or did you guys have a fight?"

Instead of answering her question, he said, ''Did you know that my parents had a little girl once?''

''No.''

''She died.''

''Oh, dear!'' This wasn't what Christy had been expecting and it took her a moment to shift gears. Then she said, ''That's terrible. What happened to her?''

''She broke away from my mother's hand and ran out in front of a Winnebago in a crowded parking lot at a restaurant. The old man driving the thing said he never even saw her.''

''Oh, my heavens.'' Christy clutched Sam's arm. ''How horrid! Poor, poor Gayle. And your poor father. And poor Sam. How old were you?''

''Five. Lila was three.''

''So she was Gayle's baby.''

''Yes. Mom had 'the boys' and then she had Lila.''

''It must have been terrible for her. No wonder she's so crazy about Meggie.''

''Yes.''

''But that is all in the past.''

She twisted again and laid a warm palm on his cheek. ''Sam, are you going to tell me what's really bothering you?''

He reached up and with one gentle finger he teased a strand of wind-blown hair away from her mouth. ''I think maybe my mother arranged for you to come and take care of Meggie so we could get acquainted. I think maybe even subconsciously, she engineered the whole thing.''

"Don't be silly. Your mother didn't know me from Adam. She'd only heard about me from the Pearsons. She was looking for a good nanny, that's all."

"That's not true." Three beats passed. Four. Somewhere across the water, a mockingbird called out. Below, they could hear Meggie singing to herself. Finally Sam said, "My mother has known you since you were in kindergarten."

"*What?*" Christy twisted fully toward him.

"After Lila died, my dad buried himself in his law practice and she immersed herself in charity work. She was delivering coats to your family for the Junior League, and when she came to your house she met you."

"Really?"

"Do you remember that?"

"I remember a lady coming to our house." Christy gave him a confused frown. "And I remember the coat. I wore it for a long time. It was the nicest coat I ever had." She looked down at her hands. "It was red."

Sam sighed. "Maybe that's why red's your favorite color." His mother couldn't have known that her influence would be so great on her first visit to Christy's childhood home.

"I had no idea that lady was your mother," Christy continued haltingly.

"She told me you looked like Lila."

Christy sucked in a breath. "Her little daughter? Oh, Sam. That is so sad."

Sam let his eyes probe Christy's, searching for

some sign that she understood how he felt. "Yes, it's sad. And it's also a little bit bizarre, don't you think?"

Christy grew thoughtful as Sam laced his fingers with hers in what she accepted as a gesture of consolation, of solidarity. "Maybe it is strange," she said quietly. "But grief can make you do strange things sometimes."

How like Christy, Sam thought, to see this situation through the filter of compassion. He felt ashamed because he could only seem to focus on his mother's tampering. "She told me she bought you other things over the years, but did it secretly."

"Over the years? You mean she was always…watching me?"

"Yes.

"Apparently, she even made sure you got a scholarship that allowed you to study music."

Christy's eyes grew huge. "Really?"

"I suppose all of this makes you feel sort of tricked…manipulated—"

"Creeped-out is more like it." Immediately, Christy wished she hadn't said it like that. It sounded ungrateful. She didn't really think Sam's mother was creepy. In fact, she had grown to love Gayle more every day. But it seemed so odd that Gayle had thrown them together this way when she'd known Christy all of her life. Christy could not help hearing the echo of Andrea Solomon's dry voice saying, *So good old Gayle has got her fingers in this,* that day out on the patio. Remembering that moment opened the door for all of the other doubts Andrea had raised to come flooding back.

What did it all mean?

How could they get past this?

She frowned at Sam, trying to gauge his reaction.

Christy could only imagine what Sam was thinking right now—that Gayle had picked out Christy and hoped for a romance between the two of them seemed far-fetched. And yet here they were. Christy examined their linked hands sadly, remembering what a thrill it had been that first time Sam had touched her fingertips.

She wondered if Sam was thinking that maybe their love wasn't real.

But Christy *knew* their love was real. She had never felt anything so strongly in all her life. *Please,* she thought, *don't take Sam away from me. Don't let him be scared off by this strange turn of events.*

She studied his profile. He was squinting into the distance, his expression suddenly alert, worried. "Where's Meggie?"

No sooner had he asked than they heard a muffled scream.

Christy's heart leapt in her throat as they scrambled to their feet.

"Meggie!" Sam bellowed. But there was no reply from below. They scurried down over the flat steps that led to the main courtyard below.

Meggie was nowhere in sight.

"We should never have taken our eyes off of her!" Christy cried.

"I should never have even let her come down here! Meggie!" Sam called out again.

They heard her then, her small voice seeming far away, with an odd echo to it.

"It sounds like it's coming from the new cistern." Sam dashed off in the direction of the recent drainage construction.

As they ran toward the manhole, Christy could already see a huge lid lying askew next to the wide hole that dropped into the deep cistern. Below, the giant drainage pipes diverged, carrying water runoff to the lake.

"Who the hell took that thing off?" Sam demanded, and ran harder. "It weighs almost two hundred pounds!"

As they lurched up to the edge and peered down they could hear the child's frightened whimpering above the gurgle of rushing water.

"Get a flashlight," Sam commanded Christy. She dashed to the Suburban.

"Meggie," Sam called down, "are you okay?"

"Dad-dee!" came Meggie's frightened plea.

Christy ran up, breathless, and Sam snatched the flashlight, aiming it down the hole. His chest exploded in terror at what he saw.

At the bottom of the ten-foot-deep manhole was Meggie, blinking up at the flashlight, soaked and covered in mud, hanging on to an eye bolt at the opening of one of the large pipes. Her skinny legs dangled knee-deep in the water as it rushed in a riverlike torrent from one pipe across the six-foot diameter of the cistern floor, swirling in a vortex before it rushed into the other pipe.

If storm debris began to plug the drainage pipe at the lake end as it had last spring, the water would rapidly rise and drown her. But Sam had had the grates removed, which meant that wouldn't happen—knowledge that brought no relief, because without the grates to stop her, if Meggie let go she would be swept down the pipe straight into the lake.

"Keep this aimed on her." Sam thrust the flashlight into Christy's hands and flipped his legs into the manhole.

After he lowered himself all the way through, Christy leaned over the edge, giving him light. "Daddy's coming!" she told Meggie.

"Hold on tight!" Sam yelled as he crawled down the inspection rungs that were embedded into the side of the concrete.

"I hode-ing on, Daddy!" Meggie yelled.

Christy shone the light at the top of Sam's head. "It's like when you were on Grandma Lorna's roof," she encouraged Meggie, trying to keep her voice calm for the child. "You just have to hold on, sweetheart." She dropped onto her stomach and straightened her arm down into the manhole to better shine the light. "You can do it. Remember how strong you are."

Sam's boot slipped on one muddy rung and he splashed onto his backside into the roiling water.

As Sam struggled to his feet, Christy said, "Hold on, Meggie!"

"I hode-ding! I hode—" Meggie's voice was cut off in a gurgle of water as she vanished into the pipe.

"Meggie!" Sam screamed, and dove into the pipe after her.

"Oh, God!" Christy cried as she pressed her chest to the edge of the manhole, aiming the light at the black hole where they had disappeared. "Oh, dear God," she begged, her voice echoing in the huge cistern, "*please.*" Her heart slammed into her ribs as she imagined the two people who had become her whole world being swept into the dark lake.

CHAPTER EIGHTEEN

INSIDE THE DARK PIPE, SAM had to fight for air. His head bobbed in and out of the muddy water as he struggled to get abreast of the current, reaching, reaching for his child. Each time he came up for another gulping breath he screamed, "Meggie!"

Sam knew the exact length of this one-hundred-and-ninety-foot pipe, which angled steadily downward until it reached a narrow finger of the lake below. Now he would give anything for some storm debris. Something, anything, to stop Meggie's progress long enough for him to get his hands on her. His head and shoulders bumped the sides of the pipe and his palms scoured the walls as he passed through. Nothing was sticking. The water was moving exceptionally fast, draining all of the undulating slopes and hollows of Moonlight Grove with impressive efficiency, just as he'd planned.

He saw light when he took his next breath and quickly came to the opening of the pipe where the turbulance spewed from the pipe like a small waterfall into the lake twelve feet below.

He clung to the edge and scanned the red-tinted surface of the water for signs of life, then he pulled his legs out of the pipe and splashed down. He plunged deep under the surface and sank into the silted bottom with outstretched arms. The lake was only ten or so feet deep here. But it was ten feet of cold, muddy, debris-filled water. He righted himself and pushed off the mushy bottom.

"Meggie!" he called when his head came up. This inlet formed a narrow trough, full of brush and overhanging trees, no more than forty feet across. But the dark water, pushed by the flow from the drainage pipe, was moving inexorably out to the larger lake. He looked beyond the inlet, toward the sun touching the surface of the lake, an eye of orange, about to slip closed. He had to find Meggie while she was still in this inlet. Again he scanned the scarlet water in a three-hundred-and-sixty-degree circle, but in the dusky light he saw no sign of her.

He wondered if he could even see anything below the surface of the freshly storm-churned waters. He took a test dive, eyes wide open, kicking downward, and saw nothing but the bloody orange-red of the sunset-lit waters, teeming with Oklahoma red earth. He touched the bottom with grasping fingers again, keeping his eyes open in vain. Down there, all was darkness.

FOR WHAT SEEMED AN ETERNITY, Christy clutched the edge of that manhole, vacillating. If she ran to get the cell phone and called for help, would Sam and Meggie appear out of the pipe, needing the light to crawl up to safety?

''Sam!'' she called, but only the sound of her echo and the rushing water answered. Even as she watched, the level of the water seemed to be rising. A bare six inches of free air space remained at the top of the pipe opening.

After several seconds of watching the filthy torrent rush past, Christy pushed herself to her feet and ran across the construction site to where the Suburban was parked. She prayed Sam did not have the cell phone in his pocket. Thanking God the vehicle was unlocked, she yanked open the door, fumbled under the papers on the seat and found the cell phone. Snatching it up, she punched 911. Waited. Nothing happened.

She experienced a moment of panic when she realized that Moonlight Grove must be too remote for 911 service. Then she remembered the highway patrol's road emergency number for cell phones. She dialed *55 and sank back against the side of the Suburban in weak relief when a dispatcher answered.

''Yes, I'm out at the Moonlight Grove construction site on Broken Arrow Lake. And we…oh, God! We need *help!*''

''All right, ma'am,'' the dispatcher answered in a level tone, ''just calm down and tell me what's happening.''

''I think—'' Christy felt lightheaded, so short of breath she could hardly say it ''—I think…two people may be drowning out here.''

SAM CONTINUED A SERIES of wild dives, each time groping along the treacherous bottom until he ran out of air and was forced to come back to the surface. He hit logs, rocks and tangles of water plants. He felt himself becoming lacerated and bruised and the whole while his mind churned.

He kept imagining Meggie below the filthy water, her pale hair floating out from her head in a ghostly pattern. Floating, floating. Waiting for him to do something. Each time he came up for air, he took one great gulp and screamed her name before going back down.

Meggie. Meggie.

CHRISTY WAS TOLD TO REMAIN on the line with the emergency dispatcher. Clutching the phone, she ran across the construction site back to the manhole. She told the dispatcher that she was going to set the phone down so she could shine the flashlight into the manhole again.

''Okay'' came the answer.

Once again, Christy flattened her belly to the ground and leaned into the manhole, shining her flashlight beam in a circle around the cavernous space.

She sat up and grabbed the phone, squatting on her heels as she talked. ''No sign of them. Should I go down to the lake?''

The dispatcher told her no, to go back out by the road and watch for a fire truck, already on its way from Claremore.

Sam had the keys to the Suburban in his pocket,

so Christy had to run all the way out to the road juncture. As she jogged up the road in the dusky light, she saw headlights swinging into the entrance to Moonlight Grove. Relief sluiced through her for one instant before she realized it was a long black car.

"Someone's coming," she told the dispatcher, "but it's not the fire department. It looks like a...a limousine."

The thing pulled up alongside her and rolled to a stop. An electric window was already sliding down. The driver, a clean-cut muscular man in a yellow golf shirt, seemed perturbed to see her. "Miss, this is private property."

"We have an emergency," Christy said, ignoring his officious attitude. "A man and a small child have fallen into the drainage pipe back at that construction site." She pointed. "I think they were swept into the lake."

The window behind the driver slowly lowered and an older man with Asian features stuck his head out, looking alarmed. It dawned on Christy then that this was Mr. Yoshida, returning to Moonlight Grove for a final consultation with Sam. "You say, someone hurt out there?" he said.

"You're Mr. Yoshida, aren't you?"

He nodded, waiting for her to explain the trouble.

"I'm Sam Solomon's...housekeeper—" she wasn't sure if he would know what a nanny was "—and it was Sam's daughter who fell into the manhole. Sam went into the drainage pipe after her."

Even in the waning light, Christy could see Mr.

Yoshida's face go pale. "Get in," he said as he opened the door.

Inside the spacious, softly lit limo were two other Japanese men. Like Mr. Yoshida, one was dressed in an expensive-looking business suit. But the other wore mud-smeared mechanic's coveralls. Not the kind of attire you'd expect to see inside a limo.

While the driver sat with the engine idling, Christy quickly told the dispatcher what had happened, then asked what they should do. They were told that someone should go back to the main highway and keep a lookout for the fire truck.

"Kazahiro and I will go with you to try to help Mr. Solomon," Mr. Yoshida said to Christy.

"Go back to the main road," he said to the man in the business suit. "When emergency people arrive, bring them to that manhole."

The man gave a quick little bow and opened the limo door.

Christy stopped his exit, clutching his arm. "Do you know where the manhole is?" she asked.

"I'm afraid he does," Mr. Yoshida said, and when Christy turned to him his brown eyes winced with regret. "You see, an hour ago, this man—" he angled a palm politely at the muscular one in coveralls "—removed the manhole so I could inspect the new cistern."

WHEN HE CAME UP FOR AIR each time, Sam continued to call Meggie's name again and again, treading water, fighting down terror, willing her to answer him. "Meggie!"

Then he thought he heard her. Far away. He grew still in the water and listened.

"Dad-dee" came the sound. Tiny. Distant.

"Meggie!" he bellowed. "Where are you?" He dog-paddled in a frantic circle, searching the dim recesses of the cove.

"Over he-e-ere!"

He took several strong strokes in the direction of her cry but still saw no sign of his child.

Was she hurt? Could she hold on?

"Meggie! Keep calling for Daddy!"

She did. Over and over, she called out the most precious word Sam had ever heard in his life, *Daddy*.

He found her near the far bank in the deep shadows of the inlet. She was hanging on again, this time clinging to a dead branch on an ancient cottonwood tree whose gnarled limbs reached down and touched the water like the arms of a gentle, rescuing angel.

He parted the water in three powerful strokes and scooped her into his arms, clutching her, breathing so hard from exertion and relief that he could not speak.

Her thin arms wound around his neck, tight, and they adjusted their hold on each other. Sam flung one arm out to find a grip on the cottonwood limb.

Meggie was shivering, and in the dwindling light Sam could see her wet blond hair snaking over her pale face, which was streaked with mud. As he looked into that little face, the face of his daughter, and felt her breath, her warm *living* breath, fanning over his cold skin, Sam Solomon thought that surely, at this moment, he had been given, as if for the second time, the greatest of all gifts.

"I swimmed, Daddy." Her little teeth chattered, but she was actually smiling at him. "I swimmed and I swimmed. Just like Christy teached me."

He pressed his lips to his child's cold forehead while his nose and the back of his eyes stung, and he wondered what he had ever done to deserve so great a blessing.

CHAPTER NINETEEN

SAM STOOD AT THE BOW WINDOW in the music room, looking out at their terraced backyard, so peaceful in its late autumn dormancy. It was time. But before he brought up the subject, Sam wanted to be sure the mood was right. Over on the bookshelves, the radio was turned low to Christy's favorite country station. At the keyboard, Christy was racking her brains trying to come up with lyrics for her new melody, but she'd have to take a break eventually.

When a slow ballad came on, Sam walked to the piano, turned her to him and took her face in his hands. He kissed her.

When he was finished he backed away an inch, studying Christy's mouth. "I can't believe," he said softly, reverently, "that I didn't ever kiss you in high school. I must have been nuts. You really do have the most beautiful mouth." He kissed her lips again, as if testing, tasting the reality of her anew.

Christy smiled against his lips. "You wouldn't have noticed this mouth in high school," she said. "I got braces in my junior year, thanks to your mother. And I had to wear them long after everybody else had their braces off. And I never, ever wore makeup. Not even lip gloss. I guess you could say I was a very late bloomer.''

''But you most certainly did bloom, didn't you?'' He looked down, this time gazing at the scooped neckline of her peasant blouse. ''I love you, Christy,'' he said hoarsely as he ran the backs of his fingers over her skin, caressing her curves gently.

Christy couldn't believe the power of such gestures could melt her, but right now she needed to work. ''I've got to have these lyrics worked out by Monday.'' She pulled a regretful face. ''Mary Jane needs one more slow song for her new CD.''

''You've been working too much. Can't you take a little break?'' Sam inclined his head toward the radio. ''We could dance.''

''I never thought you'd be the one telling me not to work so much.''

''Thank God I've changed.'' Sam smiled.

Christy swiveled on the bench, back to her music. ''What made you change, do you think?''

''Bringing Meggie to Tulsa.'' Sam sat down on the bench next to her.

Christy nodded, understanding fully. Meggie, with her wide-eyed innocence, with her selfish but trusting demands, with her poignant vulnerability. Meggie could change anyone. ''Meggie,'' she whispered with her pencil poised over the sheet music.

''When I found her out in the lake, hanging on that tree limb, after I thought I'd lost her—'' His voice choked with emotion as it usually did when they talked about that day. He swallowed. ''Sorry.''

"It's okay." Christy pecked him on the cheek. "What's important is that Meggie's okay. She's safe. And she's a wonderful child. I guess it was because of Meggie that we found each other. Did you ever think of that?"

"Every day since you first came to be with us."

"And because of your mother."

"And because of my mother," he conceded. "Mom is definitely happy that you're taking care of Meggie. And of me. We've come to an understanding. She seems to be meddling less."

"Still, without her, we wouldn't have met." They'd had this conversation before. It was like a favorite litany now. Like a private duet they sang to each other at special moments. The Amazing Way We Found Each Other.

For a long moment Sam studied Christy's face, then he reached up and stroked her fluffy hair back off her brow. Finally he whispered, "You changed me, too."

"Me?" Christy spread a palm lightly at the top of her soft bosom. "*I* changed you?"

"Don't you know that? The moment you stepped into this house—that was the day I changed."

"But I never set out to change you!" Christy protested. "I love you the way you are."

"That's exactly the point. You accepted me for who I am. You helped me accept myself, my life, the way it is. I don't know...I think before I met you I was always trying to prove something, always striving, always trying to be as impressive as my brothers.

But you..." He smiled into her eyes. "By always being yourself, by being so utterly genuine, you showed me how to be the same way."

"Wait!" Christy cried, then started scribbling furiously with the pencil. "That's it!"

"What?" Sam said, bending to look at what she was writing.

"That's my new song! 'The Day I Changed.'"

"Wow," Sam said. "How do you do that?"

"Listening to you helps." She finished writing, put down the pencil and plucked the notes on the keyboard as she sang, "Always trying to impress somebody, always trying to prove something. That was me. But then one day, I met you. You were so real, so genuine and true. That's what I learned, the day I met you. The day I met you—that was...the day I changed."

When she finished, Sam said, "Lord, you make me happy. I want to keep coming home to you...to this. To this passion, this peace, this comfort, this...this—man! I don't even know how to say it."

Christy laughed, giddy after her song breakthrough. "Happiness, Sam. It's just called happiness."

He nodded, and the look in his eyes, so calm, so perfectly content, yet burning with deep gratitude and meaning, went straight to Christy's heart.

"Christy, I want us to set the date."

"Oh, Sam!" Christy threw her arms around his neck and buried her face in his shoulder. "We've talked about this before."

"Is that another yes?" he said into her hair. Christy

could hear the smile in his voice. She'd given him nothing but yeses all these months—the problem was she kept putting off setting the date. There were other hearts involved besides theirs alone.

She clutched him tighter. Her Sam. Her Sam, who was going to live with her and pad around in his pajamas with her in winter, and sip coffee in the backyard with her on summer mornings, and reach around and snitch tidbits of whatever she was cooking, and argue aloud to the TV news shows while they cuddled on the couch. Her Sam, who inspired her song lyrics. Her Sam, who would always, each and every night, share her bed— Abruptly, she jerked back from him. "Oh, Sam." This time the words came out solemnly. "You know we can't get married right now."

"I know what you're thinking. That Meggie is vulnerable right now. But Meggie is not the one getting married here. Christy, let's be realistic." His pose became urgent and he clasped her hands between them. "Meggie has the mind of a three-year-old and she always will. She may not remember our wedding two days after it happens. As long as she has the two of us taking care of her, making her day-to-day life happy, she'll be fine."

"Sam. No. I'm not talking about Meggie. I mean we can't get married while Meggie's mother is slowly dying."

Andrea's condition had continued to seesaw for the last few months. Each setback brought fresh sorrow. Each victory brought renewed hope.

"What do you suggest? That we postpone our life

together until after Andrea is gone? That makes absolutely no sense. We are obviously in love. People know about us now. You might as well live here for all the time you spend here in this studio and taking care of Meggie and me. If we wait to get married until after Andrea's gone, it will look as if we were doing just that—waiting for her to be gone. Have you thought about it that way?''

When she didn't answer, he continued, ''And let's suppose Andrea doesn't die?''

''Sam.''

''Well? It's what we're all hoping for, isn't it? A miracle? Then what? Will we be secretly disappointed that she's still hanging on or something? When will we get married if Andrea simply continues to struggle with her disease and—''

''Sam! Stop it!''

They broke apart and he raked his fingers through his hair. ''I'm sorry. I don't mean to sound cruel. But I am not tied to Andrea. I don't love her. I love you, and I want us to be married. My life finally feels whole, sound, *right* because of you. And I want to be married to you. I want to be your husband. I want you to be my wife. I want us to be a family in this house together. We have waited long enough. We should at least set the date,'' Sam insisted. ''I *want* to set the date. We *need* to set the date.''

''What is the big hurry? Wouldn't it be best to wait and see how Andrea's next set of tests turns out?''

''No. That *wouldn't* be best. Not for me. Not for you, either. And certainly not for Meggie. And not even for Andrea. If Andrea knew we were waiting because of her illness, she'd d—'' He stopped himself short at the near gaff. A guilty frown clouded his face.

Christy clamped a warm, soothing palm over his muscular forearm. She didn't even have to say ''It's okay'' for him to know that it was. Christy had certainly taught him how to deal with his small, stupid mistakes. With her, mistakes were always instantly forgiven. Forgotten. And then a man could do better.

How long had it taken him to realize that when she said, ''I don't remember,'' about some little transgression, it was just another one of her little Christy tricks?

Oh, Lord, how he loved this woman.

Christy released his arm...and smiled. She had smiled through it all. Through the ups and downs of Andrea's illness. Even on that dark night when...his throat felt tight as he remembered again that terrible evening a couple of months ago.

''What are you thinking about?'' Christy studied him.

''You. I'm thinking of how brave you were last September when, you know, when Meggie—''

''I know. But Meggie's safe now. And right now Andrea is surviving, day by day. And we'll always be available to help them both. And you and I will always be together to make new memories—happy ones. But as far as a wedding...I think we need to take it day by day and wait until the timing is right.''

''We can't wait forever for everything to be just right, sweetheart. We need to be together. I *need* you.'' He pulled her close to him again. ''Christy...'' Just saying her name filled him with contentment, with joy. He touched his index finger under her chin and tipped her beloved face up to his. ''Please. I love you. I want you to be my wife. I'm tired of postponing our future. Let's set the date.''

Christy smiled again. She could tell he wasn't going to give up this time. ''Okay.'' She walked over and rummaged around in her overstuffed quilted bag, producing one of those little planning calendars that greeting card shops give away for free. ''Sooner or later?''

''You mean it?'' Her handsome Sam looked like a kid on Christmas morning. He walked over and studied the calendar over her shoulder.

''Yeah. So what'll it be? Now or next year?'' She grinned and flipped through the months of the calendar, pretending to concentrate on the dates, biting her lip. ''After you finish Moonlight Grove?''

''What do you think?'' He pulled the calendar away and grabbed her to him. ''Give me a kiss.''

She tiptoed, gave him a little moist smooch on the lips and tried to go back to studying her dog-eared calendar.

''No—'' he captured her waist, tilted her chin up and swooped in ''—I want a *kiss.*''

Sam pulled her lower lip between his, tasting her, her lipstick, the hint of strawberry that he'd now become habituated to. His tongue seemed to have a mind of its own when it came to Christy. A very urgent, insistent mind.

She responded to that urgency, moving the tip of her tongue in a swirl around his, with that unique, maddening pressure that was Christy's alone. The sensation sent his nerves, muscles and hormones strumming with desire. This passion was what he wanted. Always.

She broke off the kiss, much to his disappointment. "We've got to stop kissing like this every other minute."

"Yeah. If we keep it up, we're going to end up in a ranch house raising a pack of kids."

"A *ranch* house?" She made a disgusted face. "Never! *Our* house will be an immaculately restored period beauty in a historic preservation neighborhood."

"Ah, yes." He angled his mouth down to nip at hers again. "I just happen to own one of those."

"Good enough." She turned her head—and that luscious mouth—teasing him, as she went back to studying the calendar. Was she always going to have the power to drive him wild this way? Sam hoped so.

The next song on the radio caused Sam to thrust his palms out, adopting an astonished air. "Omigosh!" He pretended to hyperventilate. "That's Christy Lane's song!" It had become a standard joke with them. Every time Christy's song came on the radio, which was fairly often these days, Sam pulled this routine.

He crossed to the radio and turned up the volume. Then he slowly walked back to Christy and took her lightly in his arms for a slow dance.

''You were right,'' he said as he swirled his bride-to-be in a gentle waltz over the hardwood floor. ''The first time I heard your song, I recognized it immediately.''

She smiled. ''I figured you would.''

They danced, completely absorbed in each other, while the lyrics of ''Meggie's Song'' lilted through the open, sunny room.

When they finished dancing, Sam leaned in to study the calendar over Christy's shoulder again. ''Pick any date. I mean it.''

''How about this one?'' She pointed at a Saturday in December. ''Meggie will be out of school on Christmas break by then.''

''In December? Only a month from now?'' He felt lightheaded at the prospect. They would actually start their lives together by Christmas!

''Maybe while we're on our honeymoon, Gayle would take Meggie out to visit Andrea.''

''You mean it?''

''Why not? I expect we can keep our wedding simple. I could do a holiday theme. We could have a small reception right here at the house—right here in the music room. Nothing fancy. Although I do want to buy Meggie a fairly fancy dress.''

Now Sam smiled. ''Buy her anything you want, sweetheart.'' He scooped her off her feet and swung her around in his arms, then planted another sound, energetic kiss on her beautiful, beautiful mouth. Sam Solomon had never imagined that he could be this happy. No. Not ever.

He set her back on her feet, studying her eyes as he so loved to do. For a moment she allowed this, then she lowered her lashes, looking down at the little calendar. Gently, he slid it from her fingers. "I will marry you any day you say."

"Ooh," Christy crooned. "That sounds like another song. We are on a roll today. We may even have a future at this."

Sam wrapped his arms around her. "Maybe. How about this one?" As he lowered his head, he murmured, "My future is you."

"And my future is you—" Christy smiled as she tilted her face up to his "—and Meggie."

"And Meggie," Sam whispered, just before he kissed her again.

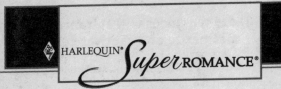

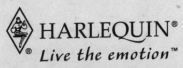

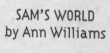

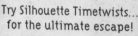

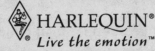

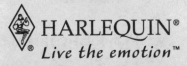

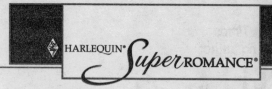

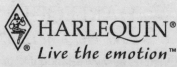